Ramadan Man

The Brendan Cleary Series, Volume 4

P.M. Heron

Published by Sirani Publishing Limited, 2019.

RAMADAN MAN

First edition. December 21, 2019.

Written by P.M. Heron.

Chapter One

BRENDAN AND LORNA SAT facing each other in the small family run cafe down a side street of Leicester's city centre. They'd been in England three days, and Brendan was already starting to relax. Away from Belfast. Away from Union Jacks and tri-colours marking out the various danger zones of the city he called home. No mentions of the IRA or UDA. No murals or portraits of dead paramilitaries who'd died fighting for their community. Brendan didn't want to see any of that ever again. He'd seen it all. His mother's three older brothers were former British soldiers who'd help form the Protestant UDA and became leaders of the Shankill Road brigade. His grandfather on his father's side and his dad's two older brothers were long serving members of the Provisional IRA army council; calling the shots for the republican movement in Belfast and the entire thirty-two-county sovereignty, having overthrown the old IRA in Dublin for failing to protect the catholic communities north of the boarder. This gave Brendan Cleary one of the most controversial names in the world.

Now twenty-seven years old, Brendan had lived with the knowledge that his bloodline had made him loved by many and hated by just as much. Having been a rebellious teenager, in with the wrong crowds, he'd watched his friends on the catholic Falls and protestant Shankill roads being subjected to punishment beatings and shootings for selling drugs and stealing cars, getting on the wrong side of the paramilitary groups that had taken on the role of judge, jury and executioner in the absence of the police and army. Belfast and Derry had many no-go areas for police and other British state forces. This gave the IRA and UDA the feeling of being the rulers of their own kingdoms. One of Brendan's greatest traumas in his young life was when his best friend Mickey Mooney hung himself after being beaten so severely, he'd lost his marbles. Being in possession of the UDA member that had done this to his friend, Brendan had returned the favour for Mickey, with little regard for the consequences. That was a dish that had yet to be served up to Brendan, if it ever would, again, the Cleary name came with it's pros and cons, perhaps it was the reason he was still alive.

Brendan had become the definition of a product of his environment: angry, hardened, an aggressive. But thanks to the late Damien Cleary, Brendan had been schooled on how to stay alive in the dangerous world that many people only believed existed on the news. He'd watched his family get torn apart because of the division between the two sides. His mother became an alcoholic and his father had disappeared, gone AWOL. After the unexpected chain of events in Belfast, he began to re-evaluate himself. The love of a woman – a stranger – was pivotal to all this.

Lorna Woodward: a twenty-nine-year-old former British MI5 agent was Brendan's only support. And he hers.

Upon discovering a corrupt government in both Ireland and Britain, Brendan and Lorna now faced a life on the run with nobody to turn to. They were real a life bonny and

Clyde. Just a little less psychotic than the infamous American couple.

'What are you staring at?' Lorna nudged Brendan with her elbow, causing him to flinch, knocking his still full-to-the-brim flat white that he'd let go cold.

He snatched up a napkin and dabbed the ring of coffee, then the bottom of his grey ceramic cup before placing it against his lips and taking a swig. 'Lukewarm coffee, almost as bad as warm piss!' He screwed up his face, showing his disgust. 'Look at that pair of twats over there.' He gestured out the window where two men stood, handing a bag to a young boy on a bicycle. The lad wasn't a day over thirteen and looked like he hadn't eaten a proper meal in weeks.

'Little shit should be in school,' Lorna said. 'Not out here on a dope run for his bum parents.'

'That's if he even has parents.' Brendan finished the rest of his coffee. 'Let's go.'

They got up and left the shop.

Stepping out into the rain, they watched as the boy peddled towards the pub at the end of the street. It wasn't a high end establishment to say the least, and that was being generous.

'Come on,' Brendan said, taking Lorna by the hand. She put a golf umbrella, large enough to shield both of them from the downpour. As they approached the run-down boozer that looked like a bulldozer would be just as useful as a refurbishment, a tall, thin guy in his middle to late thirties stood with his hands inside the pockets of his navy Adidas tracksuit bottoms. He had one foot on the ground and the other against the shop window he was leaning against. He looked up for a split second at Brendan and Lorna, only long enough for the two to see his eyes, glazed over and struggling to focus.

'Any spare change, mate?'

Brendan stopped and emptied his pocket, giving the guy about seven quid in shrapnel. 'Thank you, brother.' The guy cupped the coins in both hands as if Brendan had just given him a lifeline.

'Get yourself some food with that, mate.'

'You're Irish?' The guy said, clasping his fistful of coins tightly as if holding a precious stone. 'My grandfather was Irish. I love Ireland.'

'If you grew up in Belfast, you'd probably think different- ly.' Brendan said. 'Take care.' They made their way towards the door of the pub. The Leicester Arms could just about be read from the faded white sign above the door.

'You know he's just going to buy more drink or drugs with that?' Lorna said.

Brendan held the door open for her. 'But that's one less person who'll die on the streets tonight.' He followed Lorna inside. The dimly lit pub was complete with varnished tables, chairs with burgundy coloured cushions, navy walls with brass railings about waist height and a faded blue carpet that had stained patches sporadically throughout.

Three elderly men sat propped up on the bar stools, probably spending their pension, enjoying their retirement.

'What can I get you guys?' The lady behind the bar asked. She had chin-length mousy brown hair and ma- hogany coloured eyes. A white blouse that promoted her feminine curves in all the right places.

'Diet coke for me,' Lorna said.

'Same for me,' Brendan said. 'What time do you start serving food?'

'We can put it on now for you.' She reached under the bar and pulled out two folded menus. 'Have a look at...'

'I already know what I'm after,' Brendan said. 'All day breakfast, large.'

'I'll have the same,' Lorna said.

'It'll be around twenty minutes. That'll be fourteen pound fifty, please.'

Brendan pulled his bank card out and handed it to her.

'Thanks. Where in Ireland are you from?'

'Belfast,' Brendan said. 'You ever been?'

'No, never. Would love to go. Mind if I use the contactless?' She looked at him, he waved his hand dismissively, giving her the green light. She swiped his card and ripped the receipt from the machine. 'Maybe one day I'll go,' she smiled and handed Brendan his card and receipt just as the door flung open and three men entered the pub, making their presence known with the volume of their laughter, shaking the rain drops off their coats.

'Why don't you just ask for her number?' Lorna said, getting up from the stool and making her way towards the seating area at the back of the room.

Brendan laughed and followed her. He looked back at the lady behind the bar who was still looking at him. He smiled. She smiled back. Their view of each other became blocked by one of the rowdy men. The man turned around and looked at Brendan, his expression, one of disapproval for the brief interaction between the two. Brendan assumed he was her boyfriend and thought nothing else of it.

Lorna grinned at Brendan as he sat down beside her. 'You like her.' She nodded in the direction of the bar and nudged him with her elbow.

'I only have eyes for you.' He nudged her back then kissed her on the cheek. Then came an uproar of laughter coming from the group at the bar. Brendan looked towards them. The one who looked like the bar lady's boyfriend was still looking over at him. A smug grin written across his face.

Brendan held his stare. A few throats were heard clearing and the laughter from the rest slowly faded away until there was nothing left but the clinks of cups and cutlery from the kitchen.

'Don't start, Brendan,' Lorna said. 'We haven't even had breakfast yet.'

Lorna's words passed through Brendan's right ear and straight out his left. 'I guess we've met the local hard man, then,' Brendan said, as his phone began to ring.

'Who the hell could that be?'

He answered it. They both laughed hearing a lady with an Indian accent, telling Brendan he may be eligible for compensation after an accident Brendan and Lorna weren't aware of.

'Are you positive he comes in here?' Brendan looked at Lorna who had her laptop out, searching through files she'd saved from her former post as an upcoming agent for her majorities forces. Her MI5 badge gave her exclusive access to the criminal world that plagued the UK. This was now what Brendan and Lorna were devoted to cleaning up.

'The Leicester Arms, this is his hangout.' She slapped a few fingertips on her keypad and turned the laptop around for him to have a look at the image. An image of a short thin man, with a false tan and a blue Leicester City football top on was getting out of an electric blue BMW. His white smile sat directly below his Rayban sunglasses. His perfectly styled hair told Brendan the guy spent more time in the tanning and beauty parlours than he did in full-time employment. 'Handsome devil isn't he.' Lorna joked.

'This is him?' Brendan said. 'This is Leicester's drug king-pin and god of the local underworld?'

'He might not look dangerous, but believe me he is, and he's had many people brutally tortured and killed. He never gets his hands dirty or allows himself to have a direct link to anyone he doesn't know for a very long time. He's very smart.'

'He won't be when we're done with him.'

'Alright, tough guy.' Lorna looked at Brendan then back over at the group of hard men at the bar. 'How are we going to take down this gang, then?'

'I've got to get close to him, gain his trust.'

'Brendan, I've already told you, he's not stupid. If he doesn't know you, he'll not even give you a second thought.' She pushed a strand of hair behind her ear. 'You'll not even get a handshake from him.'

'Want to bet?' Brendan sounded confident, looking over at the three. He looked at them as if he'd just found a precious stone. 'You think those three are acting as if they can do what they want?'

Lorna looked over at them. 'Yeah, they've got that untouchable swagger, like they've...'

'Got some heavy back up from someone influential?' Brendan gestured back at the screen. 'Like they're in tight with our tangoed friend here?'

'Brendan, those guys probably work for the guy who works for the guy, that reports to...' Lorna gestured at the laptop screen. 'This guy.'

'I'm going to ask for a job,' Brendan said, as the bar lady came over with their breakfast. 'After this.' She set their plates down. 'Thanks.' He smiled at her, she smiled back, turned and walked away. She turned and smiled at him again as she walked away.

Lorna cleared her throat, breaking Brendan out of his stare. He looked at her. She gestured towards the group again who were now all staring at him. The smug grins on their faces had disappeared and been replaced by expressions of three angry pit bulls.

'That's enough eye-balling my missus, pal,' the man shouted over, finally disclosing the relationship between the two.

Brendan was about to react when Lorna kicked his foot below the table.

'Sorry, mate,' Brendan shouted back, putting his hand up in a sign of peace to the three. He looked at Lorna. 'You happy now?'

Lorna looked at Brendan, sucking a greasy mushroom into her mouth. She nodded and smiled at him. Brendan heard the group of three laugh among themselves. Feeling his neck redden in anger, he looked back at Lorna who was dipping a sausage into her egg yolk. 'Let them have their little laugh. She grinned and looked up at him. 'We'll have the last laugh.' She put the sausage in her mouth and winked at him. 'Now eat your breakfast. Perhaps their boss will make an appearance.'

They both sat quietly, listening to the group of three laughing, reminiscing their recent trip to Amsterdam. How they'd gotten "fucked up" and were made to wash their cocks before shagging the hookers. Brendan and Lorna both struggled not to laugh when they heard this. But had they burst out laughing, they'd be given away as listening in and would put them on edge. They didn't want to throw away a valuable opportunity to pick up some information on the waves.

What the group talked about next was something that caused their ears to perk up. One of them mentioned "the big boss" going to his house in the Costa Del Sol for a week and was due to return from the Spanish resort with news about the organisation. Upon his return he was holding a *cleansing* meeting for his organisation and was planning on cutting away the dead wood. One of the three was nervous about what this meant for him. Brendan looked at him like a lion spotting the easiest catch. He was the weak link in the chain and wasn't confident in his employment being extended at that meeting. Or was he involved in something he shouldn't be? Whatever it was, he wasn't looking forward to it.

'I'd like to be a part of that meeting as a new recruit for when the boss man comes back,' Brendan said. 'Who do I need to impress in order to get an invitation to this meeting? You know these streets better than I do.'

'You need to do two things, one: make them like you,' Lorna said, as she stood up, slinging her bag over her shoulder. 'And two: make one of them replaceable so that you can step in as the likely candidate.'

'Where are you going?'

'Powder my nose.'

He watched as she made her way across the bar towards the females. The music got louder. Local charts were playing. Brendan looked up at the bar, there was now a guy in a white shirt and bow tie leaning across the bar chatting up the bar lady. He was dressed in the door security uniform. Brendan grinned to himself, almost feeling like he could read his new friend's mind, he looked around at their table. The three were all looking at the guy chatting up the lady. Brendan looked back up at the bar, the well-dressed guy had straightened himself up and made his way to the front door. His sheer size said he could probably wrap all three of his new friends around his little finger, but if these guys were part of an organisation, the doorman probably wouldn't have had the balls to do anything. Brendan, on the other hand, well, he'd dealt with the IRA and the UDA in the past, groups that would look at an English gangster as nothing but the shit on the bottom of their shoe.

Brendan looked down at his hand, noticing he'd clenched his fist, as if his sub-conscious was preparing him for something. He looked at his phone, a new bulletin had talked about Ireland and the mass shooting that had taken place at the docks. The hunt was still on for the culprits.

Brendan watched as Lorna made her way back from the ladies. She was grinning, looking directly at him. Just as

Brendan was about to ask her what the smug grin was for, the building's evacuation alarm went off. Everyone in the pub was directed to calmly make their way out to the assembly point in the car park.

'What did you do that for,' Brendan asked.

'I'm giving us all a little opportunity to get to know each other.' She pulled lipstick from her bag and ran the scarlet coloured stick across her lips. 'Let's go.' She dropped it back into her bag and led the way through the sea of wooden tables and chairs.

Brendan stood up and followed her towards the front door. The doorman made his way into the pub. The girl behind the bar shouted to him to check the females.

'You okay, babe?' The bar lady's fella shouted, as he followed Brendan out through the doors.

'Probably just a false alarm,' she replied as she too followed them out. Accompanied by two chefs, a cleaner and the manager who'd been scratching his ass in his office, probably watching the TV.

The assembly point was in the pub's carpark. The homeless guy that Brendan had given money to on their way in was now vibrating on a more positive vibration with a bottle of cider in his hand, clearly being entertained by the drama that was unfolding. They all stood in the gravel covered carpark at the end of the city block. A run-down look in contrast to the high end, vibrant part of the city called the High-cross Shopping Centre.

Brendan stood with his hands in his pockets, still being stalked by the bar lady. He looked back at her. She had those wide eyes that you could fall in to. She was a gem for sure, and this local hardman would have his mind reeling at the thought of her going with someone else. Especially given the fact that she appeared to be so flirtatious.

'Who was smoking in the females?' The doorman shouted from the side exit. The group of ten men and women all looked more interested in getting back inside than giving a shit about who'd set the alarm off.

'Sorry, that was me,' Lorna said. 'It's a bad habit, I'm sorry.'

'Okay, you're barred,' the doorman said. 'The rest of you can go back in again.'

'What do mean barred? Screw you, fat neck, I've just ordered food.'

'Tough, you should have thought of that before you went for a smoke.' He looked even more smug when the manager came through the side fire exit with another three doormen. He whispered something in the manager's ear while the manager's eyes scanned the crowd, landing on Lorna.

'You stupid bitch.' The manager snatched the butt off the doorman and threw it at Lorna, Brendan swiping it away, stepping in front of Lorna.

'What did you just call her?'

Before Brendan could say another word, the manager was surrounded by the door staff. 'Piss off now, mate. You're both done here.'

'Do yourself a favour, pal,' Brendan's new mate sounded like he was passing on valuable advice. 'Fuck off, and don't come back, yeah?'

'What are you, this knob's secret protection?' Brendan spoke mockingly. 'We've paid for our food, and we're not going anywhere before we get it.'

'Clearly, your Irish accent means you're not from around here and don't know who the fuck we are,' the manager said. 'For that, I'm going to give you a pass, and let...'

'I don't give a shit who you are.' Brendan stepped closer to him.

Two of the door men lunged towards Brendan. Brendan used one their momentum to throw them headfirst in to the wall. The second grabbed Brendan but Lorna kicked him in the balls from behind. The third doorman grabbed Lorna but Brendan bearhugged him from behind. He lifted the rugby player sized guy and threw him into the red Vauxhall Corsa that was parked next to the fire exit.

'You've got some balls, Irish!' The manager said. He looked at the other three guys who'd entered the bar after Brendan and Lorna. Brendan's first mate of the day, nodded his head, gesturing in Brendan and Lorna's direction.

The guy looked at Brendan. Then he looked at his two mates. He then looked at the three door men who were standing bunched together, all of them reluctant to go in for a round two.

'This is your door security?' Brendan mocked the three.

'You'd do well, to leave now, mate.' The manager said, he pulled his phone out to take a photo of the two, but before he raised the device to point it, Brendan swung a round-house kick, sending his phone out of his hand, crashing into the wall.

'I'm calling the police,' the bar lady shouted. 'All this over a fucking smoke in the toilets?' She looked at Brendan then Lorna. 'You two, fuck off, now. Come back later when they aren't here.' She looked at the door staff. 'You three are fucking useless.'

'You come back here, and you'll be shot, you hear me? You'll be fucking shot,' the rugby player sized bouncer made another run for Brendan. Brendan spun in a circle, lifting his leg and kicking the rugby player in the side of the face, knocking him out before he hit the ground.

Lorna pulled Brendan away. 'Come on, Brendan. We'll come back later. For a refund.'

Brendan put his hood up and linked arms with Lorna as they made their way to the other side of the street, repeatedly glancing over their shoulders, making sure they weren't followed.

Getting to the Highcross Shopping Centre, they went to the third-floor car park, to section A5 where their BMW 6 Series was parked.

As Lorna jumped into the driver's seat, she started the engine and laughed. 'You get who the manager was?'

'I guess you're going to tell me, but I can have a good guess... He's someone I want to impress?'

Lorna looked at him a nodded, grinning. 'Well be back later.'

Chapter Two

AFTER SATISFYINGLY quick and easy McDonalds, followed by a drive out into the lush Leicestershire countryside, Brendan and Lorna returned to their hotel, set in the suburban area of north Leicester, convenient – only a short drive from the city centre. They decided to change into more formal attire and planned to make use of the millions left to Brendan by his late father. He joked about himself being like Bruce Wayne. Left with more than enough. Money he didn't care about, but what he did care about, was making the lives of criminals a living hell. And if the money could support that, then he'd put it to good use.

After a shower and sprucing themselves up, Brendan and Lorna left their hotel room, with nothing but a bank card and a small handgun that Lorna kept in her purse. Brendan didn't want to waste bullets on the small fish. Why would he be interested in wasting his time with the scum that worked on the streets when their time was better suited to taking down the heads. Cutting the head of a snake is how you kill it.

Passing through the foyer, they were greeted and wished a lovely evening by the receptionist, followed by the night porter as they made their way towards the front door. Brendan drove. Lorna directed him while playing around on her phone. She was distant, her eyes fixed on the screen longer than required to operate Google Maps.

'What's got your attention?' Brendan said, as he pulled onto the A6 duel carriageway, city bound. The time was shortly after six and the evening traffic was beginning to thin out.

'I think it's not just the English gangsters we need to be thinking about.' She looked at Brendan. 'I'm reading a local news report that talks about there being an influx of Italians in the Leicester area. Not only Italians, but drugs and weapons that appear to have come from Italians.'

'Our recent trip to Italy has come back to haunt us already?'

'We'll soon find out.' She put her phone in her purse and put the window down. 'If Italians have muscled in on the local gangs, then it brings the level of sophistication, and brutality of the criminal world to a new level. But right now, I just want my money back.' She laughed. 'I was looking forward to that fry today, too.'

'I'm wondering who out of that group of three clowns we can use to get close to the boss.'

'Don't think about it too much, just let it unfold naturally.'

The next fifteen minutes were spent in silence. Stopping at a red light almost every two hundred yards would have been enough to put the most patient of people in a bad mood.

King Street on the city centre was a residential area, mostly catering for students of the local De Montfort University. This meant, most of the residents didn't have cars.

What was more frightening to students than having to pay a parking fee? After parking, they made their way towards the Leicester Arms to get their money back from the breakfast they'd ordered that morning.

'Is it too late for a fry?' Lorna joked.

'Never too late for one of those,' Brendan laughed. Locking the car, he zipped his jacket closed. He was about to follow Lorna who'd already crossed the street and created an impatient distance. 'What?' he looked at her as she pointed towards the back of the car.

'You want to go in here holding nothing but your cock in your hand?'

He laughed. 'I'm pretty sure I can handle them with my hands.' He popped the boot open, grabbing his backpack. It would have passed for a school bag, but the contents of the bag were certainly not that of school materials. Two handguns, resting in their leather shoulder holsters. Brendan had confidence that the magazines had more than compressed air in them, but he pocketed fresh mags just to be safe. He unzipped his jacket and tossed one of the holsters over his left shoulder. He mirrored with the opposite arm. He threw his jacket back on and zipped it closed, crossing the road to join Lorna.

'Let's go.' She linked arms with him.

He slipped his hand into his trouser pockets.

After fifteen minutes of zig zagging through the Roman styled cobbled streets of the inner city, they rounded a corner, finding only fifty feet and about ten pedestrians between them and the door of the Leicester Arms. Two guys stood on the door, busy chatting to a group of women, obviously flirting with the pair of six-and-a-half-foot bodybuilders. One had one of those oily tans that muscle men plastered all over themselves before stepping on stage, and with thr grin on his shining face, he was feeling confident about himself. The other was paler, but just as menacing looking. Each shoulder similar in size as Brendan's head.

As Brendan and Lorna got to within ten feet, door security offered them little more than a passing glance, which was better for Brendan and Lorna, they were indulging in the bare flesh in front of them, enjoying the attention, certainly enough to not give Brendan and Lorna a second glance. The tanned on held the door open for them.

Brendan entered first, followed by Lorna. The warm air hitting their faces was welcome. The overpowering stench of stale beer and the sticky floors as they headed towards the bar was not. Brendan looked back a Lorna and smiled. She blew him a kiss. It was almost as if the two were enjoying the buzz. As he got closer to the bar, he seen the same lady serving. She caught Brendan's eye almost as fast as he caught hers. She smiled and held his gaze right up until he reached the bar.

'You've got balls, Irishman. I'll give you that.'

'And you've got money belonging to us,' Lorna said. 'Now cough up.'

The bar lady smiled at Lorna, but her expression was not half as welcoming as the one she gave Brendan. 'How about I get you both a drink, then I'll go and get you your refund?'

'Thought we were barred? How's the boss man going to feel about that?' Brendan said.

'You pissed him off, that's for sure. But he respects people with balls. And you pair,' her eyes darted from Brendan and Lorna. 'Did make our door staff look like a bunch of kids today.'

'I'll have a sparkling water, please,' Lorna said.

'White coffee.' Brendan added.

'Grab a seat. I'll bring them over to you. Louise is the name, by the way,' she reached her hand over the counter, first towards Lorna.

'Lorna.' Lorna shook her hand.

'And you?' Louise reached in Brendan's direction.

'Brendan.'

She squeezed Brendan's hand softly. 'Lovely to meet you both. Grab a seat, I'll be over in a minute.'

They both turned and made their way through the pub floor, zig zagging through clusters of people in the direction of their seats, taking the same seats as they had in the morning. Brendan took his phone out and took a photo of Lorna.

'What are you doing?' She smiled awkwardly.

'I wanted to see a real-life picture of a jealous expression.' He laughed out loud then pulled her in close to him. He kissed her, but as he moved in, he spotted someone coming up behind her. 'We may have a problem.' He whispered in her ear. He pulled her around to his side of the table.

They both stood together, shoulder to shoulder as the three guys they'd met today approached.

'Thought you two would have learned your lesson this morning.' The one who acted like Louise's boyfriend said. The other two just stood on either side of him, looking smug, in their element. Brendan looked at the one he'd sussed as the trio's weakest link. The guy broke his stare almost instantly.

Lorna sat down. Brendan did the same. Both emanating a quiet confidence. Which was at least recognised by the group.

'We're just here for a drink,' Lorna said, as she pulled her phone out and took a picture of Brendan, grinning at him, paying more attention to Brendan's silly expression towards her than the three onlookers. She looked back at the three. 'Now fuck off.'

Brendan smiled at them, then turned his attention to Lorna. 'What was that photo for?'

'I wanted to see a real example of a pissed off expression.'

He laughed then looked at the three. 'You heard her, fuck off.'

The leader of the three was about to step in closer to them when Louise interrupted.

'Look, we don't want any trouble with you. We understand we may have tread on your toes this morning, but we were tired and hungry,' Brendan said.

The nervous one of the three finally looked as if he had a mind of his own, stepping in closer to Brendan. 'He reminds me of Jonty Moore Jr. The accent. The hardman, untouchable act. It's funny, in a cute kind of way.'

Brendan stood back up again. And the guy flinched, stepping back again, with the other two acting as his bodyguards. 'What do you know about Jonty Moore Jr?' He looked at the three who all looked like they were ready to pounce.

'Just that when he and his old man came to the meet the boss, they brought with them the same swagger and cockiness as you seem to have.' The leader of the group said. 'But the difference between you and him, is that his name brings with it a notoriety.' He looked at Lorna then the other two. 'You on the other hand,' he stepped up to Brendan. 'Who the fuck are you?'

As much as Brendan wanted to plaster the guy all over the bar, mixing in his mates in with it, he bit his tongue.

'You three, fuck off and let the two of them have their drinks. This morning was just a misunderstanding. And he's done us a favour by highlighting how shit our door security is.' Louise pushed the three back. 'I won't tell you again.'

'That's it,' the one who highlighted Johnty Moore Jr said. 'You're part of the Irish MMA scene.' He nudged Louise with his elbow. 'Maybe he wants a job.'

'Well, we both know I could spread your scrawny ass around this room without much bother.'

Louise grabbed the mouthpiece and turned him around. 'Fuck off and stop starting shit then hiding behind their back.' She looked at the other two. 'You start more shit than enough.' She turned around and smiled at Brendan and Lorna. 'You two enjoy your drinks. If you need anything let me know.'

They watched as she left and went back to the bar, weaving in and out of the human traffic.

'You know Johnty Moore and his son?' Brendan took a drink.

'I've worked with British intelligence most of my adult life, Brendan. Of course, I do.' Lorna lifted her drink and looked inside the glass first before taking a drink. 'He was put out of Belfast. A former god in Ulster loyalism fallen from grace.' She spoke mockingly.

'Maybe he's decided to come down here and flex his steroid pumped muscles.' Brendan looked around the pub. The venue was filling up, people were having a normal social gathering. Cornerstone in British culture. A mixture of young and old. The older crowd perhaps desperately trying to hold onto their youth. The younger ones more reckless and adventurous. He took another drink of his coffee and smiled at Louise as she fixed her eyes on him as she wiped down the top of the bar.

'You know she's only trying to sweeten you up?' Lorna said, sounding bitter. 'She could have any guy in here, why'd she give a shit about you?'

Brendan laughed. 'Ouch!' Their attention got dragged away to the other corner of the room where a guy had fallen off his stool for trying, and failing, to hug one of his mates. There was always one in a club that would end up getting kicked out by the bouncers and it looked if it was going to be that group.

'So?' Lorna brought Brendan's attention back to their table. 'What about this scumbag Johnty.'

Brendan looked at her, fighting to contain his expression. 'Do you really need me to tell you what I'm thinking, or can you figure it out for yourself?'

'Maybe I just need some clarification.' She took another drink. 'You probably talked about it to your friends, about how much you, and perhaps most people your age, would do to be given the whereabouts of someone who was responsible for so many innocent lives in Belfast. Now, the most un-likely person in the world,' she gestured to the group of three who were still watching them from the bar. 'Just handed you a winning lottery ticket.' She finished her drink. 'And now, the only thing that's running through your head is – how do you go about cashing in.' She smiled at him. 'Did I miss anything?'

He leaned in and gave her a kiss on the cheek. 'You summed it up perfectly.' He stood up and fixed his jacket. 'I'll be back in a second. I'm going to go ask for a job.' She blew him a kiss. He responded in kind.

As Brendan made his way towards the bar, the manager whom they'd met in the carpark came to the till on Brendan's near side of the bar. He opened the drawer and started taking the cash out. 'Is it wise to do that with so many people around?' Brendan shouted across the bar. The manager didn't look at Brendan, instead keeping his eyes on the cash as he tipped the tray of notes and coins into a navy cloth pocket.

Once all the cash was in the bag, he looked up at Brendan. 'Most people wouldn't have the balls to even attempt it, mate.' He slammed the drawer closed, looking into Brendan's eyes.

'That confidence doesn't come from having a security team like yours. After this morning, we both know they aren't worth the shit wages you pay them.'

'You think you can do better?'

Brendan smiled.

'You're cocky, kid,' the manager shouted. 'What are you after?'

'A job.'

'Here,' the manager handed Brendan a twenty-pound note. 'That's for missing out on the best breakfast in Leicester this morning.'

Brendan refused the money. 'Give it to charity. What about the job?'

The manager smiled and shook his head. 'Come back tomorrow, then we'll talk.'

He offered the manager his hand. 'I'm Brendan.'

The manager respond with a firm grip. 'Richard.'

'I'll see you tomorrow, Richard.'

Brendan turned and spotted the guy who looked like Louise's boyfriend sitting down in Brendan's seat, talking to Lorna but looking at Brendan. If Brendan didn't know any better, he'd think he was trying to wind him up. The guy clearly didn't know that Lorna had impeccable taste and in her eyes, she was way out the guy's league. Brendan turned back to Richard and waved as he made his way back to their seat.

Lorna was looking at her new friend, but he held his stare on Brendan. Brendan got within five feet of the table and the guy stood up from the seat, putting his hand out to shake Brendan's. Brendan responded in kind.

The guy pulled Brendan in close and whispered in his ear. 'She's fit, mate. Watch her close.' Still in the tight handshake, he squeezed Brendan's hand, as if trying to cut off the blood supply. 'Was nice knowing you. Pity we couldn't have got to know each other a bit better.' He spoke sarcastically.

'I'll be back in the morning. Richard is meeting me about a job.' Brendan smiled, as if replacing the guy's facial expression that had now dropped. 'See you tomorrow if you'll be here.' He looked at Lorna and indicated that it was their que to leave.

Chapter Three

BRENDAN TOOK LORNA by the hand, making their way along the road towards the city's Highcross Shopping Centre. It was closed. The rain was falling, not enough to make them run, but certainly heavy enough that they decided to cut through the sheltered shopping outlet that was at that moment serving it's purpose as the abode of the city's homeless. Brendan noticed the guy he'd given the money to that morning, lying up against the shutter of Burton Menswear. His eyes were gazed, not even recognising them.

'You see what happens when you give homeless junkies money,' Lorna said, as she linked arms with Brendan, increasing their distance between them and the homeless guy.

'He would have ended up robbing someone else to get it. Then that victim would have been dragged into this shitty world.' He flicked up his jacket collar and gripped Lorna tightly. The rain was now being thrown down at an angle by some heavier wind.

'So, you made a new friend tonight? What did the manager say to you?'

'His name's Richard. He offered me twenty quid for the mix-up this morning. But I refused. I then told him I'd like to become a part of the door team.'

'You got the job?' Lorna spoke through a giggle, sounding humoured.

'Of course, I don't need the job, that's to my late father,' he cleared his throat. 'But I want to find out more about the boss of this organisation and whether or not Johnty Moore are linked to the organisation.'

'You want to cause problems for the local boss, or for the bastards that brought so much trouble to Belfast?'

'Both.' Brendan reached into his pocket and pulled out the car key. 'What about your new friend?'

Lorna paused. She approached the passenger side, waiting for Brendan to unlock it. 'His name's Charles and he's invited us to a party tonight.' She pulled the door open and got in, adjusting the heating the moment she sat. 'He's given me his contact details.'

Brendan looked at her, he tried to hide it, but the jealousy was written all over his face. 'You gave him your number?'

She laughed. 'I'm not stupid, Brendan, come on. What do you take me for? I searched for his Facebook page. I can contact him via messenger.'

'Send the message.' Brendan started the engine. 'It would be rude to refuse an offer. I'd like to get to know this Charles a bit more anyway.' He put the car in gear and took off.

AFTER A DRIVE THROUGH the city, Lorna finally got the invitation they'd been waiting on. Charles had not taken long to respond. The party was in Quorn, a quiet little village ten miles outside the city. Short for Quorndon, the village was perhaps a more popular destination for retired folk and families who'd said goodbye to the city life and were now ready to trade to concrete jungles of a city and put down roots in an area of more greenery. Not a normal hangout for a group of youngsters, but perhaps much better for them to operate more under the radar. Not mixing their business life in the city with their personal lives in amongst the surrounding green fields.

As they reached the city's outskirts, Brendan put his foot down on the A6 northbound as Lorna played with the radio, finding nothing but the news. BBC East Midlands was talking about a growing issue coming from the city of Leicester. The issue specified an increase in drug crime. According to sources within the local police force, there seemed to be an Asian influence to the increase in gangland crime. And with Ramadan approaching, the city was becoming more tense.

'Looks like the Muslim gangs are taking a piece of the criminal.' Brendan was joking, but something said there was even the slightest possibility of some truth in it.

'They have,' Lorna said. 'We sent our number five and six agents out to find out what they could.'

'And what did they find out?' Brendan slowed the car down to take the roundabout that cut the A6 in half.

'They didn't come back.' She said frankly. 'This will sound strange coming from me, considering what we've been through together…'

He flew up the car's gears. 'Go for it.'

'But Hughes tried to contact your father to send him out after them.' She cleared her throat, stroking her neck. 'When agents five and six didn't come back, we knew the Asian's were on to us, and there was only one man who'd be skilled enough to go over there and come back with something.'

'The Ghost.' Brendan spoke mockingly. He looked at Lorna. 'He was just a normal guy. There was nothing special about him.'

She laughed. 'Not according to his file. If you'd seen the amount of jobs he did. The amount of missions he took on and walked away from successfully. You certainly wouldn't think he was normal.'

Brendan was perhaps the last person that would see his father as anything more than the man whom he'd remembered at home. Damien Cleary. Not *The Ghost*. The family man.

As they approached the next roundabout, Brendan took the first left for Quorn and followed the road along the village high street. The house they'd been invited to sat just off the high-street, nestled in a private estate, a mixture of detached and semi-detached houses, all sporting the traditional British red brick styling.

Guiding the four litre BMW around the grassy roundabout with a playground in the middle, they spotted a group of three teens, all looking no older than twenty. They all wore dark baggy jeans, white Nike trainers and matching hoodies. It was as if they were part of a local team. Perhaps it was the gang uniform. All three stared into the car as it circled them and stopped outside number twelve. It was the only house with lights on. The living room window was wide open. A guy and a girl of similar age to the three hoodies stood at the window from the inside, blowing smoke out through the window as if whoever owned the house didn't want smoke circulating the inside.

Brendan pulled the car up behind a blue Audi that looked as if it had just been pimped out. He shut the engine off and laughed, gesturing towards the private plate.

Lorna looked at him. 'Please tell me you never had a car like that when you were younger?'

Brendan laughed, but didn't respond.

'You did, didn't you?' She teased.

'Piss off.' He opened the door and got out, ignoring the three in the playground, not wanting to give anyone a chance to start any unnecessary conversation. His accent stood out as much as the Audi, and he wanted to remain anonymous as much as possible.

Louise opened the front door, her cheeky smile plastered all over her face. 'Glad you could make it,' she said. The three lads from the playground shouted to Lorna, expressing their gratitude for her presence, in a less than a classy manner. 'Don't mind them. A couple of dicks who can't handle their drink. That's all they are.'

'We were all that age at one point in time,' Brendan said, as he entered the house. It was a narrow hallway with wooden floors and a sickly smell of paint. A black wooden bannister ran the whole way along the red carpet covered staircase to the right. The living room was to the left and the kitchen was at the end. All the doors were open. A low volume track from the British rap scene was being played but could barely be heard over the noise of chatter.

'Don't you get complaints from the neighbours,' Lorna asked, as she stepped inside.

'We own half of the street,' Louise said. 'I own the house next door.' She looked out the front door and pointed at the three at the playground. 'Those three over there own a house each.'

'How did you manage that?' Brendan said just as someone came running down the stairs.

'We put our names down when it was being built.' The guy stopped and eyed Brendan up. 'It's that simple. Nice to see you again, pal.' It was the scrawny of the three guys they'd seen in the pub. The one that likened Brendan to Johnty Moore Jr.

'Same to you, pal.' Brendan spoke with a humorous tone.

'Are you two going to act like adults now and get along?' Louise said. 'You may be seeing a lot of each other from now on, if Brendan here gets himself a job on the door.'

The guy looked at Brendan, his eyes wide, looking reluctant at first, but then he reached his hand out to Brendan. Brendan shook his hand without even a hint of it being genuine. The guy clearly didn't like Brendan. The feeling was mutual. 'I'm Steve.'

'Nice to meet you, Steve,' Brendan said, offering a little more than a civil response. He didn't want to be associated with any of them longer than he had to.

'Good,' Louise said, as she led the way towards the kitchen. 'What do you guys want to drink?' She went straight to the fridge. 'We have beer, alcopop or spirits?'

'Just a coffee for me, please,' Brendan said.

'Same for me.' Lorna added, as she strolled further into the kitchen, towards the window. She looked out into the garden, it looked onto the back of the pub they'd driven past on the main road. Whoever owned the pub would have something to say about the partying they were doing in the house. Logically, it should be the other way around, but that would clearly not be the case in that moment in time. 'I don't know who to feel sorry for, the owners of this house or the people who own and operate the pub,' Lorna said, as Louise excused her way passed to fill the kettle.

'We have a working agreement with the owners,' Louise said. 'We send customers to them, and they send customers to us.'

'So, you're completely open about being involved in the drugs trade?'

'Who the fuck are you, undercover drug squad?' Steve said, leaning against the fridge as if he needed it for support.

'We're not that exciting,' Brendan said. 'I wish we were.'

'You'd be wise not to talk about the people that run that pup, Irish. Trust me.' Steve spoke while focussing on the ground, his eyes scanning everywhere. 'Some nasty people operate that place. Let's just leave it there.'

'Do me a favour, don't call me Irish,' Brendan said. 'And why should I be afraid of them?'

'Because they're bringing something very barbaric to this country.'

Brendan looked at Louise.

'Some nasty, meat-cleaver-wielding Asians,' Louise said. 'And a nasty bunch of bastards they are, too.'

Brendan looked at Lorna, 'yeah we heard something on the news about them.'

Chapter Four

AFTER SPENDING A FEW hours with their newfound friends, Brendan and Lorna bid them a farewell and returned to their hotel in the city centre. Entering number thirty-four on the first floor of the Holiday Hotel, Brendan shut the door behind Lorna. He watched her figure behind as she strolled further into the room, stopping at every step to kick off each heel. Brendan approached her from behind, wrapping his arms around her. She let out a girly giggle as he kissed the side of her neck. She slowly turned to face him, kissing him. She looked into his eyes. He kissed her more passionately, picking her up and walking towards the bed, kicking his own shoes off with each step. His eyes were closed as his lips continued to run up and down the left then right sides of her neck. The lips barely touched her soft skin, but enough to make her entire body tingle with excitement. Once he felt the wooden bed frame come into contact with his shins, stopping him from going any further, he lay her on the bed. Looking down at her, he was still in awe at her beauty. This angel that had walked into his life at a time when he was about to face more turmoil than he'd perhaps be able to cope with himself. Or was she a devil, bringing it all onto him.

'Angel or demon?' He said.

'What?' She looked at him, unbuttoning her blouse.

'Are you an angel that's walked into my life or are you a demon that's brought all this mayhem into my life.'

'What do you want me to be?' She opened her blouse, her firm breasts resting in her black bra. She smiled biting her lower lip. 'I can be either for you.' She sat up and began unfastening his belt.

'A bit of both, I think,' he said, grabbing her face, cupping her head in his massive hands. He kissed her, then looked at her body again.

'Good answer.' She pulled him down on top of her.

BRENDAN'S ALARM WOKE them at five thirty the next morning. He rolled over and switched it off, Lorna complaining about constantly being woken up so early. He kissed her and laughed, telling her to go back to sleep. He got up and had a shower. After standing under the hot shower with his eyes closed trying to think about what the day was going to bring, he eventually stepped out of the cubicle to find the room filled with steam. Wiping the mirror clear, he had a shave, both his face then his head. He stood for a second, looking into his emotionless blue eyes. Then he shifted his gaze down to his bare torso. His six pack a little faded but still visible. He'd always kept himself fit and in shape through regular exercise and proper diet. He then acknowledged the tattoos. The angel on his right shoulder and the demon on his left. They represented for Brendan something much deeper than most people would have recognised. Spending his later teens and early twenties taking drugs and alcohol eventually got it's grasp on him. He then realised he was beginning to follow down the same path as his late father. Therefore, set to do exactly what his father did when he was around Brendan's age – give it all up. Go completely sober. The tattoos were a simple reminder of the man he'd once looked up to. A reminder that everyone has that angel and demon tapping on our shoulders, one tempting, the other guiding away from temptation. His life was far from perfect. He'd been given a lot to deal with in his young life. But one thing he had going for him was the strength to say no. No: a two-letter word. Yet sometimes the most difficult one to say.

He stepped back into the room, Lorna was now lying on her back, her mobile raised in the air to accommodate her gaze.

'Good morning,' she said.

'Is it?' Brendan said sarcastically, as he grabbed his jeans that hung over the desk chair.

'Well, nobody's died, yet. There haven't been any terrorised attacks anywhere. The sun's going to be out today.' She set the phone down on the bedside cabinet and sat up. 'So yes, looks like it's been a good one so far.'

'I'd rather wait to see how breakfast tastes to judge how my day's going to be.' Brendan sat on the edge of the bed. Pulling his jeans on, one leg at a time, he stood up and walked back to the seat that acted like a clothes hanger. He lifted his black T-shirt shook it, dust floating through the early morning sun rays. He fed his arms though the sleeves, then pulled it down over his head, feeling Lorna's lips touch the skin of his abs. The garment dropped over her head as she continued to kiss him. He flipped the chair around and sat on it. She straddled him. Looking deeply into his eyes. Her mahogany eyes sparkled, darting from one eye to the other.

'You should have woken me up to shower with you,' she said, drawing her face in closer to his, the tip of her button nose touched the tip of his. She rotated her head and slowly pressed her lips to the side of his neck.

'I can always come back in with you.'

She lifted her head from his neck. 'Too late,' she said, biting her lip, a cheeky schoolgirl expression on her face. 'Go and get some breakfast. Bring it up to the room. We can have breakfast here before we go get you a job.' She kissed him on the lips and stood up, making her way towards the bathroom. He watched her long slender legs, bare, with nothing but a black thong at the top of them. She turned and looked at him, still wearing that cheeky grin on her face.

He smiled back at her, half turned on and wanting to follow her in. The other half wanting to focus on the task at hand. Knowing Johnty Moore Jnr was in the area, Brendan had a bull's eye target right between the eyes of Jnr, at least strong enough for him to shrug off the temptation for now.

He stepped out into the quiet hallway. The hotel was just beginning to wake up. He could hear faded mumbles of other guests as he passed the room on his way to the lift. He stepped into the lift and pressed the button for the ground floor. Exiting out into the foyer, he stepped over the lead of the floor cleaner. The morning receptionist was just setting up for her shift, the receptionist that Brendan had seen when they came in a few hours earlier was just leaving their night-shift.

As Brendan approached the reception, the lady looked at him, smiling. She had straight blond hair that ran down beyond her shoulders. Her face was fresh and youthful, her wide blue eyes assisted her bright smile in creating a genuine, approachable appearance. Perfect for the first point of contact in a customer service role. Whoever was the hiring manager, got the recruitment right.

'Morning,' she said, sounding fresh, a steaming Starbucks cup in her hand. 'Are you checking out already?'

'Morning,' Brendan said. 'No, I'm after some breakfast. What time does the restaurant open?'

Her curled lips straightened. 'Sorry, love. It's not open until seven thirty. If you can't wait, there's a twenty-four-hour Tesco just around the corner. You can probably get some breakfast from there.'

'Great, I fancy a walk anyway. Some fresh air in the morning will work wonders. Where's the shop?'

'Just go left as soon as you step out of the front door. Cut across the carpark, and you'll find a row of shops. At the end, you'll see it. You'll not miss it, it's huge.'

'Thanks.' He smiled at her and left through the front entrance. He texted Lorna as he crossed the carpark, telling her he'd just gone to the shop for breakfast.

The morning was warm. The sky was a light shade of blue. Early morning traffic queued in the usual places. Red traffic lights turned green but queues of impatient commuters sat in the congestion, almost trying to nudge each other along. The normal life, Brendan considered. It was never meant to be for him. And judging by the look on the faces on some of the people involved in the morning rat race, he was happy it wasn't.

After buying two English breakfasts, Brendan returned to the hotel room. Lorna was sitting at the dressing table, putting on her makeup. But the second Brendan set the breakfast down on the bed, she quickly finished off what she was doing and joined him. Brendan switched on the television while they ate. The news talked about a meeting between the British ministers with local authorities, working closely together in a bid to crack down on the increase in crime in the city of Leicester and other areas in the region.

'Sure,' Brendan said sarcastically, as he cut a sausage and dipped it into the egg yolk. 'They don't give a shit, as long as their pockets are deep and full.'

'True,' Lorna said, making a bacon sandwich with her toast, smothering it with brown sauce. 'But we can't keep attacking heads of government just because we know they're bent.' She cut the sandwich in half and smiled at Brendan as she lifted half of the sandwich. 'Besides, this is what's really important. Proper food.' She took a bite and looked at him, her eyes wide, full of excitement.

Brendan watched her chew slowly. 'How do you manage to make a fry sexy?' They both laughed, sprawled across the king-size bed. 'And you're right.' He looked back up at the TV. 'We were lucky to get away with what we did in London and Belfast. We can't do that again.' He sliced the egg up and took a piece. 'That doesn't mean we stop what we're doing.'

'How about we retire to south America and build a house?' She asked with humour on her voice.

Brendan gestured at the laptop. 'With all that classified information we have? We're in a position to ease the pain for a lot of people by toying with these people. I couldn't enjoy a retirement knowing we had access to that stuff.' He took another piece of egg. 'Besides, my father's training would go to waste.'

'Okay, Batman.' She teased then looked up at the TV, her smile dropping into a frown. 'But can we turn that shit off. We don't need to watch all this.'

Chapter Five

AFTER BREAKFAST, BRENDAN and Lorna killed some time in the city centre. A bit of shopping and exploring the city. They tried to at least act as if they were a normal couple out doing normal things. Brendan bought himself new clothes – a pair of brown leather shoes, dark jeans and a jumper. Lorna took pleasure in fitting herself out with a new wardrobe, too including a few casual garments and a black dress which was made for the Ritz in London. Once they'd searched the retail outlets, they were exhausted and returned the hotel. They dropped their bags off in their room and left for the pub. Brendan had shown his enthusiasm for the job, now he wanted to display his punctuality. Richard was not only the boss of the establishment but also appeared to be a boss that led the darker side of the business. The side that was kept out of the public eye which was the side Brendan and Lorna were more interested in getting to know. Being door security wasn't something Brendan nor Lorna had any interest in pursuing, but needs must when they needed to get closer to the staff.

The time was shortly after midday and the amount of staff was in greater ratio to the number of customers, but the lunchtime rush hour would perhaps flip that around.

Brendan led the way in through the doors, walking past a sign in blackboard chalk advertising a darts night happening later in the evening. As he approached the bar, Louise was stocking the fridges. The moment she clocked eyes on him, her face lit up her eyes as wide as her smile. If she didn't have the hots for him, her expression would certainly lead one to believe that she did.

'Hello, you two,' she said, 'looks like the lads were wrong.'

'What do you mean?' Brendan asked.

'They were of the impression that we'd seen the last of you both last night when you left the party.' She lifted four bottles of coke, stacking them in neat lines along the right side of the fridge's bottom shelf. 'Like we're a little bit too rough around the edges.'

Brendan looked at Lorna, Lorna biting her lip to hide her smile. 'We're back,' Lorna said, as she pulled out one of the stools, perching herself on it.

'You guys want a drink?'

'Coffee, please,' Brendan said, planting himself down on the stool next to Lorna.

'I'll have the same,' Lorna said.

'So, you guys living here now?' Louise said, as she set the first cup under the coffee dispenser. 'You're from the south?' She asked Lorna.

'London. Yeah, I've just been transferred here to our offices just outside the city.' She looked at Brendan. 'That's why he's here, grovelling for a job.' She nudged him with her elbow. 'If he gets a job on the door team, he'll...'

'Improve the door security tenfold.' Brendan butted in. 'I'm looking for a proper full-time job, but a job on the door will do until something else comes along.'

'So, you were on the MMA circuit. Professional?' Louise handed Lorna a coffee.

'Yeah. I turned pro when I was twenty-one. I did it for the love of it, not really for the money. The money was crap anyway. Unless you're Conor McGregor.'

Louise laughed. 'Yeah, but he's more of a business-man.' She handed Brendan a coffee. 'You think you could have taken him?'

Brendan smiled, looking at Louise over the rim of his cup. 'What do you think?'

'I don't know. He's pretty handy with his fists.' She made herself a coffee. 'But the way you handled those guys yesterday. You're no push over either.'

'Him and I come from different worlds now,' Brendan said, sipping from his cup. 'What time does the boss man come in?'

'Richard should already be here,' Louise said. 'He usually sneaks in through the back door. He's a bit of grumpy bastard, unless you can do something for him.'

'Like bring some money his way?' Lorna said.

'Exactly.' Louise laughed.

'Where's his office?' Brendan stood up and finished his coffee.

'Upstairs.' Louise pointed across the room. 'But you can't just go up. It'll piss him off.'

Brendan made his way around the back of the bar. 'I'm going to help him improve his door security.' He smirked. 'He'll be glad to see me.'

Brendan made his way across the room, stepping through the doorway behind the bar, leading him into a narrow hallway. It was dimply lit and served as proof that this part of the building was not given the attention as the customer facing part. Tattered posters celebrating the city's almost impossible premier league win was splattered all over the walls. It was almost as if they ran out of wallpaper and decided to use their dated marketing material instead.

As Brendan got to the top of the stairs, he could hear Richard on the phone, his voice muffled. Brendan stopped at the door, silently trying to listen to the conversation. There was a mention that *the action man* was pissed off at the new arrangement and wasn't willing to negotiate his demands. As he continued to listen, he could hear footsteps from inside, getting closer to the door. Brendan jumped back from the door just as it opened. A look of shock sat on Richard's face seeing Brendan standing there, perhaps analysing how long he'd been there and what he'd heard. He shook his head. 'You're eager, I'll give you that.' He passed Brendan, gesturing for him to go and wait in the office.

Brendan stepped inside. It was the perfect front for a criminal underworld boss, as normal as any office he'd ever seen. A messy desk, with files open: health and safety and food hygiene documents strewn across it. Being nosy, but not so much to give himself away, Brendan strolled around the room, looking at the staff photograph. A recent day out, team building. He took a quick photo, hoping he could perhaps cross reference the photos to Lorna's intelligence data.

As he took the photo, he could hear footsteps coming back up the stairs. Richard's voice accompanied the steps. Brendan lifted the health and safety folder, scanning through it, pretending to show an interest.

Richard stepped into the room. 'You're worried about your own health and safety?'

Brendan set the folder back down on the desk and sat down in the chair. 'Not in the slightest. Should I?'

'You're a cocky little bastard, aren't you?'

'We've already established that.'

'Where does that come from?' Richard said. 'It's one thing to be confident. But you'll go much further and last a lot longer in life if you understand that being humble and putting your head down, will help much more.'

'I came here looking a job,' Brendan said, folding his arms and crossing one leg over the other. 'Not a counselling session.'

Richard laughed, turning his back to Brendan. He reached for a kettle that sat on a tray on top of a filing cabinet. 'You want a drink?'

'Coffee, please.'

Richard put the kettle on to boil and pulled two sachets of power form cappuccino, tipping one into each cup. As the kettle boiled, he poured the water in and stirred. Setting the spoon down on the tray, he lifted two cups. One was black with a cheap slogan scribbled across it. The other was blue and had the Leicester City Football Club's badge on the side. He handed Brendan the football mug.

Brendan took it in one hand and watched as the foam stirred in the cup. He tilted his head and checked out the badge on the side. 'It was an impressive year for the team.'

Richard nodded his head in agreement. 'It was. But the legacy of that incomprehensible achievement will perhaps be tarnished by what's happening on the streets of Leicester now.'

'What do you mean?' Brendan thought he was about to hit the jackpot. Thinking Richard was about to tell him more about the involvement of the criminal wing of their empire, his ears perked up, but he contained his excitement, not wanting to give anything away.

But Richard caught himself and shook his head. 'Never mind.' He took a drink. 'So, you think you can make an improvement on the door, do you?' He smiled, his eyes glazed over.

'I know I can,' Brendan said, seriously. His face straight, his posture in the chair straight and confident.

'You do seem to handle yourself pretty well.' Richard looked down at his mug, as if staring into a crystal ball. 'But being able to handle yourself in a fight and having balls to tackle someone with a knife are two different things, Brendan. Louise has told me you're a cage fighter.' He cleared his throat. 'I'm sure you're quite skilled in the ring. Or cage. But as I say, these streets are...'

'I'm pretty sure I can handle them.' Brendan was quick to assure him.

'Is your stay here permanent?'

Brendan shrugged his shoulders. 'If the missus's job keeps her here, then yes.'

Richard looked at him, swivelling a few inches to each side in his chair. 'Okay, we can give you a shot. Would you be able to start tomorrow?'

'You mean I'm going to give you a shot to see if I want to work for you?' Brendan smiled. He was joking, and hoped

Richard was able to pick up on it. He did. He stood up and offered his hand to Brendan. Brendan accepted.

'I'll look forward to working with you.' Richard pat Brendan on the shoulder. 'Can I buy you and that lovely girl-friend of yours breakfast?'

'We've already eaten, but thanks. Another time.'

Chapter Six

THE REST OF THE DAY was spent looking for an apartment. Lorna had fallen in love with the tiny village of Quorn. Brendan had wanted to be close to those druggies and the pub they lived behind. If that bar was the local hangout he wanted to float around, perhaps with the hope of finding more information on the whereabouts of Johnty Moore Jnr. He felt he was handed a winning lottery ticket when he was described as being like Moore Jnr. He should have been offended. But he wasn't. He'd found a way to kill two, or possibly 3 birds – if his father was around also – with one stone.

They found a place they'd like to look at and made an appointment with the estate agent for the next day, before Brendan's first shift was due to begin. They decided that if they were going to be in England longer than a few days, then perhaps it was better to find somewhere to at least set down roots, even temporarily.

Brendan wanted to go further afield. Perhaps Italy or Spain. Lorna wanted to go even further, like the other side of the Atlantic.

After arranging the viewing, they both strolled through the Highcross shopping centre, hungry and feeling at a crossroads to where they were going to eat.

'Maccy D's?' Brendan suggested.

'I'm not really a fan of McDonalds,' Lorna said. 'How about Chinese? There's a nice-looking place just around the corner.'

Brendan shrugged his shoulders. 'I'd eat anything.'

'You're a man, of course you would,' Lorna said, as she led the way towards the exit.

As they entered the restaurant, they were greeted by a young Asian lady, perhaps in her mid-twenties, wearing an oriental style dress, her hair as black as the broach she wore on her left side. She directed them to a two-seater table by the window. A middle-aged couple sat at the table next to them, looking like the kind of couple that had forgotten how to talk to each other. They were there more out of habit than of genuinely wanting to be spending time with each other.

Lorna looked at the couple. 'Promise me, we'll never end up like that.' She sat and pulled her seat in underneath her.

Brendan looked over his shoulder at them as he sat down but didn't stare. He just regarded them and turned back to Lorna again. 'They look bored, that's what's done that.' He grabbed a menu from the stand in the centre of their table. 'You see how he was looking at his plate? He should be looking at her that way.' He looked at the menu then back up at Lorna. 'We'll never be like that.'

'How can you be sure?'

'Because boredom is clearly what's caused the spark they once had for each other go out. We don't have that problem. Our lives aren't exactly dull, either. No chance of boredom setting in anytime soon.'

Lorna smiled and looked at her menu. 'Perhaps you're right.'

'Perhaps I'm right?' He laughed. 'We've got so much shit going on in our lives, we'd be safer to slow down a bit.'

Brendan was right. It couldn't last. How could it? Their lives were not normal, and never would be until they decided to go into hiding. With all the cash they had at their disposal, it would be easy. But the people they were, or at least had become, perhaps moulded, reshaped by recent events, were exactly the people the couple next to them wasn't.'

'What can I get you guys?' the lady said. 'Anything to drink while you choose from the menu?'

'I'll have a coke, please,' Brendan said.

'Can I have a sprite?'

The lady nodded and hummed. 'I'll bring them over. Have a look at the menus.'

Brendan glanced at the menu, but he already knew what he was having. He smiled and just set the menu back down.

'Your usual, king prawns with fried rice?' Lorna's eyes momentarily jumped up from the menu, her tiny slits sizing Brendan up. He just smiled and nodded his head. 'You're so predictable.'

'I like what I like.'

She grinned and nodded her head. She set the menu down and looked up at him. 'Be predictable is dangerous. Especially after what we did in Belfast.'

'Dimitru and his crew deserved everything they got.' Brendan's eyebrows came together, the muscles in his face tightening. He looked at his phone and checked BBC News. 'The people who'd been suffering at their hands will have the last laugh.'

The waitress came back with their drinks. She handed Lorna hers. Then Brendan his. 'You guys ready to order or do you need more time?'

'King prawns with fried rice please.' Brendan was quick to say.

'Can I have the same, please?'

'Sure. Anything else?'

Brendan looked at Lorna, she nodded her head. 'That's it. Thanks.'

'It will be about twenty minutes.'

Lorna smiled, 'Perfect.'

Chapter Seven

AFTER THEIR MEAL, THEY both sat, allowing the food to digest. Brendan had remembered the pub from Quorn. He had a feeling they'd seen it before. Or for some reason he knew there was something about it that was drawing him to it. Then he remembered what Stefano Botticelli had mentioned it. A place his father had stayed when the late Damien Cleary came to Leicester in search of Paolo Indino.

'What's on your mind?'

'The pub, in Quorn.'

'What about it?'

'My father stayed there when he came here in search of Indino.'

She thought for a second. Her expression quickly livened up, all the white of her eyes visible. 'That's right. God, how'd I not realise that. Within intelligence, obviously I was still working with them at the time, word circulated that your father was attacked by a couple of young dealers who were selling coke at the time in the area, but when they attacked your father outside in the pub's darkened car park, they quickly came to regret it.'

'What do you mean?'

'One of them pulled a knife on your father, but ended up with it in the side of his neck, bleeding out on the ground with your father looking over him, not cursing the guy, but more cursing the people that they'd worked for, who sent the lads down the road, directing them into his company. A bad idea. But they weren't to know how dangerous your father was.'

'Good old dad.' Brendan spoke sarcastically. 'How many people died at his hands?'

'Countless,' Lorna said. 'But don't forget, they died at the hands of the man your father became, at the hands of the British government.' She poured herself a glass of water from the frosty jug and took a sip. 'Anyway, let's not talk about them.' She smiled at him. 'You excited to start your new job?'

'It'll be fun, I'm sure.' He said sarcastically.

'We'll need to get you a uniform.'

'May as well do that now.'

Chapter Eight

AFTER THEY WENT INTO Next and bought Brendan a pair of black trousers, shiny black leather shoes and a couple of plain white shirts, they went back to the hotel and rested. They'd received an invitation to a party that evening by Louise and a couple of her friends, however, neither Brendan nor Lorna were in the mood to go. Instead they went for a swim in the hotel's pool and spent an hour in the health suite, jumping from the sauna to the steam room.

Finishing a bottle of water, replacing the liquids she'd just released through her pores, Lorna nudged Brendan. 'You're quiet.'

'I'm thinking about Diana and Teodoro.'

Lorna moved onto the bench on Brendan's side of the steam room and kissed him on the cheek. 'They're okay. Try not to think about them. We've given them a new chance at life. Better than they could have possibly dreamed of having had they stayed with Dimitru.'

'Yeah but I could have...'

Lorna pressed her finger across Brendan's lip. Then she moved in, replacing her index finger with her lips. They kissed for a few moments. He ran his finger through her hair and pulled her over onto his lap. Nothing but skimpy underwear shielded her private parts. He began to kiss her neck, travelling down her neck onto her chest.

Lorna looked at him, smiling cheekily. 'Ever made love in a public place?'

'Like a sauna?' He grinned, as he untied her bra from the back, releasing her perky breasts. 'There's a first time for everything.'

After one hour, they returned to their room and showered together again. Brendan was much more relaxed than he had been when they'd went for a swim.

'Sex really does loosen up tense muscles.' Lorna joked as she mounted him on the bed. 'You feel better?'

'I'm just eager to find out if that bastard Moore Jnr and his old man are running around with these scumbags. If he is, I'm going to send their heads back to Belfast.'

'If they are working with local organised crime, why wouldn't your father have taken them out when he was here?'

'Maybe he didn't know. He's very good at staying focussed. And if Indino was his sole focus, then everything else would have simply been blocked out.'

'We'll soon find out.' Lorna grabbed a purple silk robe and pulled it on over her naked body. 'Just so you know, I'm coming to watch you work. I don't want some little skanks flirting with you.'

'I thought you were more confident than that?' Brendan stood up, pulling her in close to him. 'There isn't a lady alive as beautiful as you are.'

She wrapped her arms around him and whispered in his ear. 'I'd better make sure your pretty blue eyes remain only for me.' She kissed him softly. 'I love you, Brendan.'

'I love you, too. More than life itself.'

They were interrupted by Brendan's phone sounding.

He grabbed the phone and looked at the number. A mobile number but he didn't recognise it. 'Hello?' He said, as Lorna continued to kiss his neck.

'Brendan, it's Richard. I know you're not due to start work until tomorrow night, but we have a bit of a staffing issue this evening.' Richard said. 'I don't suppose you could start tonight? One of our guys has phoned in sick and has let us down. Can you help at all?'

Brendan closed his eyes, embracing the sensation of Lorna's soft lips still on his neck. He paused for a moment.

'Brendan are you there?'

'I'll see you in thirty minutes.'

'Nice one, mate. You're a life saver. We'll pay you double time for it.'

'Good. See you soon.'

'Cheers, mate.'

Brendan ended the call and dropped the phone down on the bed beside him. He sighed, as Lorna's lips began to make their way back up his neck towards his face.

'Tell me you're not going in to work tonight?'

'I could say that, but I'll never lie to you.'

She groaned. 'Okay. Well, let's get dressed then.'

'You don't have to go. You can stay here and keep the bed warm for me coming back.'

'No chance. What if something happens?' She got off the bed. 'Where you go, I go. Together, remember?'

'Are you worried in case I get involved with another woman, or if I get into a fight and don't know how to get out of it?' He tossed a pillow at her as she stood over him, enticing him with her slender figure. Her perky breasts made the thought of leaving the hotel room much less appealing to him. She looked at him, tilting her head. 'You're really sexy. I mean, look at you...how the hell did I land a lady so beautiful...and classy.'

She smiled, showing all her teeth. 'You're such a flatterer.' She stepped off the bed. 'But it's nothing to do with the local ladies, *or* your ability to handle yourself. But after what happened in Italy, we should be together always. She fastened the silk robe around her. She stood alongside him. 'I don't ever want to lose you, sweetheart. What we're doing is very dangerous. And I can understand both of our reasons for taking down as many of these scumbags as possible.' She paused, her eyes darting from his left to the right. 'But not at the expense of either of our lives.'

'After this, we're going to take a long holiday. It's definitely overdue.'

'I agree.' She turned and made her way towards the ensuite. 'Now come and join me in the shower. I want to loosen you up before you go to work.'

Chapter Nine

LORNA DROVE, BRENDAN had responded to the call that he'd missed when they went for the shower. It was Stefano Botticelli calling to find out if they'd managed to stay out of trouble since what happened in Italy.

'How's our friends who've seen the light?' Lorna spoke mockingly. 'Has he joined the cloth?'

Brendan sniggered, his eyes glued to the phone. 'Stefano Botticelli, a priest?' He laughed. 'I think he'd probably burst into flames if he put the robes on.' He finished his text and locked the phone. 'But if it weren't for him, we'd both probably be dead.'

'You don't owe him a dame thing, Brendan.' Lorna's tone became more aggressive. She reached across him and opened the glove compartment, pulling out a Sig Saur, cradled nicely, dangling from it's brown leather holster. 'And that's exactly what this kind of people try to do. They do something nice for you, thinking they've got you in their grasps, then they'll exploit you for whatever they want.' She looked at him. 'Luckily you're not like the rest of the people who's gotten involved with them.' She turned back to the road as she negotiated the car through the city's one-way system. Pulling up outside the pub, they witnessed an altercation at the entrance. Three youngsters, dressed in short sleeved checked shirts and stonewash jeans were all stood defensively, delivering some verbal abuse to the door staff.

Brendan looked at Lorna and laughed. 'Looks like we're going to be in for an interesting night.' He reached into the back of the car and grabbed their jackets.

Lorna shut the engine off and took her coat from Brendan. She dressed herself with the holster first, then put the long leather coat on to cover up the weapon. She looked at Brendan. 'I'm not taking my eyes off you tonight. We can't trust these people. And let's be honest, they'd be stupid to trust us, too.'

'I don't think they trust us, they see me as their lap dog that will tear through people like those three over there.' He gestured towards the entrance. Two of them were yelling at the single doorman, while the third was looking at his phone, perhaps calling for backup.

Brendan stepped out of the car, slamming the door behind him, signalling their arrival. The single doorman and the three looked around. Brendan met their gaze while fixing his jacket. He approached the entrance, and the three's confidence in their numbers slowly began to disappear.

As they approached the entrance, Louise came out, as if to back up the doorman. She looked at Brendan and Lorna as they approached.

'The three of you need to fuck off now, before you get regret it,' Louise said, her arms folded, as if in guard of the door.

'What's happening?' Lorna said, as she overtook Brendan, looking as if she wanted to take on the role.

'Who the fuck are you, sweet cheeks?' The one on the phone said, looking Lorna up and down then back as his two mates. 'I'd let her beat seven shades of shit out of me, any day.' He turned back to Lorna and blew her a kiss.

'Watch your mouth, mate,' Brendan said.

'Do you know I am?' He walked up to Brendan, blanking Lorna.

'I don't a shit a shit who you are, pal. Unless you want to be on your way to A and E to get your toothless gums looked at, you'll take you're two amigos over there,' Brendan looked at the other two, 'and disappear before I embarrass the three of you.'

The guy pulled a knife out. 'Fuck you, paddie,' he stepped up to Brendan, knife by his side. 'You've got some balls...'

Brendan cut the guy's sentence short by spearing his hand into his throat, cutting off the circulation and knocking him out. He dropped to his knees, then face first into the ground. Brendan looked at the other two. Both had quietened down, as if their courage his disappeared along with their friend's consciousness.

'First night on the job and you're already making friends,' Louise said.

'Now you two, take your mate, and fuck off.' The bouncer yelled in the face of the one who'd looked as if he wanted to take the bouncer on.

'Come on in, you two,' Louise said, gesturing for Brendan and Lorna to follower her inside. 'Richard wants to brief you, Brendan on what's kicked off down here.'

Brendan turned and looked at the guy he'd just knocked out, being assisted to his feet by his two mates. He handed the knife to the door man. 'I think I can pretty much sum up what's happened.' He gestured to the knife as the doorman handed it to Louise. 'I'd get that thing disposed of. It's probably got someone's DNA on it.'

'We don't deal with the police here.' The doorman said. 'We deal with the shit on the street ourselves.'

'Fair enough, either way, if these guys are part of a gang, I'd be closing these doors and asking for more help over the weekend.' Brendan turned and followed Lorna and Louise inside.

As they stepped through the entry, the warm air and odour of stale ale almost sent them back out the door again.

'Where's your boyfriend and his mates?' Brendan said.

'Steve's not my boyfriend,' Louise said, as she stood holding the inner door open for them to enter. The noise of the pub made communication almost impossible. Unless they wanted a sore throat.

Lorna spotted the guy in question, hanging over the bar, his two mates beside him. The three turned and watched as Brendan and Lorna made their way across the bar, weaving in and out of the sporadically placed groups of two, three, four, and five. A mixture of old and young, male and female, were the evening patrons of the establishment.

'Here he is,' Steve shouted. 'You look nice in your uniform don't you.' He teased. His two mates laughed.

Lorna kissed Brendan on the cheek. 'He's fucking gorgeous, isn't he?' She shouted, 'and the fact he could mop the floor with you three twats, is the reason why he doesn't need to say a word.' She gave the three of them the finger. Steve laughed and blew her a kiss.

From the other end of the bar, Richard appeared from the back, looking stressed, scruffy – his tie loosened from his neck and twisted, his sleeves rolled up, his shirt more yellow than white, pulled out from the waist of his black trousers. He waved them to come over.

Louise led the way, following Richard into the back. Brendan, then Lorna followed. They all went up to the office on the first floor, where Brendan had been the day before.

As they got to the top of the stairs, Lorna produced her weapon as if they were about to walk into something. Arriving at the doorway to the office, Brendan stood, blocking Lorna's way in.

'Come on in, Brendan,' Richard said. 'Thanks for coming in.'

'As long as you're paying. It's a job, right?' Brendan spoke casually, walking in with his hands in his pockets. He stood in the middle of the room, watching Louise on her knees with her head stuck inside the safe in the corner.

'That's right. But I might have a bit of extra work for you, Brendan.' He turned and looked at Louise. 'You got them?'

'Got them.' Louise groaned, getting back up to her feet again. Two silver pistols sat in her hands. 'Brendan, now's your time to walk away from this company.' Louise took the attention of the room, as if she were the boss.

'You think this is the first time I've seen a gun?' Brendan laughed. He looked at Lorna. 'I'm feeling like a child again.'

'We know who you are, Brendan Cleary,' Louise said. She handed Richard the weapons, and sat on the edge of the desk, folding her arms. 'Those guys outside...' She cleared her throat. 'They've been sent here by someone, trying to muscle in on our territory. We know you come from a family whose seen a lot of bloodshed, Brendan.'

'More than any of you lot could ever imagine.' Brendan spoke sharply, imitating Louise's body language.

'That's why we know,' Louise looked at Lorna, then back to Brendan, 'neither of you are going to run to the authorities. Not when you're both still considered public enemies 1 and 2. And it just happens that you've come into our lives when we're attracting far too much attention from the wrong people.'

Richard took over. 'It's not as if either of you can just go and get normal jobs.' He ejected the magazine from the handle of one of the pistols, checked it, and slid it back in again. 'If you want to earn some money,' he handed the gun back to Louise. 'You two can earn more money in the next week than you'll be able to earn in the next ten years.'

'Doing what?' Lorna said. She sat on the edge of the desk, next to Brendan, mirroring his posture.

'We have a plan to shatter someone else's plan to take us out,' Louise said.

Richard continued. 'Brendan, Lorna – we've got a group of good lads working for us. But, seeing the way you made those three look like children out in the carpark, was not only embarrassing, but highlighted we need better people working for us, stop us all getting fucking killed.'

Louise stood up off the desk and turned to face the wall behind the desk. She pointed at the framed photo. 'The guy in that photo, that's my father.' She walked around the desk and lifted it. 'He was making a lot of money. A very wealthy man.' She kissed the tip of her index finger and pressed it onto the glass. She then set it down again. 'But this life has taken him too soon. Stupid bastard was stingy with his money and didn't hire good help. Instead, he hired a bunch of wannabe hard men who were more interested in getting high than actually making some money.' She looked at Brendan, then Lorna. 'This is my business, and I want the proper people working with me. Not people that are going to run a mile when it starts to get real. And what I mean by real is...'

'I think we can guess what you mean,' Lorna said.

Chapter Ten

'SO, HAVE I PASSED THE test, then?' Brendan said, looking at Richard, who was looking towards Louise. 'I'm guessing you're the one running things in here, then?'

Richard shook his head and nodded towards Louise.

'I've taken over from my father's business.' Louise spoke with confidence in her words. An unshakable self-assurance. She certainly was not what either Brendan or Lorna had imagined when they'd first met her. 'I'm interested in building a team of loyal people, who will be rewarded for their services.'

Lorna laughed. 'Christ, you make it sound like a real job. Should I send you my CV?'

'No, it's fine.' She smiled. 'I'm a good judge of character. I can tell you're both of good stock.'

'Okay, what's about to kick off tonight?' Brendan said. 'If those clowns that I met outside are part of a rival gang, then there's a good chance they'll be coming back. And I don't want to be standing on the front door with the possibility of being involved in a drive-by.'

'We operate the bar as normal,' Richard said. 'We don't let the bastards effect the business. But we've got ideas of where we can find a few of their informants.'

'Where?' Lorna said. 'Leicester's not London. Everyone knows everyone in a small city like this.' She looked at Brendan. 'More like Belfast.'

'It's funny you should mention Belfast,' Louise said. 'Look at this.' She walked around the desk, taking the seat behind the monitor. She tapped on a few keys and swivelled the screen around.

Brendan stood up. Looking at the screen, his eyes almost popping out of their sockets. 'You dirty bastard.' He looked at Lorna, then back at the screen again. 'Billy Moore.'

'You know him?' Louise said.

'That bastards been responsible for the lives of countless innocent Catholics on the streets of Belfast.'

'Yes, and even his own side got sick of his bullshit and put him out of the city.' Lorna added.

'He's got some very nasty connections in these parts,' Louise said. She looked back at the screen and tapped a few more keys. 'And this piece of shit tried it on with me a few weeks ago.'

Brendan grinned, shaking his head. 'Well, when you grow up in Belfast, and your dad's Billy Moore, you can pretty much get away with whatever you want.' His face straightened and he clenched his jaws. 'He's Billy Moore Jnr.'

'And you're the notorious Brendan Cleary.' Louise spoke amusingly, a far cry from the lady that had taken control of the conversation a moment ago. She looked up at Brendan, then at Lorna. 'And you're the former MI5 agent, Lorna Woodward.'

'You're definitely surprising,' Lorna said. She looked at Brendan, then sat back down on the edge of the desk. 'You're not stupid, are you?'

'No, I'm definitely not,' Louise said. 'I knew when you two walked into this pub, you'd both somehow play an important role in what we're about to do.'

'And what are you about to do?' Brendan said.

'We're about to go to war with the group that's being led by this piece of shit. Britain First meets former UDA leader. That bastard is responsible for my father's death. Now he's trying to muscle in on our territory.' Louise looked at Brendan and Lorna.

Brendan stepped behind Louise and brought up the image of Billy Moore again. 'Nobody but me gets their hands on him.' He looked at Richard, then Louise. 'And I'll help you take out this entire group.'

'Great.' Louise smiled. Standing up, she extended her hand out to shake Brendan's. 'Welcome to the family.'

'I've got to go and help out on the floor, it's getting busy down there.' Richard shouted, as he looked at the CCTV monitors. He pulled the door open and left the office.

Louise handed her pistol to Brendan, but he raised his hand in refusal. 'I've got my own.'

'Is this the famous pistol of Damien Cleary?'

It was unsettling how much Louise knew about Brendan's background. He wasn't happy about it. But he was now close to being the person who'd exact revenge for many innocent lives that were lost on the streets of Belfast.

'You need help in the bar?' Lorna said.

'Have you pulled pints before?'

'It got me through university.'

Louise's phone rang. She answered it. With the smartphone pressed to her ear, she walked back to the computer. She shut it down and smiled. 'Great. I'll see you there. We'll be about half an hour, forty-five minutes.' She hung up. 'Change of plan. How'd you pair like to join me on a night out? My treat. We can get to know each other a bit better.'

'Where?' Brendan said.

'Nottingham. There's a nightclub called Black and White. A friend of ours has been keeping an eye on one of Moore's mates, and he's just walked into the VIP room, walking around like he owns the place.'

'It's been a long time since I was last in a nightclub,' Brendan said.

'Who's your informant?' Lorna asked. 'Informants are the least trustworthy people you could work with.' She folded her arms, as if she'd gone back into agent mode. 'It could be a trap, if they're feeding information to Moore, too.'

'He has no reason to side with Moore,' Louise said. She walked around to the back side of the desk and lifted her grey coat. She swung it around her back, inserting her left arm, then the right. Flicking down the collar, she looked at the photo of her father. A sinister look flashed across her face. She was certainly a far cry from the lady they'd met. 'You guys want to come or stay here? There's a substantial amount of money to be rewarded if you help us.'

Brendan looked at Lorna. 'We'll come. And as long as I can get my hands on the two Moores, then that's all I want.'

'Great. Let's go.' Louise marched passed them towards the door, slotting her pistol inside her handbag.

Brendan turned and watched her leave. He looked at Lorna. 'Bet you're glad you came to work with me now?'

'Come on, handsome. Let's go clubbing.' Lorna followed Louise out.

Brendan followed. As he approached the door, he spotted a group of six monitors behind the door. One of them was displaying Richard behind the bar. He was emptying the till drawers into a bag. Brendan took this as strange. A little too early. He closed the door and headed down the stairs. Entering the bar, the room was packed. Groups of people were scattered throughout the main room.

The moment he walked along the side of the bar, Brendan met Richard's gaze. He was smiling, but the expression lacked sincerity.

'What's with the early cash up?' Brendan said to Louise, as he joined them outside. 'Isn't it a bit early to be closing the tills?'

'We've been expecting company the last few nights,' she said, leading them towards a black Mercedes parked in one of the staff parking spaces to the right of the door. 'Moore has employed a tax man to do the rounds.' She pulled a key out of her coat pocket and pointed it at the car, unlocking it. 'One of his ex UDA colleagues in Belfast, is quite notorious for being a deadly man. A hitman who takes new meaning to the word evil.'

'Davy English?' Brendan said. He pulled open the front passenger seat and got in. Lorna got in the back. Louise got behind the wheel. 'He was Moore's number one hitman. Wherever Moore pointed his steroid pumped, tattooed index finger, that bastard would send a bullet.' Brendan fastened his seatbelt.

'From where MI5 was concerned, he did more than fire bullets,' Lorna said, shuffling around in her seat. 'He was the one who worked as a butcher on the Shankill?'

Brendan nodded. 'Yes. He liked to carve people up.' He cleared his throat as Louise started the engine. 'He'll not be doing any more of that.'

'Not if he's still involved with Moore. I'll personally chop the bastards balls off.' Louise spoke calmly, as if unphased by the words that came out of her mouth.

'You've got a face butter wouldn't melt in your mouth, Louise,' Lorna said. 'You talk a good game.' She folded her arms. 'Let's see if you walk the walk as well.' She pulled her pistol out of her handbag and checked it was loaded.

Brendan seen this as Lorna perhaps being a little nervous. Given the fact she'd already checked the weapon. Either that or she was indirectly showing Louise she wasn't going to instil any fear in either of them. Either way, whatever her methods, innocent or not, it left an awkward silence in the car as Louise fitted her smartphone to the centre console and thumbed in the postcode to the club. Brendan put the window down to let some of the city's nighttime atmosphere in.

The noise of people on the streets, shouting, cars tooting and driving by all helped kill the tension until Louise put on the radio.

'This might be a stupid question, but does the Moore clan or any of it's associates know you, Brendan?' Louise said.

She looked in the rear-view mirror. 'Or you, Agent Woodward?'

'They know the Brendan Cleary who looked like a fucking caveman, with long hair and a beard that covered everything but my eyes.' Brendan looked at Louise. 'They wouldn't recognise me now.'

'Not the handsome devil you are now then?' She said. 'What about you?' She repeated her question to Lorna.

'The waist length blondie who'd worked in British intelligence was washed down the shower drain along with the hair I'd trimmed off.'

'You're much hotter with short black hair, anyway,' Louise said. She looked at Brendan briefly then turned her gaze back to the road. 'If I was a lesbian, I'd definitely fuck you.'

Lorna exploded into a fit of laughter, as did Brendan.

'You're such a flatterer,' Lorna said sarcastically. 'Like I said, I hope it's not all talk.'

'I could say the same to you pair.' Louise brought the car to a gradual stop at a set of traffic lights.

'I've got nothing to prove.' Brendan sighed, folding his arms. He was getting the impression that the journey to Nottingham, although only a thirty-minute journey, was going to be a long one.

Chapter Eleven

ELEVEN TWENTY-FIVE, they'd reached the club. Black and White was a swanky joint that looked better suited to the upper middle-class who perhaps spend the evening sipping one glass of wine over dinner. But the queue outside the venue, said something else. Underdressed females, with skirts that left nothing to the imagination, and men who looked better suited to a football hooligan setting – stonewash jeans, bright white trainers and zip-up hoodies.

Louise parked the car along the road directly outside. Two cars away, a male was crouched down, leaning on a car bonnet, his dinner was now being worn on his jeans, the rest of it was on the ground.

'There's our friend.' Louise gestured to the front of the queue. A tall thin male with an Asian complexion was waving them to come over. 'Let's go.'

They got out of the car, and walked over to the front, passing a queue of twenty to thirty waiting to be granted access. They drew some aggressive looks from those who'd perhaps been standing there for a while.

'That's why you don't go out dressed in almost nothing,' Lorna said, 'you could be standing out in the cold for long enough to give nipple pleasing access.'

'That's right,' Louise laughed. 'Sam,' she reached out her hand to shake hands with the Asian guy who'd looked like anything but a Sam. 'Thanks for your call.'

'Good to see you again,' Sam said. 'How's the lovely Louise doing?'

'I'm good.'

'I see you've got re-enforcements with you tonight.' He looked at Brendan, then Lorna. 'What happened the other guys?'

'Needed an upgrade.'

Sam laughed, reaching his hand out to shake Brendan's 'Suhag, but everyone calls me Sam.'

'Brendan.' He gripped Sam's hand, receiving a dry, cold texture. 'Nice to meet you.'

'You're Irish,' his eyebrows narrowed, he looked at Louise. 'He's not part of...'

'I've got fuck all to do with Moore,' Brendan stopped him mid-sentence. 'We just happen to be from the same city.'

There was an awkward silence, Louise cleared her throat. She looked at Brendan. 'Come on, handsome.' She pulled him by the cuff, leading the way towards the door security. Little more than a quick nod of the head was needed to grant them the access they needed.

Brendan reached back a felt for Lorna as he followed Louise in the door. She linked her fingers with his as they entered the club. The doors opened. The heavy bass could alter even the fittest person's heart rate.

Brendan felt Lorna grip his hand tighter as they made their way through the middle of the club. The music was a mix of noughties club trance, with some contemporary spin on it, strobe lights zapping all around the room, in and out of their vision.

Louise looked over her shoulder, at Brendan, then passed him to Lorna. Her cheeky grin came across off-putting, perhaps reckless, like she didn't care about the consequences of her actions. She turned and made her way passed the bar, through a set of double doors manned by two bouncers almost as big the doors. One of them, a black guy who looked like he was ready to step right onto a bodybuilding stage, smiled at her and let her in before she had a chance to speak.

Brendan gripped Lorna's hand from behind him again and nodded at the bouncers as they followed Louise on through. The bouncers closed the door, and the music disappeared back into the main dance hall. They were in an emergency exit: a long corridor, with green walls and a red carpet. Fifteen yards down the corridor, the door was open, light and shadows spilled out into the hallway.

The bouncers opened the doors and Sam stepped in from the dance hall. 'Go on in.'

Louise stepped inside. Brendan and Lorna followed. They were in a darkened room. Lights were on, but they were very dim. Along the left wall, was a mahogany bench, with a cluster of monitors, each showing a different location in the club.

Brendan looked around the room, it was a typical security hut, too warm and not enough light, perfect for falling asleep in.

'Make yourselves comfortable, get ready to watch the show,' Louise said. She grabbed one of the office chairs and wheeled it towards the bench, paying attention to the one marked – VIP.

'Our VIP is just being brought in now by one of the bar girls,' Sam said, sitting down beside Louise, crossing his left leg over the right. 'He's been acting quite the big man.'

'Not for long,' Louise said, chewing on her thumb nail, her eyes almost cutting holes onto the screens.

Brendan looked two monitors to the left. He stepped up to the bench, crouching down, looking into the screen. A tall, slender lady, around the same age as Lorna – mid to late twenties – was making her way, tall and confidently through the crowd. In spite of the lady's true beauty, Brendan was more interested in who the male was. And it confirmed what Louise had been saying so far: Davy English was there, in the club. In the same club as Brendan. He turned and looked at Lorna, then at Louise. 'Here's the bastard.'

Lorna stepped closer to the screen and crouched down to look. 'It is, too.' She stood up. 'He's fatter than he was on the documents MI5 have on file. Obviously since he went into hiding, with Moore and the rest of his clan, he was harder to keep track of, but I'd recognise that fat head anywhere.'

They both stood and watched as he was led into the VIP room, jumping from the screen they were looking at, to the one Louise was still sitting gawking at.

In her seat, waiting for the blockbuster to start, Louise said, 'have a seat.'

Lorna and Brendan both ignored her, and moved closer to that monitor, staying on their feet.

Through the monitor, they could see English, being pushed down onto a cream leather sofa, with the lady straddling him. She moved in for a kiss, and as they both grew more intimate, a group of three Asian guys could be seen entering the room, their expression much too serious to be in for a lap dance. Without any sound from the monitors, it would have been difficult to understand the language, or the atmosphere in the room, but the reaction from English the moment he clocked eyes on the three, was enough to compensate for the lack of sound.

The dancer jumped off his lap, and English found himself seated alone, his hands in the air as two of the three new arrivals had pistols pointed at him. The third pulled his phone out of his pocket, hit a few buttons, and pressed it to his ear.

Sam's phone rang and he answered in Arabic. He quickly said a few words, then hung up again. Simultaneously, the guy in the video dropped his phone back into his pocket.

English was on his feet, shouting, pointing his finger at the two, probably delivering threats which would usually come from someone with his connections. But the three were not fazed by the response they've received.

'Let's go,' Louise said, standing up and making her way towards the emergency door. Brendan followed her, an extra spring in his step. Lorna cleared her throat and accompanied Sam out after Brendan and Louise.

A cold, concrete stairway led them down to a below ground level, towards another evacuation door. Louise thumped on the door. After a few muffled words from the other side, it opened. One of the three males they'd watched popped his head out.

'Alright sexy!' He looked at Louise, grinning like a cheshire cat. 'Got a little surprise for...'

'Shut your mouth and move out of the way.' Louise cut him off, pulling the door open. She stepped around him, into the room.

Brendan followed, then Lorna, and finally Sam. The door was closed.

Brendan and Lorna both stood at the door. Sam and Louise stepped further into the room.

'You stupid bitch, you know what's going to happen to you if you fuck with me?' English's Belfast accent sounded broader than normal, which usually happened when a voice was raised in anger.

'Less of the crying, don't panic.' Louise spoke through a sigh. 'We're not going to kill you. Haven't made that decision yet.' She sat down on the seat and crossed her right leg over her left. 'Where's Moore, and his pain in the ass son, who're running around the midlands starting more wildfires that the Australian outback.'

He laughed and sat back down on the sofa facing her. He looked straight at Brendan, not recognising his new appearance, shaven head and bearded. He then looked at Lorna, and back at Louise again. 'You know who Moore's in tight with now.' He tried to sound confident, imitating Louise's relaxed posture, almost a mirror image. But his trembling vocal cords would lead one to believe something else. He cleared his throat and shuffled in his chair.

Sam sat down next to him on the sofa. He pulled out a flick knife, throwing it open. He ran the blade down English's cheek. 'With this I'd like to just cut the eyes out of this piece of Irish shit. Fucking paddy.'

'Check your use of language, friend,' Brendan said. 'I don't like this piece of shit any more than you do but mention anything Irish again and you and I are going to have problems.'

Sam looked up and Brendan, raising his hands. 'My apologies.'

'Who the fuck does this guy think he is?' the guy who opened the emergency door to let them in said. 'You better check your tone, mate.' He squared up to Brendan, his gun clasped in his hand, down by his side. He looked into Brendan's eyes, searching for a sign of weakness.

Lorna pressed her gun to the back of the guy's head. 'He may be the rugged one of us two, but trust me, I'm not afraid spread your brains all over this fucking room. And I wouldn't lose a night of sleep over it.'

His two accomplices then drew their weapons, pointed them at Lorna.

'You're out numbered here, sweetheart,' he stepped up to Lorna, his gun pointed to her temple.'

'All of you stop fucking about,' Louse said. 'Can we please put our dicks away and get back to our common enemy over here.' She stood up and looked at Sam's three men. 'Trust me, you three twats could do well to have this pair on your side.'

They all lowered their weapons and took a seat. Brendan and Lorna both stood behind the sofa facing English, who was sitting on the sofa, his arms folded, grinning with entertainment.

'Moore is not someone you want to be pissing off right now,' English said. 'He's not been in a very good mood recently. And if I were you bunch of wannabe gangstas,' his Belfast accent coming through his weak imitation of an English accent. 'I'd be more careful about...'

'Fuck what Moore's feeling right now,' Louise shouted, sitting back down on the sofa facing him, Brendan and Lorna stood over her shoulder. 'You may think you got one over on my father, but I'm not the pretty little fragile thing that he used to bring with him on his little business deals.'

'I wouldn't be so sure about that,' the guy who squared up to Brendan mumbled to his mate. 'Still a cute piece of ass over there.'

Louise took a pistol out of her handbag and shot him in the foot. He dropped to the ground, screaming, clutching the wound. She stood up and walked over to him, pointing her gun at him, slowly moving in closer, placing the end of the barrel on his forehead. 'Would you like to repeat that?' She looked around the room. 'Any of the rest of you like to say something?'

Sam sniggered. 'Just that I've never been so attracted to you.'

Louise lowered her weapon. She looked over at Brendan and Lorna. 'What do you think we should do with this piece of shit?'

Brendan stepped closer to English, looking down at him, English looking back up and Brendan, an antagonising expression. 'He's not going to tell us anything.' He looked back at Louise, then Lorna. 'We take him with us. If we send him back to them, we may as well send them a text disclosing what we're doing.'

'Do you have somewhere we can keep him for a while?' Lorna said.

'We've got a place,' Louise said. 'And if he doesn't want it to be his final resting place, then he'll be delivering me some information.'

Lorna reached into her handbag. She walked straight over to him, raising her hand towards him, clasping a gun.

He raised his hands, and broke out into a scream, as if begging for mercy. She shot him in the neck. He went limp, closed his eyes and dropped back against the chair.

'Tranquillizer,' Louise said.

'And if you want him to spill his guts, you'll get your hands on some truth serum,' Lorna said, dropping the gun back into her bag.

'Tesh, Reg, you two get a side each.' Sam ordered the two that were still assisting their wounded mate. 'We've a van out the back.' He looked at Brendan, 'it was nice to meet you.' He shook his hand, and then offered the same to Lorna, his eyes fixed on the monitors. 'I've got to go. The club needs me.' His phone rang. 'But I'll see you all soon.' He winked at Louise and made his way towards the door.

'Thanks, Sam,' Louise shouted after him. She turned and looked at English. 'Right, get him into the van.' She looked at the one she'd shot in the foot. 'Better get him to A & E after.'

Chapter Twelve

NORTH LEICESTER WAS a cluster of residential areas, with a few industrial estates dotted around. A car mechanics was situated deep in one of those industrial estates, just off the Fox Road. Surrounded by a twelve feet tall pointed steel fence, guarding the perimeter. The repairs garage had been closed for business for many years but was still under tenancy to the same. Louise's father, and now Louise.

'This is us,' Louise said, as she pulled up to the chained gates. She jumped out, and ran to the gates, pulling a set of keys out of her pocket. Inserting one into the brass padlock, she released the chains then separated the gates. She jumped back into the car and led the convoy into the grounds, pulling up at the reception. The transit driven by Sam's two guys reversed in, stopping directly outside the rusty blue roller door. Louise jumped out of the car again and went to raise the door. The van reversed into the garage. Louise quickly dropped the door again. She made her way towards the car, indicating for Brendan and Lorna to accompany her inside.

They both got out. Rain was never far away, and judging from the expression on Lorna's face, she was about ready for a break, perhaps somewhere warmer. 'We should make a return to Italy again,' she laughed. 'Or maybe somewhere further south, closer to the equator.'

'After we're finished here, we're going to San Andreas,' Brendan said, pulling his head into the collar of his top, shoving his hands into his pockets.

'You know any Spanish?' Lorna said.

'Enough to get by,' he said in Spanish.

'Smartass,' Lorna provided him with the Spanish translation.

'Come on in and I'll show you guys around.' Louise stood, holding the door open for them. Looking past them, up at the sky, her expression less than enthusiastic. 'And I think I might join you two on the plane across the Atlantic.' She closed the door and switched on the lights.

The office was small and smelled fusty. The counter was three feet high, mahogany and so tidy, it looked like it wasn't used in a long time. Brendan looked at the old calendar on the wall behind them, an old Max Power calendar, with an attractive big breasted lady bending over the bonnet of a green supercar.

'Bet you had that, didn't you?' Lorna said to him.

He smiled. 'Think I still have it somewhere at home.'

Louise laughed. 'You're all perverts.' She walked around the back of the counter, pulling the drawer below the computer open. She pulled out a key and walked to a grey wall-mounted key cupboard. Inserting the key, she took out a key that looked older than the three of them put together.

'Where's the safe?' Brendan said, gesturing towards the long thin key, with a five-inch-long stem.

Louise made her way towards a red door, beside the calendar. 'In here,' she said. 'Come on in.'

'They followed her into the office. The safe was under a black rug below the desk. She inserted the key then typed in a four-digit combination. She dropped the handle and pulled the door open.

She pulled out a wad of notes, all thousands. She tossed a fat bundle to Brendan, then another to Lorna. 'Everything in here is yours if you help me bring these guys down.'

Brendan tossed the bundle back to her. 'Keep your money. I said I'd do it for free.'

'There's over two million pounds in here.' She looked at them, astonished. 'In diamonds and cash.'

Lorna tossed her bundle back into the safe. 'Give it to charity then.'

Louise stood up and looked at them both, slightly taken aback. 'You're for real? You realise nobody who's worked for us has ever seen inside this before?'

'And yet you let two people you've met a few days know it's location?' Brendan said, seeming astonished. 'What's to stop us from walking away with the entire stash right now?'

'Because I know enough about you that you've got bigger ideas than to rob a little criminal organisation like this.' She looked at Brendan, then Lorna. 'And I know you both would make great additions to my local team.' She laughed. 'You've both seen my local group of clowns.' She sniggered. 'You made three of them look like kids when they went for you outside the pub.'

'I just wanted my breakfast,' Brendan joked.

'Yeah, he's a grumpy bastard when he's not eaten, especially first thing in the morning.'

'Look who's talking,' Brendan protested. 'Little miss can't stand the alarm at five thirty in the morning.'

Sam's associate Reg entered the room from the main garage area. 'Where will we leave sleeping beauty?'

'Leave him in the van,' Louise said. 'Someone's on their way to keep an eye on him. You and Tesh should probably get going, take your stupid ass friend to the hospital and get his foot sorted out.'

Reg looked across the room at Brendan then Lorna, nodded at Brendan and the same to Lorna. He closed the door again.

'Charming guy, isn't he?' Louise said.

Brendan looked at Lorna. 'Yeah I feel a bit worried. He might try and steal her from me.'

Lorna folded her arms, smirking. 'You want to get your hands on some of that truth serum. Then we can find out some more info about that scumbag.'

'Forget about it for the rest of the evening, we've got our blackmailing token.' She slammed the safe shut and locked it. 'Let's get back to Leicester.'

Brendan and Lorna follower her out of the room, getting soaked in the rain. Brendan looked at Lorna. 'San Andreas it is, then.' He pulled the door open and got in.

Chapter Thirteen

THE TIME WAS TWO THIRTY in the morning when they'd arrived back in Leicester. Brendan and Lorna were both happy to be dropped off at the hotel again, but Louise insisted they stay with her. She lived on a private estate on the outskirts of the city. Growing tired of the hotel life, Brendan and Lorna didn't need much convincing.

'You've got a beautiful home,' Lorna said, as they pulled up to the imposing white pillars supporting a shiny black gate. 'It's clear crime pays well.'

'Get off your high horse. It's not as if you're whiter than white,' Louise said, pointing a remote control at the gates. 'You worked for MI5, the shadiest bunch of bastards around.'

Brendan cleared his throat. 'You two need to start getting along, even if only for as long as we need to work together. Then we can all happily go our own way.'

Louise guided the car through the gates and along the tree-lined driveway, approaching the sandstone covered side of the house towards the five-garage block. The rain had stopped, but that rain smell lingered in the rain.

'As long as you've got a warm bed, and some food in the fridge for breakfast in the morning, we'll all get along fine,' Brendan said, getting out of the car. He stepped into the stones, crunching with every step.

'Of course, you're a man,' Lorna said, slamming the door shut.

Louise laughed. 'Come on in and we'll grab something to eat before I show you guys your room.' She led them around the side of the house, towards the front door. The exterior lights illuminated the grounds. The front garden was almost big enough to host one half of a football field. The perimeter was lined with a ten-foot-tall wall, promoting a feeling of security and seclusion.

'This reminds me painfully of the summer house,' Brendan said. He looked at Lorna. 'If we had a freezing sea spray of the Atlantic Ocean, I could close my eyes and imagine I was there right now.'

Lorna stepped onto the doorstep, behind Louise. 'And how does that make you feel.'

'Hungry,' Brendan joked.

They followed Louise into the house. Lights came on automatically to greet them. A white spiralling staircase stood to their right, a black piano sat beneath where it began it's sprout out of the ground up to the next floor. Louise's phone sounded. She didn't respond, instead taking her jacket off and throwing it down over the bannister. 'Come on into the kitchen, I'll make us something to eat.'

The house was empty. Huge, but empty.

'You live here on your own?' Lorna said.

Louise nodded, walking along the marble floored hallway, toward a set of double white doors. 'This was my father's house. This is where I grew up. I have many happy memories here, especially in here,' she pushed the kitchen door open.

'Doing my homework at the table was the most time I got to spend with him.'

The kitchen lights came into. The room was a dizzying mass of black and white squares, almost like a life-sized chess board. She pressed a button on the wall, next to a light switch. An electronic blind dropped to cover the floor to ceiling windows that made up three of the room's four walls.

'What would you guys like?'

'What have you got?' Brendan said.

'I love it when people ask that question.' She pulled the fridge's double doors open. 'Ham and cheese sandwich?'

'How about putting that ham and cheese into a toastie instead?' Lorna said.

Louise was interrupted by her phone ringing a second time. 'Be back in a second, but yes a toastie would be a great idea.' She spoke hurriedly as she left the kitchen.

Brendan went to the fridge. 'I'll get started.' He pulled out the ham and cheese. Setting it down on the work surface, he grabbed a stainless-steel knife from the stack and grabbed a chopping board that was hooked to the black and white tiles that matched the floor. He started cutting the red Leicester local cheese when Louise came back in.

'Moore's been seen at the club we just left.'

'That's good,' Lorna said, 'he now knows we have his boyfriend and will come looking for him.'

'What's he doing there?' Brendan said. 'Is he making a racket or just there acting like a hardman?' He spoke mockingly. 'He's really good at that.' He cut the cheese into thin slices, leaving them on the plate and moving on to buttering the bread.

'Whatever he's doing, he won't be doing it for much longer,' Louise said, strutting towards Brendan. 'I'd cut the bastards throat without thinking twice about it.'

Brendan looked at her. 'I told you, Louise.' He held her gaze as she approached him. 'We'll help you as much as we can, but when the time comes, I get my hands on both him and the son.' He turned and looked back at the worktop, slapping butter on the bread. 'You can do whatever you want, but every person in Belfast who died at his hands will be able to rest easy knowing one of their own has put them to sleep.'

Louise didn't reply. She just walked past him, lifting the kettle. 'As you wish.'

'Have you got anyone who can get their hands on that truth serum?' Lorna said. 'We can get some very useful information from English, get us a step ahead of Moore and son.'

'I know a few people who might be able to get their hands on it,' Louise said, setting the kettle back down and switching it on. 'For tonight, I just want to chill out, and get some rest.' She strolled across the kitchen and sat down on one of the stools beside Lorna. 'It's been a long few days.'

'Who've they been involved with?' Lorna said, and what's giving them so much power in England?'

'Apart from being a Loyalist godfather, complete fucking badass in the name of queen and country, maybe his ability to gather support from other criminal outfits, he'd get a job anywhere he'd go. Trust me,' Brendan said. 'Someone who'll go down in history for firing a rocket launcher at the Sinn Fein offices in broad daylight, he's got balls. He's a nasty bastard, and most people wouldn't want to bump into him when he's pissed off.'

'Except you,' Louise said.

'I'm different.'

'What do you mean?' She interrogated him. 'What makes you the person that must right all the wrongs that he's done?'

'I didn't choose to be the person I am.' He looked at Louise, then at Lorna. 'Because everything single shitty thing that's happened to me in my life was meant to bring me to this point.' He lifted the ham and began piecing the sandwich together.

'I've heard about your father,' Louise said, making a pot of coffee. 'He's made his mark around here, you know, only very recently.'

Brendan looked at her, stopping everything he was doing. 'What do you mean?'

'You know he was working with the Italians that have recently set up shop here?'

'My father lived an...let's just say, a controversial life.'

Louise looked at Lorna. Being an agent in MI5, you must have studied Mr Cleary a lot?'

'No,' Lorna said. 'Nothing was ever mentioned in the office. But his business was never discussed. It was highly classified. Only the head of British Intelligence and the Prime Minister ever discussed *The Ghost*.'

'What do you know about my father's links with the Italians here, in Leicester?'

'Well, perhaps you can speak to them yourself some time,' Louise said, as she reached into the cupboard beneath the coffee machine. Pulling out three espresso cups, and three tall transparent glasses, she set one down under the dispenser. She pressed the button on the side of the machine that had begun to flash green. The brown stuff began to pour, steaming from the cup. 'But one thing's for sure, the Italian's fucking hate the Moore clan.' Louise said. 'It's more of a fact that the scumbag made his name by butchering Catholics simply because they were that.'

Brendan brought the sandwiches to the table. Louise did the same with the drinks.

Chapter Fourteen

AT FIVE THIRTY, BRENDAN'S alarm sounded, much to the annoyance of Lorna who groaned at him to shut it off.

'I'm growing tired of this bloody thing, waking me up every morning,' she complained.

Brendan laughed, and rolled over to kiss her. 'Rise and shine, sweet cheeks.'

She pushed him back onto his side of the bed. 'Don't call me sweet cheeks, I hate it.'

He switched the alarm off and got up off the bed. 'I know you hate it, that's why I said it.' He trudged bare foot across the thick white carpet towards the bow style windows. He pulled the curtains open, then opened the window. The cool morning air biting into his topless skin, sending him back to the bed. Lorna pulled the duvet over her head.

Brendan sat back down on the bed and lifted his phone. He unlocked the screen and opened his messages. One was from Richard.

We had a bit of trouble last night. Some of those guys came back, looking for the hard man from Ireland. You're lucky you weren't here mate.

'Yes, I feel very fortunate,' Brendan mumbled.

'What are you talking about now?' Lorna said.

'Apparently those guys came back to the pub looking for me last night, and I'm lucky that I wasn't there.'

Lorna pulled the duvet off her head, revealing her face. Her eyes mostly closed, tiny slits.

He smiled at her, then lay back down on the bed again. 'You're so cute when you're sleepy.' He lifted her soft hand and kissed her knuckles.

'You're such a cheese-ball, Brendan Cleary.' She rolled over facing him, her eyes open slightly more, but her deep voice was still evident she hadn't yet regained full consciousness. She placed her head on his chest, twirling the tip of her index finger on his chest hairs. 'Feels weird waking up in this house, and not a hotel room.'

Brendan nodded his head. 'One day, we'll have our own house, just the two of us, and a family.'

Lorna's eyes shot open. Brendan's words appeared to wake her up fully. 'You want to be a father? You think you've got what it takes?'

'How hard could it be?'

'You're joking, right?'

'I'd never joke about something as serious as that.'

Lorna looked at him. 'It's a big commitment, Brendan.' She sat up.

'I know, maybe it's something we need to bring us some kind of normality in a life that's not going to last.' He got up off the bed. 'I'm going for a run. Go back to sleep. I'll see you when I get back.'

Chapter Fifteen

BRENDAN TOOK TO THE hills of the English country-side, and by the time he'd arrived back to Louise's house, his calves were hanging off him. Drenched in sweat, he pressed the buzzer at the gate to get back in. After announcing himself to Louise, the gate crept open. He jogged up the drive-way, and in the house. As he stepped inside, he could hear the radio playing, blurring out from the kitchen. As he got to the doorway, Lorna was standing at the hob, holding the frying pan in one hand, and a fork in the other. Louise was just walking in through the set of double patio doors. She smiled at Brendan.

'We're all up early,' Brendan said, as he stepped into the kitchen. 'Although I'm not complaining, the smell of that food is great.'

'Go and get a wash,' Lorna said, 'this'll not be ready for another while.'

'You're the boss.' Brendan quickly turned around and left the kitchen, making his way upstairs to the bathroom, grab-bing himself some clothes from the wardrobe. He checked his phone. Nothing. No news was good news. He went into the bathroom and put the shower on. He put on the yellow duck radio that dangled from the shower hose. The last thing he wanted to listen to was the news, half of it was bollocks anyway so he settled for some mediocre pop music. He lowered the temperature of the water, so that it shocked him awake. After a three-minute blast and rub around with the Imperial shower gel, he grabbed the towel that hung over the cubicle door and stepped out.

He wrapped the towel around his waist and went back into the room. He sat down on the edge of the bed, looking around the room. Spotting a set of Samuri Swords crossed on the wall next to the door, and a shotgun taped to the back of the door, he sniggered as he got up and inspected the swords more closely. 'Crazy bitch would chop you up no doubt.' He mumbled.

A knock came at the door. 'Breakfast is ready.' Louise shouted.

'Be down in a minute.' He dropped the towel and let the room's cool air dry his skin. He quickly got dressed and went back into the kitchen.

Lorna was sat at the table, her laptop open. Her expression was one of deep focus, not even recognising Brendan had returned. When she had the serious expression on her face, it usually meant she was doing some work.

'Checking the old intelligence documents?' Brendan said, sitting down next to her.

'We did have people watching him for years,' she grabbed a piece of toast and took a bite, scanning the screen. 'We know his address in Scotland, then he moved to Manchester. Then...' she trailed off and looked closer at the screen. 'There you are, you bastard.' She flipped the screen towards Brendan. 'He's running a gym up in Nottingham.'

Brendan had a look at the laptop. 'McGregor's Health Club and Spa.' He pulled the laptop closer. 'He always did love the gym, pumping steroids in his ass inside the Maze.'

Lorna sniggered and shook her head.

'That part of Nottingham has been a hotbed for recent racial attacks,' Louise said, as she sat down to join them. 'People in the Asian community are getting targeted because of the Islamic extremists. All the old National Front and Combat Eighteen slap heads are tooling up and are planning to take matters into their own hands.'

'It's not like they need a reason to start killing non-whites,' Lorna said.

'Yeah and Moore's merry men in the UDA and UFF all those years ago were in tight with them. I wouldn't be surprised if he's looking to nominate himself as the supreme commander and muscle his way in to this. One thing he loves more than anything is being feared. Being a leader and ever since being kicked out of Belfast, he will be dying to get that feeling again.' He lifted a sausage off his plate and took a bite. 'Think I might go for a wee training session in Nottingham today.'

'You sure it's wise?' Louise said, 'Brendan Cleary, son of The Ghost.'

'They'll not recognise me from the old days.' Brendan dipped his sausage into the yellow egg yolk and folded a slice of toast around it. 'There's a reason my father told me to grow my hair and beard so long...'

'So you could easily and quickly change your appearance,' Lorna said.

Brendan nodded and took a drink of tea. 'I never knew why. Until you walked into my cell that day, I'd no idea what he was involved in.'

Lorna smirked, 'yeah you looked like nothing more than a drunken bum that day.' She looked at Louise then back at Brendan. 'He scrubs up alright now doesn't he?'

'Stop it, you're going to give me a big head.'

'Right, well, I'm going to go and speak with our friend English this morning. You two are welcome to come along with me, or you can go off and do your own thing.' She took a piece of toast and slapped two bacon rashers onto it, then sandwiched it with another slice of toast. 'You're going to make an appearance on the door in the pub tonight?' She looked at Brendan as she took a bite of the sandwich.'

'I'll go to Nottingham by myself,' Brendan said. 'You two go and see English, try and get some information out of him.'

'You sure you want to go on your own?' Lorna looked at him.

'I'm just going to use the pool. Go for a swim, see if I can see any of the old faces from home.'

Chapter Sixteen

MCGREGOR'S HEALTH CLUB and Spa was situated in the Long Eaton suburb of Nottingham. Close enough to the city centre, but without being right in the thick of it all. As Brendan stepped in through the double doors, he was met with a steel barrier running all the way up to the oak effect reception desk where two ladies, looking no older than late teens early twenties both wearing the white t-shirts, with the black McGregor's names splashed across the chest. One of the two was busy taking a phone call whilst the other was focussed on the screen of her computer on the opposite side of the reception.

Approaching the reception desk, the girl on the phone looked at him and smiled, alerting her colleague that he was coming. The other girl looked up. She smiled Brendan, perhaps thinking he was her next membership sign up.

'It's busy in here,' Brendan said, sarcastically, looking around the foyer, one guy stood at the vending machine wiping sweat off his face with a towel in his right hand and holding a protein shake in his left hand.

'This is usually our quiet time of the day.' The girl said.

'Can I have a look around?' Brendan said.

'Before the girl had a chance to say another word, the lady that was on the phone stopped her.

'I'll show you around, Sir.' She ended the call and set the phone back down. 'I'm Michelle.' She pressed a button on the counter and the red light on the turnstile changed to green. 'Come on through, have a seat and I'll be over in a second.'

Brendan stepped through and took a seat in the waiting area next to the vending machines. He looked at the wide screen tv mounted a few feet above his line of sight. The news was displaying a life protest coming from Leicester City Centre from a group calling themselves the New Britain First. The volume was turned down on the tv, but the anti-Islamic and get out of Britain banners in amongst the crowd, he could pretty much catch the tone of what was being said.

Michelle came over to him, taking a seat at the table. 'You've come at a good time. We have an end of the month offer on where you get the joining fee knocked off and the first month for free. You save yourself forty pound if you sign up to the yearly membership, today.'

'I'm actually here to speak with a cousin of mine. His father owns the place. Billy Moore.'

Michelle looked at him. 'I thought you wanted to have a look around?'

'I did, I was hoping to catch my muscle-bound uncle pumping some iron in the weights room.'

Michelle, although a little knocked off her stride, quickly found her composure. 'I don't think Billy's here this week, I haven't seen him.'

'What about my crazy cousin, Jnr?'

'Billy Jnr,' Michelle checked her phone. 'I think he said he's having new artwork done today.' Her tone lowered, sounding bitter. 'He's been dating this goth and spends most of his time down in the bar she works in. Think that's where he'll be.'

'Where is this?'

'Down in Leicester, a pub called the Red, White and Blue.' Michelle's interest in Brendan had dissolved with the sale she thought she was about to make.

Brendan was about to make a quick exit but didn't want to raise too many suspicions. Moore and Moore Jnr would soon be put on alert if they knew someone was asking questions about them. 'You know what? Can I have a look around and see what my uncle's managed to accomplish since he left Belfast.'

Michelle grinned, a twinkle appearing in her eye. 'Let's go.'

As Brendan stood up, he could feel his phone buzzing in his pocket. He pulled it out. It was Louise. 'Sorry, I've got to take this.'

'Tell you what, just have a look around yourself, if you have any questions come and get me.'

'Thanks,' Brendan said, shaking her hand.

'What's your name?'

'Gary Moore,' Brendan said. 'And by the way, I want to surprise them, so don't mention anything to them about me coming in. If I don't find my cousin, I'll come back this evening, and I'll sign up. I'll be around here for a while anyway.' He lied, as he made his way towards a row of six cardio machines. Louise had ended the call. He called back straight away.

'Brendan,' Louise sounded disturbed. 'It's Lorna, she's taken sick. I'm taking her to hospital.'

'What, what the hell's happened to her?' Brendan stopped and looked around. 'We went to meet Sam. He's said he'd some information for me. About the Moore clan.'

'And what, he's done something to Lorna?'

'I don't know, Brendan. She just collapsed. When she came around, she started vomiting uncontrollably. She went into a fit, we've managed to calm her down, but I don't know if she's ingested something she shouldn't have.'

'I'm on my way.'

'Wait, Brendan. Don't.' Louise shouted.

'What?'

'If Lorna has been attacked, it means she's in danger and that will also mean you.'

'I don't give a shit if I'm in danger, where are you taking her to?'

'You're going to have to trust me that you're better off not knowing.' Louise didn't sound as confident as she usually had. 'Please, this is bad, Brendan. If someone knows who Lorna is, then they'll know who you are and that means trouble for us all.'

Brendan didn't respond, but he felt himself go into a blind rage. 'If someone in your organisation, or your mate Suhags lays a finger on her, Louise, I can promise you every last one of them will die. I don't care if I die in the process.'

'That's why I think I've met the best person to help me. Now please, let me take care of Lorna. I'll get her checked out and to a safe location where only I and my father knew about. When she's there, I'll contact you and you can come meet us.'

'I'm on my way to Leicester. Check out a hangout of Moore Jnr.'

Chapter Seventeen

BRENDAN WALKED INTO The Red White and Blue , a rundown pub in the centre of Leicester city centre. It was dark and fusty, reminding him of The Black Ball, an old snooker club he played in back in Belfast, where he spent much of his teen years. It was in that snooker club where someone had first punched him. This just happened to be after his third summer of training in Donegal with his father. Little did the poor guy that punched him know that Brendan was not only overflowing with anger at the time, but he was now in the possession the skills his father had beaten into him. Brendan's response to his first physical encounter with someone other than his father sent out a clear message to everyone in that snooker hall that day that he'd best be left alone. Quickly word had spread like wildfire around the school and the local neighbourhood that Brendan wasn't just protected by having the Cleary name, but his hands were more than able to defend him.

As he approached the bar, the rattle of cutlery coming from the kitchen made him hungry. The spit of the frying pan oil made his mouth water. And the smell of fried bread sealed the deal for what he was going to have for his second breakfast of the day.

The union jacks draped on every wall was unsettling. He felt as if he'd just walked into the Crown bar on the Shankill

Road. A clear sign that the scars of growing up in Belfast hadn't fully gone away.

He fixed his shirt collar and pulled his cuffs through his jacket sleeves, progressing towards the bar. A tall thin lady of around the same age, looked directly at him, her white face was, although plastered in makeup, beautiful. Her black sleeveless T-shirt was tight and advertised her perfectly toned body. Tattoo sleeves on both arms were, as Brendan thought, stunning works of art. He was impressed. The lady carried a certain level of confidence. Perhaps the manager, or certainly capable of running the place.

In spite of his current mood, Brendan managed to smile as she walked around from the serving side of the bar and handed him a menu.

'Morning. On your own?'

'Yes.' Brendan glanced down at the menu, then back up at her.

She pointed towards a table in the corner. 'I'll be with you in five minutes. Have a look at the menu. What would you like to drink?

'Bottle of still water please,' Brendan said.

He went and took a seat. The seat was hard and uncomfortable. The table wobbled. Three coasters sat under one of the table legs, trying to counteract the issue but wasn't doing a very good job. He watched the lady absentmindedly strut around to the serving end of the pub, catch a sneaky glance over at him then look away immediately when they made eye contact. She cleared her throat and hummed a melody, as she reached down and grabbed his bottle of water from the fridge. She came back over to him. He watched her the entire way. She bit her lip, trying to hide her grin. To no effect. He grinned at her and didn't give a shit if the entire city seen it. Lorna was the only thing on his mind.

'Full English, all day breakfast, please,' he said, as he took the water. 'Can I have a pot of tea with it, too, please.'

'You're accent tells me you don't have many full English breakfasts. Maybe more full Irish breakfasts. Belfast, right?'

'Good guess,' Brendan said, 'how'd you know I was from Belfast?' Like he didn't already know.

'My boyfriend's from Belfast.'

'That's a shame,' Brendan said, 'that means you wouldn't let this charming Irishman buy you breakfast.' His anger and frustration over the lady he loved was making him become reckless.

She pushed a strand of hair out of her big green eyes. 'Sorry. I'd join you, but he's not the type you'd want to upset.' She winked at him.

'I'm sure he's not,' Brendan said, under his breath. He'd now met the girlfriend of Billy Moore Jnr. The Moores had evidently brought their hardman image to England, and perhaps relished the fact people were growing afraid of them.

Brendan always wondered what it was that made such a beautiful lady like this one be attracted to that bad boy image. She was gorgeous and could have the pick of most men in Leicester. But something about the Billy Moore Jnr type just caught her eye.

Had he not been with Lorna, Brendan would have pursued her, but as it stood, former British Agent Woodward was the only person that had Brendan's attention. He checked his phone to see if he'd any news about her yet.

Nothing. Had she been poisoned? or was she suffering a bug, or food poison?

Brendan hoped that for the sake of Louise and her group of people that it wasn't an attempt on her life. Louise and her people were the only ones who'd been in contact with both Brendan and Lorna, therefore if it was an attack, he wouldn't have to go far to find out who was responsible.

Feeling distracted, Brendan sat scrolling through his phone when he heard a familiar accent from home. Three men walked into the pub, one of them was Billy Moore Jnr. Brendan didn't recognise the other two. But all three of them were sporting new tattoos. The Neo-Nazi mark. Moore Jnr just helped himself, walking around the back of the bar, grabbing three glasses and helped himself to the taps.

Brendan put his head down and waited for his food to come. He only hoped the lady wasn't going to tell her boyfriend she'd just been asked out by a man with the same accent.

FINISH THIS!!!

Chapter Eighteen

AT SIX THIRTY-FIVE, after exploring the city and it's unique features, Brendan returned to the Leicester Arms. Early and smartly dressed in a black suit and shiny black shoes, it was obvious Brendan was a man who took pride in both his appearance and his punctuality. It was almost as if he were trying to impress someone, but the only person whom he'd want to look good for was laying up in a hospital bed, vomiting her guts up.

As he was early for his shift, he decided to grab a seat in the main lounge. He sat at the empty corner table, with a clear view of the exit and everyone else. Steve walked in with that usual untouchable swagger he strolled about with, his two mates trailing in behind him, not noticing Brendan in his discreet location. Their swagger and "we own the place" persona, again to Brendan's amusement disappeared as he approached them at the bar, wanting a glass of water.

Steve looked shocked, his face was riddled with guilt, or some similar emotion that appeared to be running through his head at that moment. 'Brendan. You're early.'

'Is that okay with you?'

'Don't know, depends.' Steve laughed, as if trying to make the situation humorous. 'What are you doing here? Thought you'd be in the hospital with your beautiful...'

'Tonight, I'm helping keep these doors safe, then I'll make sure the lovely Louise over there gets home safely.' He looked at himself in the mirror, fixing his shirt collar. 'Tomorrow, I'm not sure. I might take a drive up to Nottingham and do your entire business a favour.'

'I wouldn't go bothering them if I were...'

'Don't you worry about me, Steve. I'm pretty sure I'll be fine.' Brendan looked at Louise. He took his glass, half water, half ice cubes. 'Thanks.' He looked at the trio who were looking around the lounge, perhaps wondering where there any spectators.

Brendan returned to his seat and sat back down again. He looked at his phone. He'd received a text from someone. Somebody from a part of his life which he'd not wanted to hear from, but was grateful all the same.

Brendan, It's your aunty Mary, love. Give me a call when you get this message. It's important.

Staring at the message, Brendan's intrigue begged him to respond. But the beautiful lady making her way across the lounge in a tight purple and black dress won the struggle with his mind and he decided to drop his phone back into his pocket, standing up to greet her.

'Where is she?'

'Lorna's safe. She's at my home. I've had a family friend look at her. She's been spiked something that's made her have a reaction to it. The doctor doesn't know what it is, but she's stable.' Louise stroked Brendan on the right shoulder. 'She's going to be fine.'

'Thank god for that.' Brendan exhaled a gap, looking down at the ground as if in silent prayer. He wiped his eye with the knuckles of his right fist. He looked at Louise. 'You look beautiful. What's the occasion?'

Louise smiled. 'Thanks. We've got a private evening planned tonight. You're not going to waste standing on that door. The staff can look after the place. We're having dinner over in Nottingham.' She tugged on his shirt collar. She shouted back to the guy serving the drinks, deep in conversation with Steve. 'Don't forget to do the banking before you go home tonight. All cash goes in the safe before you lock these doors. I don't want a repeat of what happened the last time.'

'Place is in good hands, Louise. Have a nice evening.'

Louise looked at Brendan. 'Let's go.' They both exited.

The evening was warm and dry. The summer was well and truly in full swing.

'Why do you let them hang around in there?' Brendan looked back through the window of the entrance door as it closed behind them. Steve looked as if he were more excited at the prospect that the boss lady was gone. Now they could start pretending the place was theirs.

'Who, them?' She spoke dismissively. 'They're not to be taken seriously.'

'I don't trust them. And if I find out any of them have something to do with Lorna's sudden bout of sickness, your crew is going to be three men down.'

She nodded her head and hummed to agree as she led the way to her grey Jaguar XK. 'Let's not talk about them for tonight. Let's have dinner first and then get to know each other a bit more.' She looked at him and smiled. Her smile was not the one he'd seen in the photos. It was about as genuine as a handshake between Northern Ireland's First and Deputy First Ministers. He didn't know if he could trust her or not.

.

ENTERING THE BUSTLING restaurant, the heat was as welcoming as the atmosphere. Everything from the warm smile and greetings from the smartly dressed staff, to the romantically dimmed lighting and easy on the ears Arabic style music was somewhere the establishments customer's could wash away their daily stress. And the bright white smiles from the majority of already seated individuals was proof that's what was on offer in addition to the food.

Like an old-fashioned gentleman, Brendan pulled out Louise's chair. He took his seat, again in clear view of his entire surroundings and hung his suit jacket over the back of his chair. Before either of their brains had time to process anything, a tall brunette with a figure that wouldn't be any less out of place on one of the local catwalks introduced herself.

'Good evening, welcome to Tarboush.'

'Evening.' Louise greeted the waitress first while Brendan tried not to look too intently at the lady's impressive figure.

She handed them a menu each and told them she'd be back to take their orders. Brendan glanced quickly at the menu, then set it down on the table.

'You've got good taste of restaurants, I think it'll be a kebab for me.' He looked at Louise. Her brown eyes softly scanning the menu, smiling as she did so, listening to Brendan.

'I like your accent.' She managed to pull her eyes up from the menu, long enough for Brendan to smile back at her then they dropped back to the menu. 'That lovely Irish accent.'

'You ever been to Ireland? It's a beautiful, pity about the trouble that's made it more infamous, than famous.'

Louise's smile dropped, she set the menu back down. 'I've never been to Ireland. My father always wanted to go, but never got the opportunity.' She looked up at him, stroking her neck. 'You can't have had a lot of good experiences over there?'

'Jesus, I could talk to you until next week about my experiences over there. But I don't want to ruin your night. But, in spite of all that bollocks, my father made me the man I am today. He knew he wouldn't be around forever, and he obviously knew his only son was someone he wanted to become the biggest pain in the ass for any criminal or corrupt body in the world.'

'You can't be happy, Brendan.'

He looked at her. 'I'm not sad either. I don't feel anything about it. But if I can help some people out, good people who deserve it, then I'll find some form of happiness.' He cleared his throat. 'I like being able to cause problems to some of the bad people of the world. God knows they deserve it.'

'I'm sorry, let's have dinner first. Then we can talk serious,' Louise said, as the lady arrived back at the table. She ordered a glass of sparkling water and a bottle of still for

Brendan. They both ordered the soup of the day as a starter. Louise had a chicken kebab and Brendan had the lamb. Both chose the fruit salad for dessert.

After the meal, they both avoided the conversation they both had buried in the back of their minds, hidden behind the small talk about who they were dating, and the big *if things had of been different*. Coffee was served, but they took them to the lough area where the burgundy coloured soft seats were more comfortable that the dining furniture.

'I wonder are they employing here,' Brendan joked, as he looked around his surroundings. A shiny white piano sat in the corner next to old fashioned writing burrow with a bookshelf above it. The walls were draped in old Renaissance period art. Sculptures were systematically placed close to the windows allowing visitors to appreciate the view of the gardens along with the artwork.

'Brendan, I don't think you were meant to be a waiter or a chef. I think you're a *little* bit more skilled than that,' Louise said. She set down her cup and slid closer to his side of the sofa. Placing her hand on his knee, she smiled at him. 'I'm sure you can find something better to do. With better pay.'

'It's not about the money. I've millions stashed away in various different off-shore accounts. My father ensured money was something I'd never have worry about. But the funny thing is, all those digits don't get used for what I would have wanted to use it for. Or at least what I thought I would have wanted to do with them.'

'Let me guess, supercars, nice clothes,' Louise said, 'let me tell you something, Brendan, it's all a load of bollocks.' She sat forward and set her cup down on the table. 'If I could give up everything I have, go back and live in a tiny little flat in a rundown part of Leicester, with not a penny to my name, and have my father back...' she paused for a second a looked around the room. 'I'd give it back in a heartbeat.'

Brendan finished his coffee and set it down on the table. 'Looks like we have something in common then.'

She reached over towards him and went to kiss him.

He looked into her eyes, about to kiss her. 'I'm sorry. I can't do that on Lorna.'

She paused, then smirked, her gaze falling to the ground. 'Ah yes.' She put more distance between them, straightening herself up. She cleared her throat. 'The lovely Lorna.' She looked at him. 'I'm sorry, Brendan.'

'Don't be, I'm flattered. You're gorgeous.' Brendan smiled at her, stroking her face. 'Lorna and I have been through a lot together. I thought I'd lost her in Italy, that's when I knew I couldn't live without her.' He clenched his jaws. 'But I'm starting to think this vigilante life that we've both dived into isn't going to last. I'm thinking of just pissing off and starting a business on a remote island.' He sniggered. 'Maybe a fishing business.'

'What about the rest of your family? Your family in Belfast?'

'Like my father, I think it's better they think I'm dead. I'll just bring too much trouble home.'

'Why don't you just contact them? I'm sure there are some over there hoping that you're okay.'

'They've survived long enough without me being around.'

'So, what are you going to do? Get a job serving three courses to couples who are out trying to find love before they get too old and die alone?'

'You really paint a picture, don't you?' He laughed. 'But I really don't know what I want. I know a lot of people out there suffer. There are some nasty people that operate all over the world, getting rich by exploiting of others. Greedy bastards who take all, and leave others with nothing, I know.'

She broke eye contact and looked at the ground, a look of shame written across her face. She looked down at the diamond bracelet around her wrist.

'Hey,' Brendan grabbed her hand. 'I didn't mean you. Your father did what we did. You don't have to do the same.' He smiled. 'From what Lorna has told me – she knows more about my father's last few years than I do – he's got an endless list of bodies under his name. The Ghost, Damien Cleary,' he spoke mockingly of the title the underworld had given to his father, 'became so good at killing people that he became the most sought-after problem solver the world over. Apparently he took the contracts so I could have those healthy bank accounts. And I don't feel guilty about using the money to fund our little campaigns.' He gestured at her bracelet, 'so don't feel guilty about that, sell it and give it to charity or something.'

She laughed. 'Are you perhaps going to imitate your father and become another Ghost.'

He smiled. 'My life's very complicated, and I guess I'll always have to fly below the radar. Maybe I am a ghost. I travel from town to town, city to city, country to country avoiding people that would love to bring an end to my travels.' He paused for a second. 'Okay...' he sat up and finished his coffee. 'Tell me about your father.'

'Well, my mother died giving birth to me. It broke his heart. I was the only part of her left in the world. So you can imagine how much he treasured me. But her death also made him very angry. Angry at the world. He used this anger to fuel himself into climbing to the top of the local drugs trade. He became widely known for his drugs empire. Then he started moving weapons and running streets. The last five years of his life he wanted to go legit. He bought a few restaurants, some property and a few nightclubs around the midlands and started to make even more money. Something very interesting happened to him when he lost my mother. He developed a focus so razor sharp, whatever he put his attention to, he worked and worked until he got what he was aiming for. Perhaps it was his coping mechanism for losing my mother. He was a very brilliant man. Very intelligent.'

'Where are you originally from? It's hard to pin down your accent.'

'Leicester. He'd heard of a new club that had opened in the city. Very profitable for the family, the Qamar family. He was supportive on an honest Muslim family coming to this country and making a better life for themselves. But when the Neo-Nazi movement heard of his betrayal to his own kind, they seen that as something that carried a penalty of death. None of those fucking skinheads would have had the balls to start a war.' She smirked. 'Until of course, an urban war veteran from your part of the world appeared on the scene sympathetic to their cause...'

'Billy Moore and his merry men.'

'Exactly. A new commander of the Combat 18 movement has come to town as they say. A devil who's got an army of equally terrifying men behind him. Moore himself is known to have fired an RPG through the window of a shop just to make his presence known.' She sniggered. 'Although a don't know how much truth there is to that tale. It seems a bit too much.'

'He did that in Belfast, that's true,' Brendan said. 'I'm not sure if he's done it over here. But he's crazy. If he could do it once, he can do it again.'

'Now he's bringing drugs and guns into England. It's a new era for organised crime in the relatively timid English underworld. I think it's about to get very bloody on these streets.'

Brendan laughed. 'How about we all just close up shop. Pull the shutters down and let them kill themselves.'

'There's a club in Leicester where they all hangout. Sharpen their knives, clean their guns, make their bombs.'

'Do you know the name of this club?'

'The Eagle Eye. The style of doormen dressed in tuxedos, fancy black and white theme interior and the best drug supplier in that part of the country.'

'Interesting name.'

Louise nodded. 'The Eagle is one of the images or markings of the RVF.'

'Racial Volunteer Force.' Brendan shook his head. 'Christ it's like being back in Belfast. 'Okay. If I decide to go down here and use their services, what am I likely to find?'

'They have a lot of eyes on the place. They have a cellar beneath. That's where they make their bombs. They have a few weapons dumps. That's one of them. But I get the feeling something very big is going to take place there in the next few months.'

'Christ, it's coming very close to Ramadan. A lot of hungry, tired and unstable Muslims around the country,' Brendan said. 'Wish I hadn't of shaved all my hair off now. I could have passed as a Muslim and paid a visit to one of their mosques.'

'That's what our friends who own this place are for.'

Brendan looked around the room, then back at Louise. 'Can I be honest with you?'

Louise pushed her hair over her shoulder and shuffled in her seat. 'I thought you already were.'

'The people in your crew? And the others you work with – Suhag and the rest, I don't trust them as far as I can throw them. I've got quite good intuition, and I see something trustworthy in you, Louise. Simply because I know what it's like to lose a parent to this dirty world we find ourselves in.'

Louise stared at him. Speechless.

'I nearly lost Lorna once. I won't go through that again. Part of me wants to take her away and forget all about this country, as much as I want to forget Belfast.' He took a deep breath, then finished his coffee. 'But I now find myself in the company of someone who knows first-hand, exactly what I've been going through recently. And with that, I want to help you...'

'But?' Louise said.

'No buts, Louise. If I didn't trust you, I would have demanded I come see Lorna when you called me today. I know you've helped her. Now I want to help you.' Brendan received a text. He gabbed his phone off the coffee table and looked at it. 'Richard's wondering where we've gotten to. He said he's tried to call you, but your phone is switched off.'

'I don't want to be disturbed.' Louise looked at her phone, indicating that it was switched off. 'What's he saying?'

Brendan smirked, shaking his head. 'That's got Moore written all over it.' He handed Louise the phone.

'A pipe bomb? Exploded under a car outside his house.' Louise looked up at Brendan. 'Jesus Christ.' She handed the phone back to Brendan.

'He's sending out a message.' Brendan took his phone and dropped it back into his pocket.

'But why the house, why not one of the businesses?'

Brendan looked around the room. 'Like I said, it was just a warning. He wasn't planning on hurting anyone with that attack. And if he's looking to take over your father's businesses, he's not stupid enough to start exploding bombs outside a place where he believes he could make some money.'

'These crazy bastards,' Louise said, shaking her head. She dropped her head and ran her fingers through her hair. 'Okay, so we've got their message. How do we compete with people who are bringing bombs to the table?'

'Simple. We take out the one who's brought this knowledge into the group,' Brendan said. 'We take out the bomb maker, as soon as we get our hands on them.' Brendan stood up. 'But as of this moment, all of our cars need to be taken as marked.' Brendan grabbed his jacket. 'Can you get your hands on a few extra cars?'

Louise stood up and grabbed her bag, slinging it over her forearm along with her coat. 'I've got a place with a few cars. It's an hour north, in the middle of nowhere.' She strolled past him. 'It'd suggest we grab Lorna before we go,' she'll be safe there, too.'

Brendan followed her out of the restaurant.

'Don't worry,' Louise said. 'She'll be safe there. It's a secret cabin where my father used to take me on holiday. It was the only place he and went together.' She laughed. 'I used to think he was crazy. We changed cars like five times in underground carparks, obviously he was trying to shake any tails that would have been on him.'

Chapter Nineteen

ARRIVING BACK AT LOUISE'S safe house where she'd left Lorna, Brendan began to feel confident about her safety. The security of the estate was like nothing he'd ever seen before. Fully functional security system from the front gate and within. Just arriving at the gate was intimidating enough. Until Louise deactivated the system and the gate began to open.

The time was twenty minutes after midnight. The house was quiet. From inside the grounds, the perimeter walls were lit up by tiny blue lights, drawing a blue outline of the private land.

'We left the lights on in Lorna's room,' Louise said.

Brendan looked up at the room in question, now in complete darkness.

Louise got out, throwing her bag over her shoulder. 'Don't panic, the lights are censored. She's probably asleep and the lights have just turned themselves off.' She shut the door and headed passed Brendan, making her way towards the house. Within fifteen feet of the front door, the lights illuminated the area. Louise pulled the key out of her pocket. Brendan was weary of the place. If C18 could fit a pipe-bomb to Richard's car, then, they could certainly attempt an attack on Louise's, if it wasn't as private as she thought.

He pulled his gun out.

'There's nobody watching this house, Brendan.' Louise opened the door and stepped inside. 'Don't worry, she's safe.' She hit the switch and the hallway lit up.

Brendan holstered the pistol and went straight up the stairs.

'I'm putting the kettle on.' Louise shouted. 'We'll have a quick cup of tea then we'll be away.'

Brendan entered the room. The lights came on as the movement of the door activated the motion sensors. Lorna was still asleep. He walked over to the bed. A grey bucket that was left on the floor by her side had contents inside it that would put anyone of their dinner. He sat on the edge of the bed. She was turned facing the other way. He placed his hand on her shoulder. She flinched the moment he touched.

'It's okay, it's only me,' Brendan said. 'How are you feeling?'

'Like I've been hit by a bus.' Lorna groaned. She rolled over towards him. 'Hand me that water, would you?'

Brendan grabbed a glass of water sat on the bedside cabinet next to her phone. She took it and sipped. Barely able to open her eyes, she handed the glass back to him, her arm trembling.

'We've got to move,' Brendan said, as he lay down on the bed beside her, looking up at the ceiling. 'Richard's found a pipe-bomb under his car.'

'Jesus,' Lorna groaned, her palm resting across her forehead. 'Moore?'

'Looks like he's taken over the RVF,' Brendan spoke humourlessly. 'The Racial Volunteer Force.'

'That doesn't surprise me with the amount of support them skin heads supported him back in Belfast.'

'Which is why we're moving somewhere safer.' Brendan put his arm around her.

'Does Louise know what these guys are planning?'

'Well, it's coming very close to Ramadan, I'm hoping we're wrong but maybe they plan on wrecking some Mosques and dishing out a few hidings.'

Lorna rolled the opposite way again. 'Wake me up when it's over.'

Brendan laughed. 'I'll go and help Louise with whatever she's taking with her. I'll be back for you when the car's full and we're about to leave.' He rolled over towards her and kissed her on the shoulder from behind.

He went back down to the kitchen, hearing the very distinctive sound of firearms being loaded. The metal slide of a clip into it's chamber was something Brendan could tell a mile off. As he stepped into the kitchen, Louise had a large grey suitcase opened out on top of the dinner table. The contents were certainly not what you'd get onto a plane. He walked across the room, closer to her. She was loading bullets into a magazine, a certain look of relaxation on her face. Almost as if she found some therapeutic benefits from it.

'We planning for World War Three?' Brendan stood next to her, looking into the pockets of the travel bag. 'Tell me those aren't what I know they are?'

Louise smirked, still focussed on her task at hand. 'Yes, they are what you think they are, and we may be going to war.' She slammed the magazine into the black Beretta she was loading. She looked at him and smiled. 'For my father, I'll take them all out.'

Brendan took the pistol off her, inspecting it closely. 'Where did you get these weapons from?'

'Why?'

'We may need more.'

'Jesus, I've just met the Irish Rambo.' She teased. 'We can get our hands on more if we need some. Our Asian friends in Nottingham can get their hands on pretty much anything.' She walked over to the fridge. 'You want a drink?'

'Anything cool, and fizzy?'

'Pepsi Max?'

'That'll do,' Brendan shouted, as he rummaged through the stack of weapons, finding some pretty nasty looking knives. 'Jesus Christ, you plan on getting medieval on some of these guys?' He pulled a meat cleaver out, inspecting it more closely.'

She turned, and brought him over his drink, cracking one open for herself.' Moore took away the man that I loved more than life itself.' She took a drink, taking the blade from Brendan. 'This will connect with his head.'

'Don't forget,' Brendan said. 'There are thousands of Catholics back home who'd be expecting one of their own to do the job.' Brendan didn't sound like he was having a debate, more like delivering a matter of fact, as he seen it.'

'How's Lorna?' Louise said, setting the cleaver back in with the rest and closing the case.'

'Still feels rough,' Brendan said, cracking open the can of Pepsi.

'Is she okay to travel?'

'She's going to have to be.' Brendan grabbed the suitcase by the handle. 'We can't stay here.' He pulled the case off the table, the weight almost pulling him to the ground. 'Which car are we taking? I'll load this in the boot. You can go and get the rest of your stuff.'

'There are two Mercedes around the side of the house in the garages,' Louise walked over to the sink, pulling open the top drawer to the left. 'Here are the keys.'

As he stepped out through the front door, Brendan got that uneasy feeling like he was being watched. He didn't know why he just felt on edge. With such an arsenal in his hand, he knew at any moment he'd have to use it. That pipe-bomb had all the capacity to tear that car into ribbons, along with anyone inside it. Having seen first-hand in Belfast the damage such devices could do, he was lucky enough only his hearing was what felt the impact from it. Had he been a little closer, he'd certainly have been less able bodied.

Reaching the block of garages, separate to the house, he rolled up one of the doors. There sat the Mercedes. Having received tips on how to check vehicles for such devices that had wrecked Richard's car, he set the suitcase down just outside the garage and proceeded with the inspection. Getting down on the ground, he slowly moved himself under the car, checking the usual spots for fitted bombs. Nothing there. None of the doors looked as if they'd been tampered with.

Feeling confident it wasn't boobie trapped, Brendan opened the boot and set the case inside. He got behind the driver's seat and started the engine. The AMG C63 roared beneath the bonnet. Brendan drove it out of the garage and reverse parked it at the front door. Leaving the engine running, he jumped out and went back in through the front door. Lorna was making her way down the stairs, wearing nothing but a cream t-shirt, a pair of jogging bottoms and grey trainers.

'You ready to go?' Brendan said, as he approached her.

She looked at him, dark circles around her bloodshot eyes. 'Let's go.' She forced a smile. 'I'll be fine.' She squeezed his hand, as she walked passed him. Heading out the front door.

'Where's your laptop?' He shouted after her.

'I've got all of her stuff here,' Louise shouted, trudging down the stairs, Lorna's laptop and two gym bags in one hand, and another suitcase in the other hand. 'Here, take these.' She handed Brendan the bags. 'I've just one more thing to get. I'll be out in a second.'

Brendan dumped the stuff in the boot of the car. He ran around to the garages and quickly checked the second Mercedes for any surprises. Nothing there. He jumped into the driver's seat and started the car. He connected his phone through the car's sound system and left the garage. As he guided the car around to the front, Louise was just getting into the other car.

Louise led them down the drive, through the gates and out on the A6 duel-carriageway northbound.

Chapter Twenty

ASHFORD-IN-THE-WATER was a quiet little village in the heart of Derbyshire and the picturesque peak district. Built with old stone houses, romantic village inns and a thirteenth century church, it was a world away from the lives they'd all left behind. Louise led the way over the charming Sheepwash Bridge that looked more suited to a 1930s Rolls Royce than two modern Mercedes C class AMGs with roaring engines.

The stillness of the night air was broken as the two cars passed through the high street and left onto the beacon hill road, an almost vertical climb. One mile up the hill, Brendan followed Louise right onto another road, then sharply left onto another gated estate. The gates slowly dragged themselves open and Louise entered first. Brendan followed. They parked next to a fountain that was spewing water through the mouth of a ramping unicorn.

Brendan got out of the car, stretching out all his joints. He went straight to the boot of the other car and started lifting out the bags. 'This is some place, you've got here. But are you sure nobody else knows about it?'

Louise slammed the door closed. 'Positive. Trust me. Safe enough to keep our British agent here safe until we can fix the mess down in Leicester.'

'Former British agent,' Lorna said, getting out of the rear of the car, slamming the door shut.

'How are you feeling?' Louise said.

'I'll be alright,' Lorna said. 'It's probably just some dodgy food we've eaten. I'll be alright in the morning when I get a good night sleep.'

Louise led them into the house, an old fusty smell lingered. Everything in the house was wooden and created a smell as such. The bucket of logs sat beside the fire ready to be set ablaze was as welcoming as a hot shower and warm bed.

Brendan set the bags in the dining area and opened Lorna's laptop.

'Just get some rest tonight,' Louise said. 'Chill out even for a moment. Trust me, this is the only place in the world where I can truly switch off. Make use of it.' She made her way towards the stairs with one of the gym bags. 'I'm going to get a quick shower and get changed into something more comfortable. Make yourselves at home.'

Brendan sat down on the sofa, sinking into it. Lorna sat down behind him, kicked off her trainers and brought her knees up into her chest. Curling into a ball, she lowered her head onto his lap.

Brendan stopped what he was doing and gently stroked her head.

'What are you thinking?' Lorna said.

'What do you mean?'

'What's going through that complex brain of yours?' She spoke in a feeble tone, indicating her reduced strength. 'I know when you're thoughtful.'

'I've been thinking on the drive up here about...' He paused for a second.

'About what?'

'Joining the ranks of the C18.'

Lorna sniggered in her drained state. 'You like getting your hands dirty, don't you?' Usually she would protest about Brendan doing things that were perhaps dangerous and would be likely to get him killed. 'You've really got your mind set on Moore and his son, haven't you?' But now her tone and response were different.

He nodded and hummed in agreement. 'The moment I heard his name, my entire body tingled. It's hard to describe.' He stroked her face. 'It's an opportunity of a lifetime and I'm not going to pass it up. Imagine being homeless, living on the street, and seeing a winning lottery ticket blow up the street right in front of you. Your opportunity to do something really big but in a flash it could be gone again.'

'Promise me something?' Lorna said, sounding as if she were slipping further away from Brendan's level of consciousness. 'Be careful, and don't be stupid. Your father taught you well.'

'Lorna, shut up. Why am I getting the feeling your saying goodbye to me?' Brendan felt his eyes water up, his stomach churn. Her breathing deepened. She was asleep. 'Let's get you to bed.' He stood up and lifted her into his arms, making his way towards the stairs. Slowly he ascended the stairs, looking at her asleep, curled into him. The bedroom to the right had the light on. He stood at the doorway and looked in. The sound of the shower running from the ensuite.

He turned and went further down the hallway. The next room to the left had the door open with a small red lamp lit up on the wooden beside cabinet. He laid Lorna down on the bed and put the duvet over her. He looked at her, peaceful.

'Right, let's get us away from this life. I've had enough.'

Chapter Twenty-One

BRENDAN STEPPED INTO the living room, the fire now ablaze. The room was cosy, almost warm enough to send him to sleep. He grabbed the laptop case and pulled out the computer. He sat down and opened it. Accessing the documents, he was again reminded why Lorna was perhaps the most valuable person on the planet. She was in possession of the most detailed set of documents on every major threat to the world. Every terrorist organisation. Every organized crime syndicate. Every anti-government movement. British intelligence had agents working within all of these, and the data the agents collected was now in the hands of a former agent, and Brendan. He knew not to disclose any of this information to Louise. He'd got the impression, deep down beneath all the tough lady, aire to her father's criminal throne was a lady who wanted nothing more than to avenge her own father's murder. But all that aside, this information was too valuable. As it stood, Lorna was the only person on the planet Brendan trusted completely. Perhaps Louise could prove just as trustworthy in time, but for the moment, she was to be kept at arms-length.

Opening the file titled: C18, Brendan scrolled down through a collection of documents. Finding a document under the name of McGregor's Health Club and Spa, Brendan scanned through it. Looking at the list of staff, Brendan recognised three names from home. All Belfast born and raised lads. Willy Ferguson, David Montgomery and Ian Greystone. All three were activists in the UFF, the militant wing of the UDA. Greystone was known as a bit of a loaner with no real people skills. But what he lacked in social ability, he more than made up for in his skills in bomb making. Brendan now knew who the bomber of the group was. Ferguson and Montgomery were, on the other hand, less thinkers and more bruisers. Always there at the Drumcrea Orange parade disputes in Portadown, and first to shake Moore Snr's hands upon his release under the Good Friday Agreement. They were more likes Moore's faithful dogs. Not the sharpest knives in the kitchen, but certainly willing to die for their faithful leader. They'd be led into the fires of hell if that's were their supreme commander was headed.

Opening a photograph of Greystone, Montgomery and Ferguson together, Brendan didn't see any change in them whatsoever. Greystone was a few inches over six foot tall, thin and had long dark hair tied up in a ponytail. His brown glasses looked like they were manufactured before the British troops first set foot on the streets of Derry. His baggy jeans and plain white T-shirt only supported his fashion, or lack thereof. Ferguson was similar in height to Greystone, but with boulders for shoulders. His pencil moustache was as fashionable and Greystone's glasses and looked out of place given the fact it was the only hair on his face and head. His white T-shirt with Simply The Best across the chest region was stretched to the limit, with his inflated torso bursting to get out. His bulging arms would be slow at throwing a punch but if he caught you, he'd be more likely to mimic

a zoo gorilla and pound his victim to death. The smallest of
the three was Montgomery, also known as Monty Python as
he had snake skin sleeves tattooed on both arms. He relished
this name, and Brendan and his mates at home had always
joked about him dying at the hands of a serpent.

'You look like you're having fun?' Louise said, dragging
Brendan's attention away from the laptop. 'You fancy a
drink?'

He looked up at her. She was standing next to the sofa,
wearing black nightdress, the silk clinging to her toned body
like another layer of skin. He tried not to look but her slightly toned skin glistened off the artificial lighting coming
down from the light directly above her. *Wow, you look gorgeous,* he thought in his head, not wanting to encourage a
progression that she was after, he just replied. 'Yeah, just a
glass of coke please.'

She smirked, pushing a strand of hair behind her ear. 'I
was thinking of something a bit more relaxing like a glass of
wine?'

'I'm good thanks, coke will do.'

'The badass Brendan Cleary, sitting at his laptop with his
can of coke. Doesn't really sit right.' She joked. 'But that's
fine. You don't mind if I have a glass of the red stuff?'

'It's your house.' Brendan shouted after her as she made
her way towards the kitchen.

He looked back at the laptop. Flipping through the documents, he found a photo of Greystone leaving a house. A
note was attached to the photo stating that it was his last
known address. He took a photograph of the address and
saved it to his phone A small university town called Lough-

borough, not a likely place for recruitment in the C18 or any kind of radical group.

'Who's the weakest link in the chain?' He said, as Louise came back. She handed him his coke and sat down on the sofa next to him. Turning towards him, she pulled her feet up and curled her legs in towards her but, tucking them in under the cover she'd pulled down. Brendan got an overpowering smell of shampoo, and mint scented oil. 'My money is on it being Steve's little laptop dog.'

She took a sip of her wine, holding his gaze over the rim of the glass. She took the glass away from her bright red lips, leaving a smudge of lipstick on the side. 'Yes, I would say he is, too.' She brushed a strand of hair out of her eyes again. 'You think the weakest link is the one on the inside, firing info about us to Moore's men?'

Brendan took a drink of his coke, the bubbles causing a tingling sensation on the back of his throat. 'Someone is.'

Louise looked around the room. She took in a depth breath through her nose, looking softly at Brendan. 'What do you suggest we do?'

'I want to learn more about the Moore's gang and what exactly their planning. See if I can become a member. Impress people and perhaps get an introduction, meet the heads.'

'They're protesting in Nottingham tomorrow at an Anti-Islam rally. If you want to ruffle a few feathers. There would be a good way to create a bit of a stir.'

'Okay.' Brendan closed the laptop and set it to the side. He took another drink of his coke. He set the drink down on the coffee table in front of him. He turned his body towards Louise and crossed his left leg over his right. 'You want to find out who's the rat in your organisation?'

'Of course.'

Brendan took out his mobile and sent her the photograph of Greystones address. 'Give this address to your crew. Tell them it's the bombmakers house. Make sure all your suspected rats hear this. Tell them you want him alive. It's very important to take him alive. They're not allowed to kill him, under no circumstances is he to be touched.'

'Very clever.' Louise took another drink. 'The rat will feedback to Moore's men and Greystone won't be in the house when they go in.'

'Hopefully it'll work. And tomorrow, it looks like I'll be going to a rally in Nottingham.'

She finished off her glass of wine and reached towards the coffee table, setting the empty glass down, her tanned, perky breasts became more visible in the move, showing everything but the nipples. She sat back in her position. 'So, tell me why you wouldn't have a drink with me?' She brought her legs out from under her and crossed her right over her left, turning her body in his direction.

'Don't take it personally.' Brendan's eyes went from Louise's, down to her sultry lips, further down her neck over her exposed chest. Her breasts pushed tightly together, the silk glistening under the lights. 'Christ you're hot.' He looked at her shapely legs. His animalistic state almost taking over. What he wanted to do was the last thing he could morally do. He'd never forgive himself for cheating on Lorna. He shook his head and sat forward. 'You could have anyone you want. There's nothing special about me.'

'Yes, there is,' she said. She covered herself up. 'And the fact you've just done what you've done, for the lady upstairs proves you're special.' She laughed. 'I've wanted you since the moment I heard your accent. And when you toyed around in the carpark with our trained door staff, I couldn't resist you.' She stoked his face. 'But I know love when I see it. And you love that lady upstairs.'

'I do,' Brendan said. 'And the reason I don't drink, is because I despise it. My mother drank herself to death, tormented with the worry of what had happened to my father. I tried to help her, but it got a hold of her and she slowly drunk herself into the ground.'

'I'm sorry,' Louise said. 'If I had of known I wouldn't have joked about it.'

'It's fine,' Brendan said. 'I know what I can do and I know what I can't do. I won't ever allow my mind to become intoxicated. I keep my mind healthy and stimulated. Sharp. I have a focus in life that keeps my past where it is: in the past.'

'And your focus?'

'To become the biggest menace to anyone out there who gets off on hurting those less fortunate.'

She laughed softly, playing with her hair. 'Fair enough.' She stood up and grabbed her glass. 'Are you tired?'

'Not really.'

'Me neither. 'I'm getting another glass. You want another drink.'

'Cup of tea, please.'

Chapter Twenty-Two

BRENDAN WOKE THE NEXT morning at six thirty. He fought off the temptation he was tempted to do the previous night – bed the beautiful Louise. She should have had more respect for Lorna, and for Brendan. He massaged his temples then rubbed his eyes. Looking around the room, purple velvet curtains and matching bedsheets reminded him of the hotel him and Lorna had stayed in on the Italian/Swiss border.

Quickly scrubbing the nostalgia, he sprung up off the bed. Keeping the lights off, he reached around for his clothes, gathering them into a ball, making his way towards the door. He gently lowered the handle and slowly opened the bedroom door, closing it with the same discretion. He walked into the bathroom, black and white tiled floor, walls and ceiling. He switched on the shower, waited for a few seconds for the water to heat up, then stepped in.

After he got dressed, Brendan went downstairs. Entering the kitchen, Louise was already up, sitting at the open patio door, a cigarette between her lips as she read from her phone.

'Did you sleep?' Brendan said.

'Like a baby, after that bottle of wine.'

'You should perhaps look for more healthy ways to get yourself to sleep.'

'Usually a good shag would be enough, but I haven't had one of those for a while.'

'Get yourself online,' Brendan joked, lifting the kettle. He walked over to the sink and filled it. 'I hear those dating apps are the popular thing to do these days.' He set the kettle back down and switched it on. He walked over to the table and grabbed a seat.

Louise closed the patio door and brought her seat back over to the table. 'There's a shop in Nottingham that sells a lot of C18 and other anti-Islamic merchandise. But if you want my honest opinion, you just get yourself a black bomber jacket, some Dr Martin's and a pair of stonewash jeans and you're good to go.'

'How I look is not massively important.' Brendan set two cups out on the table. 'You want tea or coffee?'

'Tea, please.' Louise walked passed him, leaving the smell of cigarette smoke in the air. 'I'm going to grab a quick shower, I never feel fresh enough until I've had my morning shower, I just came down for a smoke.'

Brendan looked for a Moka pot, grateful to find that it wasn't just kettle brewed coffee in this house. He put the TV on and watched BBC News that was talking about the anti-Islam rally in Nottingham. The journalist said how police were expecting there to be a clash between members of the Muslim community and the rally's organisers.

Brendan brought Lorna up some toast with jam and coffee. As he stepped into the room, tray in hand, the cool air coming in the wide-open window was refreshing. She was curled up in a ball, shivering. Wrapped in the heavy duvet, yet still acting as if she was lying on top of a block of ice. He set the tray down on the bedside cabinet and sat on the edge of the bed. He placed his hand on top of the only part of her body exposed – her head. She was burning hot and clammy. He could only imagine how wet it was beneath the duvet.

The moment he touched her head, Lorna flinched and turned around. She could barely open her eyes. 'Is that coffee I smell?' She grinned weakly.

'And toast with strawberry jam.' Brendan brought his legs up onto the bed and put his arm around her, lying alongside her. 'I didn't know if you'd be able to stomach any food or not, but I'll leave it here for you until I come back.'

'Joining the C18 today then?'

'There's an anti-Islam rally in Nottingham City Centre today, I'm going to go down there and see if I can be of assistance, maybe help out a few people.'

'Those things have a tendency to become violent, Brendan. Be careful.'

He reached over and gave her a kiss.

After fifteen minutes of just lying there, neither of them saying a word, Brendan rolled off the bed, the deep breathing of Lorna letting him know she'd fallen back to sleep. He left her food there, going cold, but there all the same if she were to wake up hungry and not wishing to move too far to get something.

As he gently closed the bedroom door, he me Louise coming out of her bedroom.

'How is she?' She whispered, pulling on a brown leather jacket.

'She's asleep. I've left her some food.' Brendan followed Louise along the hallway and down the stairs, noticing a bulge under the arm of her coat he smiled. 'Maybe a different coloured jacket would conceal that thing under your arm better.'

'My primary weapon is in my handbag.' Louise was quick to respond. 'This,' she tapped on the bulge, 'and this,' she pulled the coat open, revealing another pistol, holstered to her brown Luis Vuitton belt, 'simply just extras in case my bag is ever too far to reach.'

'You're planning for a gunfight today?' Brendan grabbed his jacket that was hanging over the bannister at the bottom of the stairs.

'Ever since my father left this world, I've been waiting on the chance to blow away the bastards responsible.' She made her way towards the front door, grabbing a black umbrella that leant against the patterned glass window surrounded the entrance. She pulled the door open and stepped outside. 'You mind if I come with you to Nottingham?'

'I thought you were going to call a meeting with your team, try and get some information about what we're doing.'

'Well, I get the feeling we have an opportunity to see our Belfast friends at the rally today, and if we can follow them, we might find our inside man.' She tossed Brendan the key. 'You can drive.'

Brendan unlocked the AMG and got in behind the wheel. Adjusting the seat, he pulled the door closed. 'These doors are very heavy.'

'Bullet proof,' Louise said, as she got in the front passenger seat and fastened her seatbelt. She lowered the window. 'My father's paranoia was just,' she spoke humorously, 'even if it didn't save his life in the end.

Brendan started the engine. 'Well, between you and me, we can perhaps get revenge for him.' He put the car in gear and took off down the driveway.

Louise looked at him. 'Why are you doing this, really?'

'I know what it's like to lose my father. And I also know the sense of accomplishment I felt when I put my father's killer to sleep.'

'I look forward to feeling the same.' She coughed. 'Our Asian friends have a nice clothes shop in Nottingham. Let's go and change your wardrobe, make you look like some C18 headcase.' She ran her hand along the top of Brendan's head, still being flirtatious with him. 'You've got short hair already, would you take it all the way down to a skinhead?'

He shook his head. 'No chance.'

'Are you hungry?'

'What time does the rally start at?'

'Around midday. We've plenty of time.'

'I could eat.'

'Okay, I know just the place.' She pulled a cigarette box out of her handbag. 'You mind if I smoke in here?'

'It's your car.'

Chapter Twenty-three

THE TIME WAS ELEVEN thirty. Brendan stood looking at himself in the mirror of the booth in Salim's Urban Outfit store down a narrow alleyway off one of Nottingham's central streets. The clothes appeared to be a good quality and an affordable price. He felt awkward, looking at himself in his stonewash jeans, heavy black boots and black bomber jacket. He gathered his own clothes up and exited the booth. Louise and Salim stood speaking in a low tone, Louise had her eyes focussed solely on Brendan, whereas Salim's glazed brown eyes were darting all around the shop, as if expecting someone to be listening in on their conversation.

'You look...' Louise paused, her face struggling not to expand into a huge grin.

'Like a member of Combat 18.' Salim was quick to finish Louise's sentence.

'Then our work here is done,' Brendan said. 'How much?'

Salim offered Brendan his hand. 'For you, sir, and for what you're doing, it is on the house.'

Brendan shook Salim's hand. The Asian towered over Brendan at least seven inches and his glove of a hand made Brendan's hand look more child-like than he was used to.

'Salim here said there are many eyes watching us in Nottingham today,'

'So, I hope when they see someone like me leaving this shop, they'll understand the reason for this?' Brendan let go of Salim's hand.

'I hope Allah is kind to us all and allows us all to get on with our lives and not have any bloodshed. I wish we can all live in peace and harmony together.'

'I guess it's up to Billy Moore and whatever they're planning, but only time will tell.' Brendan looked at Louise, then back at Salim. 'I wish the same, but one thing growing up in Belfast has taught me, is that wishful thinking is not always to only option, and sometimes you have to stand up for yourself.'

'Mr Cleary, I like to let Allah...'

'With all due respect Salim, Allah is not going to stop them scumbags wrecking your homes, injuring or killing people you love. The world is not a fair place, and you sometimes have to fight back.' Brendan gestured towards the ball of clothes he was holding under his arm. 'Can I have a bag for these?'

'Yes of course.' Salim turned and made his way towards the counter.

The three of them were shocked when a brick came crashing through the display window next to the front door. A group of men could be heard shouting racial slogans whilst running off.

Salim threw the bag to Brendan and rushed to the door. Brendan looked at Louise.

'Looks like that's what we can expect from today then.' Brendan put the clothes in the bag and followed Louise towards the front door.

'Salim, thank you for your help,' Louise stroked his arm affectionately as the Asian stood, arms folded, staring down at the headless manakin, the head rolling away.

Brendan stepped outside, a bunch of onlookers gawking in their direction. A tub of red paint was lay half empty next to the window. The sign that ran along the shop's entrance now had a red blotch along with a nice big dent, thanks to the impact of the tin. Brendan looked up the street in the direction of where the men had run, a group of Asians were now walking towards the shop, all glaring at Brendan. They certainly didn't look pleased to see him standing there. Brendan was as equally pleased to see them.

'What are you looking...' Louise stopped, as she seen the group of Asians getting closer. 'Shit.'

'It's alright,' Brendan said, looking at the three.

'Christ!' Louise said.

One of the three pulled a knife. Another produced a hammer.

'We knew scum like you were coming into our city today, but we didn't realise you'd be that stupid that attack one of our shops, and stand around...'

'Unless you're going to butter me some bread with that knife or help with nailing a board to this broken window, put those away,' Brendan said. 'We're not here...'

'Irish?' The one with the hammer shouted. 'You're the Irish bastard that's causing all the....'

'He's not...' Louise didn't have a chance to finish, when the one with a knife, lifted his hand, pointing the knife a Brendan.

'I'm going to cut your fucking throat, mate!' He stepped within five feet of Brendan, but before he had a chance to take another step, Louise's pistol pressed into the side of his cheek.

'Look, everyone just calm down,' Brendan said. 'Salim.' He shouted into the shop. No response. 'Salim.'

The sound of feet crunching over broken glass grew louder as Salim appeared at the shop's entrance. He shouted something in Arabic. The group relaxed. He then looked at Brendan then Louise. 'Whatever you are doing, I wish the both of you the best of luck. But if your methods don't work, ours will.'

The hammer wielding Asian approached the shop, looking at the damage. He looked back at Brendan. 'I'm ready to kill some of these bastards.' His local accent got thicker with the increase in aggression in his voice.

'And with Ramadan soon approaching, there are going to be a lot of angry Muslim's around here,' the one with the knife said.

'Let's go,' Brendan said, taking Louise by the hand, making their way passed the group.

They both hurried up the street, the sun was breaking through behind the thick grey clouds. Brendan looked up at the sky. 'Looks like it's a good day for a rally.' He looked at Louise, her stare fixed on her phone. 'Anything interesting?'

'Davy English has said there's a lot of C18 recruitment going on in every major city in the UK. They've got an army of four thousand strong. After the recent bombings in London and at the pop concert, they've had loads of people flock to join their ranks.'

'Moore and Moore Jr will love having their little army growing again. I wouldn't be surprised if they start recruiting back in Belfast again.'

'It's funny you should say that,' Louise said. 'Apparently they've been back and forward to Belfast.'

'OId Davy English is proving to be quite useful then,' Brendan said, as they walked past an armed patrol, a group of police officers ready for whatever might kick off. The cop closest to them looked to be of Asian origin and was having a good stare at Brendan.

'There's going to be police all over the city today,' Louise said. She looked at Brendan. 'Let's not get ourselves arrested. That might be hard for us to get out of.' She shoved her phone back in her pocket. 'I'd say you and Lorna are still quite high up on the local wanted lists.'

Brendan smiled, then laughed without humour. He took his phone out of his pocket. 'I'm just going to check up on the other public enemy.' He called Lorna. The phone rang once before she answered. 'Glad you're feeling better.'

'I was just about to call you,' Lorna said, sounding tired.

'You okay?'

'Feel very weak and tired. Every time I stand up I feel like I'm going to fall over. '

'Just stay in bed then.' Brendan looked ahead as they got closer to the protest.

Lorna coughed then cleared her throat. 'You having fun?'

'Well I'm walking around Nottingham dressed as a C18 recruit, about to join in with the rally.'

Lorna laughed. 'I'd love to see you in your little bomber jacket and big dumb looking boots.'

Brendan laughed. 'I'll send you a photo after.'

'Seen anyone you recognise?'

'No.' Brendan looked at Louise. 'But I'm hoping to find a particular person. If these guys are making bombs, I think I've got an idea who the bomb maker might be.'

'Who?'

'A scruffy looking guy call Greystone,' Brendan said. 'He was the top bomb maker for the UFF and UDA. He's not really to usual type you'd find in the ranks, not like a lot of the other bruisers.'

'Most of them were knuckle draggers,' Lorna scoffed.

'Greystone was slightly more sophisticated than that, more of a thinking man. Smart.'

'Not smart enough to get a real job and live a normal life.' Lorna joked.

'Touche!' Brendan joked.

'Will a guy like that be at a rally?' Lorna said. 'Guys like him usually stay behind the scenes. Bomb makers are usually quite like snippers. Loners by default.'

'Probably not,' Brendan agreed. 'But if Moore and any of his comrades are attending, they'll stand out like a sore thumb.'

Chapter Twenty-Four

THE RALLY LOOKED SURPRISINGLY well organised. And well turned out. Brendan and Louise approached the crowd with caution, blending into the aggressive sea of skinheads, black coats, and rowdy adults who, by the way some were acting, seemed to be a few genes behind on the evolutionary track. Police were heavy and armed. Batons and shields, full riot gear was worn. Officers on horseback, in cars and on foot. It appeared that the local officials knew the possibility of violence was real and a high probability. The fact there were almost the same amount of law enforcement on the streets of Nottingham as protestors, the taxpayer was forking out quite a bit pound for controlling ring-wing element calling itself the New C18.

Brendan scanned the crowd, stepping into it, looking around, hoping to spot someone worth noting. Nobody. Towards the front of the crowd, outside the local Muslim cross-community centre, were a group of six men, standing facing an equal number of police officers, blocking the entrance to the centre. The fact there were a number of furious looking Muslims, being forced to stay inside, it was evident that what was advertised as a peaceful protest, was close to erupting into chaos.

Brendan couldn't be sure, but from the back, one of the leaders, who, judging from the side to side bobbing of the head, and overly aggressive stance, that was Billy Moore Jnr, and the man to the left, was his father. They were two peas in a pod and were rarely separated.

Brendan pulled Louise close, and shouted in her ear. 'I think that's Moore and Moore Jnr at the front.'

'How can you tell, from the back?'

'Their size and body language,' Brendan shouted. He turned and moved closer, taking Louise by the hand to follow him. They pushed their way through the crowd, almost reaching the front.

Louise stopped and pulled Brendan to stop. 'We're getting too close to the police.'

Brendan turned and looked at her. Her eyes were glazed, her gaze fixed on the group. He felt her hand squeeze his hand tighter, perhaps imagining her grip being around the neck of her father's murderer. 'You'll get your revenge,' he said. He turned and looked back at the front, just as the group turned to face the crowd. An uproar of cheers blared across the street as the people in question, stood egging the crowd on. Moore Jnr started chanting. Muslims Out. Get out of Britain. Muslims out. Get out of Britain. Muslims out. Get out of Britain.

Moore Snr started waving a Union Jack and shouted. 'When do we want it?'

The crowd shouted. 'NOW, NOW, NOW!'

Brendan looked at Louise, she looked at him. 'Do you recognise anyone else here?' She shouted in his ear.

Brendan looked around the crowd. He shook his head. Then he caught the eye of Moore Jnr's girlfriend, she was looking directly at Brendan. A smug grin slowly stretched across her face. A sultry smile from someone that wanted more than just a kiss. Brendan held her gaze for a second. She kept staring at him. He kept his sight fixed on her. The chants continued. Muslims out. Muslims out. Muslims out. Muslims out!

'Looks like someone's caught your attention,' Louise shouted. 'But that nasty little bitch will cut your balls given half a chance.'

Brendan smirked, still looking at her. 'I've met girls like her before, I know how to work my way around them.' The moment he said this, her gaze was snatched away from Brendan's as Moore Jnr grabbed her, mouthing something to her. He then looked straight at Brendan. Brendan couldn't understand what he'd mouthed to him, but he got the message.

The aggressive chants were blown out by a large group of Muslim counter protestors making their way down the street, stretching the limits of the police resources.

Moore Jnr, being led by his father, made his way, dragging his girlfriend with him towards the oncoming opposition. Things were beginning to heat up. Brendan continued to look for anymore of the old paramilitaries from home, but they all looked and sounded like locals. But the crowd was an extreme bunch of individuals. Both male and female. There was barely room to move. The crowd had grown more condensed. Moore had managed to fill the street to a five hundred strong crowd of angry, skin head, Union Jack, anti-Islam totting individuals, that believed in what they were doing. Their hate woven deeply into them, perhaps from a young age. And a notorious superstar and loyalist folk hero like Moore as their new leader, these thugs were not only fired up, but were being directed down a road which there was no turning back from.

The aggressive chants from both Moore's crowd and the Muslim opposition grew louder and louder. They got closer to each other. News reports stood at a distance. Police stood in a line separating the two groups. The expression on the face of some of the officers was not one that inspired confidence in their ability to maintain control if things were to get out of hand.

Brendan looked at a young female officer. Her fresh face, and nervous stance made her look not only incapable of executing her authority, but would cave in if any of the crowds were to test the strength of the officers. As much as Brendan disliked the police force and any government body, he understood that the individuals working within, were, to the most, just there to earn a living and go home to their families at night. The officer flinched nervously as a firework went off in the crowd of Muslims. Whoever threw it, was in the side Brendan and Louise currently stood. Next came a red flare, launched into the crowd of Muslims. Someone directly behind Brendan shouted kill the dirty murdering bastards. Burn them all.

The Muslim crowd grew more aggressive, trying to get through the police line. The noise was now deafening. Brendan and Louise both stood watching as bricks and bottles began to be launched into the crowd of Muslims.

Brendan looked Louise. 'This is about to get out of control.'

'Look,' Louise shouted, pointing into the air.

Brendan turned the direction she was pointing a flaming missile was soaring through the air. A petrol bomb. Straight into the crowd of Muslims, igniting a number of them. The Muslim crowd dispersed, trying to get as far away from the flames as possible. Fellow protestors, including police officers ran to help put the flames out.

Louise screamed in terror along with many others. She grabbed Brendan's forearm, digging her claws into his skin. He grimaced, not at the stabbing finger nails, but at the sickening cries of those on fire. The sound of them screaming was something a person would have great trouble getting out of their mind. Moore and Moore Jnr disappeared. Brendan caught a glimpse of something he could use in Moore Jnr's girlfriend. She was shouting at him, and judging from her body language, she was more interested in going to help those on fire than disappear. With an aggressive tug of her arm, Moore Jnr dragged her along with him as he followed his father, back through the crowd, creating more distance between them and the still human fireballs.

Brendan dropped his head and turned as Moore and his crew filtered through their crowd of supporters, coming in towards them. Brendan looked at Louise, she was reaching into her handbag.

'You produce that here, and innocent people will get hurt.' Brendan grabbed her hand that was now inside the bag, forcing it to stay inside. 'Let the gun go. Here is not the place for this.'

'They've planned this whole thing.'

'You get caught shooting them here, and you go to prison,' Brendan shouted, as the sound of sirens pierced the air. 'Look, the police are swarming the place now, and there are camera's everywhere. Let's go, I've got everything I need from today.' He grabbed her arm. 'Come on hurry up, they're going to start lifting people.' They rushed back through the crowd in the direction they came.

Two police vans roared down the street towards them, skidding. The doors flew open and the back-up dis-embarked. The crowd of Muslims were shouting hysterically for the police to do something, but they were outnumbered ten to one by Moore's followers who were now running in all directions. The armed troops chasing whoever was at their closest, knocking the protestors to the ground.

One of the cops made a beeline for Brendan and Louise. Brendan grabbed Louise by the hand, dragging her in the opposite direction towards a narrow entry. The officer was fast, catching up with them in no time, it was either risk a baton in the back of the head, or put the cop down.

'Bastard's catching us,' Louise shouted.

Brendan let go of her hand. He stopped, allowing the officer to charge right into him. His baton in the air. Brendan put his right forearm up to block the blow that was coming straight for his head. The officer swung the baton, it bounced off Brendan's forearm, sending an agonising sharp pain run all the way down his arm.

'Don't fucking move, you piece of shit,' the officer shouted, 'you're under arrest.'

Brendan grabbed the officer's hand, whipped the wrist in a snapping motion. The sound of bone breaking caused the officer to scream in agony. Brendan quickly followed up by sending his right foot into the inside of the officer left knee, sending the joint in the opposite way, shattering the ligaments, tearing every tendon holding the bone in place. The officer dropped to the ground.

'Brendan let's go,' Louise shouted. 'There's more coming.' She fired a shot in the air. A male and female officer coming to the aid of their wounded colleague, instinctively ducked. Brendan turned and ran into the alleyway. 'Love your moves.' Louise shouted.

'We can't get caught now.' He looked behind him, as the two officers helped their colleague back up to his feet, both of them watching as Brendan and Louise got further into the distance.

As they reached the end of the alley, they both slowed to a jog, then a fast walk. The sound of a chopper in the air meant they'd all be on the evening news. Either caught on one of the cameras on the ground, or from the helicopter's birds-eye-view.

'Do you know...' Brendan was cut off as a blue Rolls Royce skidded to a halt right alongside them. The black tinted windows wouldn't reveal who was on the inside, but the rear door opened. A middle-aged Asian man, holding a gun, indicated he wanted them to get in,

'Thank god, Omar. Get us out of here,' Louise shouted, rushing towards the car. She looked back towards Brendan. 'It's okay, Brendan, he's a friend.'

Brendan looked back up the alley way, the police were gone. But for how long? He turned and looked in the car. The guy Louise had called Omar did not long like the type of person people said no to, and he also didn't look like the kind of person you'd want to get into the back of a car with, especially with the weapon he was holding.

Louise got in. She turned and looked at Brendan. 'Come on.'

'I'm closing the door, Mr Cleary,' Omar said. 'Let's go.'

Reluctantly, Brendan jumped into the car. At the press of a button, the car door closed and they took off.

Chapter Twenty-Five

'WELCOME TO THE INCREASINGLY dangerous streets inner city Nottingham, Mr Cleary,' Omar said. 'I'd advise you not to be too concerned, but judging from the city you call home, I'm sure you've seen it all before.'

'Unfortunately, that's true. And call me Brendan.'

'Very well. Brendan.' Omar holstered set his weapon down and extended his over-sized paw of a hand out for Brendan to shake. His navy suit glistened under the shine of the star effect on the roof of the inner cabin. His white gold bracelet on the hand offered out, made him look like one of those lords of the bling. His swollen knuckles and disfigured bone structure of his hands meant he didn't always live such a life of luxury. His cauliflower ears and fat nose that ran in two different directions down the centre of his face was also a sign he was perhaps a scrapper, who's hard-man image was what helped him climb to the level in society that provided him with the expensive suits and jewellery.

Brendan accepted his hand. It was clammy and uncomfortable. Brendan didn't think Omar the nervous type, perhaps the sweaty palms were more of a side-effect of a drug that he was taking, which made him look like a hypocrite, given his religion.

'I've heard we both have a common enemy,' Omar said, looking at Brendan, then at Louise. He smiled at her, showing two gold teeth at the front. 'We're in the presence of a superstar, an enemy of the state.' He looked back at Brendan. 'I remember watching you on the news, throwing Prime Minister Thorn out of a British Army helicopter like he was nothing but a common criminal.'

'That's what he was,' Brendan said.

Omar nodded his head, holding his gaze. 'The notorious Brendan Cleary,' he laughed. 'Now here to help the Muslim community, you're such a kind man.' Omar spoke mockingly.

'Yeah, I know. I'm thinking of starting a charity.' Brendan matched Omar's sarcasm with his own.

'You calling my people charity cases?'

'That's your description, not mine.'

Omar leaned forward in his seat, glaring right at Brendan. 'Smart.' He looked at Louise. 'But smart people aren't bullet proof, are they?'

'If you were going to shoot me, you certainly wouldn't be doing it in this nice car, you wouldn't want my blood messing up this fancy white interior.'

Omar sat back in his chair.

'Are you both done measuring your dicks?' Louise sighed. Brendan and Omar kept looking at each other. Omar broke the stare first. It wasn't a victory to Brendan in the sense he felt like he'd won anything, but in the world he'd just stepped into, he'd perhaps gained at least a little bit of respect from Omar. 'Brendan's the best help we've got to stop this lunatic Moore, before there's an all-out war on the streets.'

'After what's just happened, that war may have already started.' Brendan sat back in his chair. Crossing one leg over the other, he joined his hands and set them on his lap. He looked at Omar. 'I get the feeling petrol bombs are just the start of it. There will be a whole lot more to come.'

'Our people can be pretty explosive when they want to be, and considering the new wave of violence is coming from bastards from your part of the world, give me one good reason why I shouldn't crucify you like your fucking Jesus Christ and offer you up as a painful example of what is coming to these right wing inbreeds if their attacks continue.'

Brendan uncrossed his legs and sat forward. 'Because, dead, I'm useless to you. But alive, I'm the best chance you have of saving some Muslim lives coming up to your most important time of the year.'

'You're the Muslim saviour we've all been waiting for,' Omar chuckled.

Brendan sat back, crossing his leg over again, 'You can call me Ramadan Man if it makes you feel better.'

Omar burst into a fit of laughter. He looked at Louise. His smile dropping. He cleared his throat. 'I'm sorry to hear what happened to your father. He was always a fair man.'

'Thank you.' Louise cleared her throat and shuffled in her seat.

'I knew when I heard from Salim, and that you were in the city with a certain notorious Irishman, you might need some help.' He looked at Brendan. 'Where's your other lady friend? The gorgeous MI5 agent you wrecked Belfast with?'

'She's gone.' Brendan was quick to answer. 'She got fed up with the life and disappeared. Left nothing but a note and apology.'

Omar winced. 'Ouch. Nasty bitch.'

Brendan nodded his head. 'That she is.' He looked at Louise. 'I'm interested in helping Louise level the score for her father, and then I'll be off, too.' He smirked. 'I've had enough rain to last a lifetime. Time for a new start in a warmer climate.'

'So how can you help your Muslim brothers?'

'By doing the same thing that's going to help Louise get closer to her father's killers.' Brendan gestured to his clothes. 'My current appearance, the tone of my skin, and my knowledge of the new leaders of these inbred right wing bastards is an advantage I wouldn't have if I was any of the rest of your crew.'

Omar pursed his lip, nodding his head. 'And you have a way of getting close to these ex UFF and UDA soldiers from Belfast? Does the fact you are who you are not cause an issue? Brendan Cleary!'

'I don't need to get close to Moore or Moore Jnr. I know who in their group that I should focus on.'

'Who?' Omar said.

'Just let me take care of them,' Brendan said.

'And what is your asking price for the heads of these bastards?' Omar asked.

'I've already offered him a shit load of cash,' Louise said. 'He's refused. Said he's happy to help as long as he gets his hands on Moore and Moore Jnr.'

'They must have really upset you?' Omar's eyebrows met in the middle, he tilted his head slightly to the side, as if searching for a glimmer of deception.

'Not me personally. But for every innocent person they tortured and killed in my neighbourhood. My father would be turning in his grave if he knew I had an opportunity and didn't take it.'

'Best not upset your father, then.'

'His father made him the man he is,' Louise said, looking at Brendan, slightly stroking her neck. She looked at Omar who was shaking his head, unaware who she was talking about. 'The Ghost!'

Omar's eyes almost popped out of their sockets. He slowly turned his head back towards Brendan. 'Of course, Cleary. Damien Cleary is your father.'

'The one and only,' Brendan said.

'Boss the news,' the driver shouted.

A silence fell over the car as the driver increased the volume of a report from BBC Radio Nottingham. The reporter spoke about how five men and two women were being taken to the local hospital. Three of the men and the two women had been ignited by the petrol bomb. The others had injured themselves trying to help. The centre of Nottingham has become a battle ground of rioting. The heavily populated Muslim community have taken to the streets. A number of protestors who'd came out to show support for Moore Jnr had been arrested. Police have started an investigation. They want anyone with information about who may have been behind the petrol bombing to contact the police. Moore and Moore Jnr were wanted for questioning. Moore was said to be the one who organised the event. Police have issued warrants for the arrest of a male supporter of the protest and his female accomplice who'd discharged a weapon while resisting arrest.

Brendan looked at Louise. 'Looks like we need to lie low for a while.'

'I don't plan on staying in this country any longer than I have to anyway.' Louise spat. She looked at Omar. 'I'm guessing this city is about to ignite into chaos.'

Omar was deep in thought. He grunted to acknowledge he'd heard Louise.

'How much of an influence do you have on the local Muslims?' Brendan said.

'Quite substantial, why?'

'I think you should try and tell them not to go getting themselves lifted and making things worse. Billy Moore is an animal. He'll come at you with everything he's got.'

'My Irish brother, if any of my fellow Muslims die because of this stunt, this fucking city is going to burn to the ground.' He looked at Louise. 'It's not safe for any non-Muslim to be around here right now. If they don't know you, or Brendan, they'll batter you then ask questions later. Where can I take you?' He looked at Brendan, 'I'll take you both to safety.'

Before she had a chance to reply, Brendan spoke. 'Take us to Leicester. We've got to have that meeting with your guys,' he looked at Louise. She looked at Brendan, then at Omar.

'Mohammad,' Omar shouted up front to the driver. 'Take us to Leicester.' His phone rang. He lifted it off the white leather seat, looking at Brendan as he answered it. He spoke in Arabic. He spoke fast, and with a tone that only enhanced his angry expression. After a few seconds he hung up. 'People are very angry.'

Chapter Twenty-Six

BRENDAN AND LOUISE were dropped off in Leicester City Centre outside the Leicester Arms. Omar had left them with a promise that a lot of people were going to be hurt after what happened today in Nottingham.

'Fancy grabbing a quick cup of coffee?' Louise said, flipping the collar up of her jacket. Taking cover from the rain that had begun to pour.

Brendan nodded his head and followed as Louise led the way further down the street towards a bustling Costa. Louise ignored the shop and continued around the corner.

'Why'd you not want Omar to take us back to the safe house?' Louise said, forcing her hands into her pockets as the rain got heavier. The summer time shower was heavy, yet the blinding sun, piercing out from the edge of the black cloud that was quickly passing over the sky asked for sunglasses in the rain. Part of the strange weather in this part of the world.

'Two reasons,' Brendan said. 'One, it's your safe house, and it would be stupid having more people than needed know about it, and two and most importantly...'

'The lady you love is there, maybe still defenceless, and you don't want something to happen to her?'

'Exactly.'

Louise stopped outside a small coffee shop called Greenwood's. The Green sign above the entrance still reeked of paint. The brown tables and chairs outside gave that natural forest type effect. A good idea, given the name. Louise held the door open, letting Brendan go in first. She had a grin smeared across her face, looking at him.

'What?' Brendan said, as he stepped into the shop.

'I'd love to see you get angry.'

Brendan shook his head. 'Why?'

'This city and all the scumbags wouldn't know what hit them.' She brushed passed him, stroking his arm, still playing the flirtatious game.

'Let's hope it doesn't come to that.' Brendan followed her towards the counter. The shop had that homely mix of ground coffee beans and freshly baked scones just out of the oven.

A young lady who didn't look a day older than eighteen stood at the till, a guy who looked old enough to be her father was stood over her. The girl wore a white green and white shirt, and the guy had a plain white shirt. He looked as if he was the manager, and or owner, and was training up a new recruit. The girl spoke as if reading from the company script, upselling them to a large cappuccino each.

As they took their seats, Louise gestured back at the girl. 'I remember feeling like that, my father training to me to work on the bar.'

'So you actually worked for a living?' Brendan joked, as he took his jacket off. He hung it over the back of his chair, looking at the girl. He picked up his cappuccino and took a drink of it. 'Thanks for the drink the way.'

'I worked for my father since I was fourteen years old. I've earned everything I own.' She took a sip of her coffee, looking at Brendan over the rim of her cup. 'There was a time when I held my father's entire empire together. And I'll die before I let some scumbags bring it down.'

'Are you talking about external or internal?'

'Both, but disloyal bastards are worse. You can understand your enemy wanting to screw you over, but someone who's already on your side,' she shook her head while taking another sip. 'I'll happily fry them in a bath of acid. Which is why I've wanted to come here for a quiet coffee first.'

Brendan looked at her, sitting forward in his seat. 'Go on.'

'What if they'd fed back to Moore and co that a certain Mr Cleary is helping us out?'

'It won't matter.'

'Why won't it?'

'Because they won't recognise me like this.' Brendan indicated at the way he was dressed and looked in the mirror, rubbing his hand over his cropped hair. 'I was a scruff bag back in Belfast. Long hair and equally long beard.'

'Very handsome.' Louise joked. 'You look better now I'm guessing.'

'It was one of the things my father drilled into me with serious importance. He made sure I knew that I had to be able to change my appearance as quickly as possible, if I wanted to get through the tough times that were to come.' He took another drink of his coffee. 'I never knew what those times were until the day Lorna walked into my life.' He pulled his phone from his pocket. 'Speaking of which.' He unlocked it and gave her a call.

She answered after the second ring. 'Brendan,' she sounded more upbeat.

'You're feeling better, then?'

'Much better,' Lorna said. 'I feel useless all cooped up.'

'Have you tried getting up?'

'I did. I don't know what's wrong. I get dizzy and feel like I'm about to fall over every time I try to walk.'

'It sounds like your motor skills are up the left.' Brendan looked at Louise. 'What about the sickness?'

'Stomach's settled. Where are you?'

'In Leicester. I'm guessing you've heard about what happened in Nottingham?'

'Heard all about it. Word is spreading through social media that it's a retaliation for English being taken.'

'Fuck,' Brendan said. 'That's our fault.'

'There's definitely a dirty rat in Louise's group. She needs to find out who it is before this gets worse.'

'I know, petrol bombings will be the beginning, it'll get a lot worse.' He finished his coffee. 'I've found a weak link in Moore Jnr's armoury, I think. I'm going to pay her a visit.'

'Who is she?' Lorna said.

'His girlfriend. She was at the rally today and didn't exactly look too supportive of their cause. When the petrol bomb was chucked into the crowd, she was more interested in helping those on fire than standing and cheering with the rest of them.'

'Be careful, Brendan.'

Brendan smirked. 'Careful's my middle name.'

'See you soon, Brendan. I love you.'

His smirk dropped. 'I love you, too.' He hung up the phone. Louise was staring at her phone.

She pocketed the phone and finished her coffee. 'I've just sent out a group message to all our guys. We're having a meeting to see if we can sniff out the rat.' She stood up.

Brendan grabbed his coat and stood up with her.

Louise zipped her coat up and thanked the new recruit who was still looking out of place behind the counter.

'I'll see you in a couple of hours,' Brendan said, as he followed Louise out of the shop.

'God luck,' she said. She turned to the left, and Brendan took off to the right. 'The first place he was going was to get a change of clothes. He didn't want to be in the C18 style attire a moment longer.

Making his way along King Street, Brendan spotted a clothing shop that reminded him of Milan and the shop close to the Via Paulo Sarpi where he and Lorna had changed their clothes. As he passed the front window, a small, middle-aged Asian lady was washing the shop's front window. He stopped and looked at his reflection of the gleaming glass. He shook his head and thought – I'm not walking another foot dressed like this.

He stepped inside.

'Good afternoon, sir,' the lady said, she seemed to be in high spirits, taking great pride in her job.

'Good afternoon.' Brendan walked past the suits and other formal clothing, feeling like something more casual. He eyed a pair of stretch fit jeans and a black and white shirt. A pair of heeled ankle shoes and a hooded leather jacket. He had his new wardrobe. After he'd tried on the clothes, he paid for them then asked for a pair of scissors to cut the tags. The lady was happy to dispose of the other clothes he'd been wearing.

He stepped out of the shop like a new man. Grateful to have a hood on the jacket, he threw it up as another shower had arrived. His phone had been vibrating while in the shop, but he'd ignored it. He checked who the call was from. It was Lorna. He was about to call her back, when she beat him to it.

'Lorna, you okay?'

'I've been looking at the symptoms I've been having, it's some new drug that's on the streets. In small doses, it's meant to give you a buzz like you get from cocaine. An overdose of it caused what I've had.'

Brendan stopped. Looking around him, clenching his jaws. 'So, one of those bastards have drugged you.'

'Looks like it,' she cleared her throat. 'Where are you now?'

'I'm still in Leicester. I've just changed out of those cheap looking C18 clothes.'

'Where is Louise?'

'She's gone back to the pub. She's going to try and find out who the rat is.'

'Good idea.' Lorna's tone sounded suspicious. 'You sure we can trust her?'

'If I wasn't, I wouldn't have left you up there on your own.'

'Okay. According to what I've learned about this drug, it's symptoms pass after a day or two. After the sickness, it's supposed to make you feel dizzy and you're advised to not operate any machinery.'

'No guns either?' Brendan joked.

Lorna cleared her throat. 'Listen, Brendan. I know family is a touchy thing for both of us, but...'

'But you've been thinking about your sister in Chelmsford?'

'She's my only sister.'

'You miss her, don't you?'

'I do.' Lorna paused for a second. 'I'm sorry, I know it would be stupid to try and contact her,'

'Hey,' Brendan stopped her. 'If you want to see her, we'll figure it out.' The rain had gotten heavier. 'Listen, I'll call you back later, it's pissing down don't want to wreck the phone.'

'Get back here as soon as you can, I can't wait until I get my hands on you.'

Brendan smiled. 'Me too.' He hung up and dropped the phone in his jeans pocket. He put his head down and continued at a fast pace.

Chapter Twenty-Seven

GOING ON NOTHING BUT hope that Moore Jnr's girl-friend was going to be at the shop, Brendan entered, glancing around. The girl he was hoping to meet was not there, in-stead there was a male, around Brendan's age. He looked at Brendan through glazed red eyes. His hair was long and greasy, the shop lights shining off the top. His beard was black a had more of a matte complexion.

'White coffee, please,' Brendan said. He looked around the shop, in addition to him, three other people were seated together. They looked and dressed to the way Moore Jnr's girlfriend had. 'Quiet in here today, mate.' Trying to make some small talk with the guy was hard for someone who gen-erally wasn't was for up it himself. But Brendan thought he may as well try and make a friend.

'Yeah, a lot of our usual crowd are in Nottingham today, there's been a support rally for our cause.'

'What cause is that?'

The guy looked up at Brendan a little smirk appearing on his face. 'If you don't know then, maybe you're in the wrong club, mate.'

Brendan looked at the guy's tattoos, his sleeveless t-shirt showed bulging arms with zero skin visible. The guy looked like a biker. Or a tattoo artist.

'I've just arrived in Leicester today,' Brendan said.

'Not really a holiday spot, pal,' the guy made the coffee and began to loosen up.

'Neither is Belfast, but it still has tourists every year.'

The guy handed Brendan the cup. 'One eighty, please.'

Brendan handed the guy his card. 'You ever been to Belfast?'

He shook his head, 'no, but my sister's been going back and forward there a lot, her boyfriend's from there.'

Brendan's eyes lit up. 'Really, what part of Belfast is he from? I'm from the Shankill.' He lied.

The guy looked at Brendan. 'Small world. He's from there, too.' He looked around him, then craned his head across the counter. 'But he's not the type you'd want to cross. Bit of a wanker if you ask me.'

Brendan laughed. He didn't want to make the guy too suspicious, so he didn't press him for any more information. 'Thanks for the coffee.'

'Cheers, pal. Welcome to the glorious city of Leicester.' He spoke mockingly.

Brendan took a seat in the corner, where he'd sat the last time, the best view of the entire shop. He looked at his phone. Checking the news, there was still rioting going on in Nottingham. It had gotten much worse. And now it was the Muslim community out wrecking the place. Omar was right. His people were very angry and would only get worse if any of those injured were to die due to their wounds.

Brendan looked up at his new mate, the brother of the girl he'd hoped to get chatting to. He knew she'd be the best person to get more information from. If not her the big guy with the tats would be second best. Or had he already given Brendan something. Why was she going back and forward to Belfast? Was there reason for going back there, other than to see the sights. Brendan was right, Belfast was about as attractive as Leicester. Unless you were interested in the recent conflict that had taken place. But why would Billy Moore Jnr be going back and forward? He had to be gathering more foot soldiers, and or weapons. It was widely known that Moore had not only left a very thick fan base and support network back in Belfast, but he'd also left a heavy arsenal, stashed for the day he come back for it.

Brendan still wanted to get his hands on the girl. She could prove very useful. Omar appeared to be quite an influential person, and he was about to start killing all around them, and if they were to start bringing guns, perhaps even bombs onto the streets of England, then it was going to end badly for a lot of people. And innocent people would be the ones that would suffer the most.

Brendan sat watching the TV, a mind numbing daytime talk show that interviewed troubled adults in front of an audience, finding out why they'd cheated in their relationships, or why they'd not found the strength to come of the drugs or alcohol that had plagued their lives and the lives of those closest to them. Brendan watched on, and, regardless of how beyond the norm his life was, he still managed to feel normal in comparison to the people he was watching. His cup was clasped in his hand and he watched on, amazed. He also felt a new wave of gratitude that he never had to spend his days watching such mindless dribble. Brendan was much happier living life close to death, on the run, mixing with some of the most ruthless people on the planet. At least he felt alive. Like he had a purpose. A purpose that he'd inherited from his late father.

'You don't want to get sucked into that nonsense,' the guy shouted over to Brendan. 'Trust me, it will drag you in.' He laughed, as he came around the serving counter, clearing the tables. He started on the far end of the room to where Brendan was sat, putting the crockery into a black basin, lifting rubbish and brushing crumbs off the tabletops.

'You sound like you're talking from experience.'

He walked closer to Brendan, grinning as he watched the screen. 'Standing in here serving all day, you tend to get quite bored, and you do tend to look for anything to stimulate the mind.' He looked around the shop, the last two customers – an elderly couple – had just left. 'I mean the day shift in this place could bore anyone to death. I'm just glad my shift finishes at five. My sister will have a livelier shift later.'

'You've only a couple of hours to go then,' Brendan said. He took a drink. 'Is business suffering?'

The guy pulled out a chair and sat down facing Brendan. 'This is usually a member's only club.'

'Members of what?'

'You ever heard of Combat Eighteen and Britain First? Two groups that are trying to rid the country of Muslims. Combat Eighteen and Britain First have had a bit of a revival in the past year or so. New leadership. From your part of the world. The leadership had brought them both together.' He didn't speak with the spit of deadly venom that would usually come from someone dedicated to their cause.

'I've seen stuff on the news about it, but never really paid attention to it that much.' Brendan took another drink.

'Personally, nobody bothers me. I think they can all live here if they want to. I think the C18 and Britain First supporters are a bunch of scumbags.'

'You're not going to ask me to become a member?'

He laughed at Brendan. 'Nope.'

'Why are you working here, then?'

I'm just helping my sister. And it's a bit of extra cash. What do you do?'

'I work in insurance.'

'Sounds exciting.'

Brendan smiled. 'It's not, but it pays.'

The guy extended his hand. 'I'm Mark, Mark Berry.'

Brendan was about to give him his real name but managed to stop himself. 'Simon McCarthy.' He shook Mark's hand. 'Cool tattoos.'

'Thanks,' Mark looked down at his arms, rotating them, giving Brendan a full view of the artwork. 'I have my own tattoo studio, just around the corner. You should pop around sometime.' He pulled his phone out of his pocket and pulled a black card out, skull and crossbones on the back of it. He handed it to Brendan. 'I'll do you a twenty-five percent discount on your first tattoo, any size.'

Brendan took the card. 'Thanks. Not really one for tattoos, but I'll come and check it out sometime.'

'It just opened last month so I'm looking for as much business as I can get.'

'I'm sure a lot of the C18 and Britain First skin heads will bring you a lot of business.' Brendan looked over Mark's shoulder as a couple walked in. 'You must have lots of practice at drawing Nazi symbols.' He pointed at the couple. 'You've got some business.'

As Mark got up to go and serve the couple, his sister stormed in, Moore Jnr following her in.

'Fuck.' Brendan stood up and sat on the other side of the table, his back to the rest of the room. But from what he heard, loud words coming from the girl and Moore Jnr, he'd stormed back out of the shop, telling her to go fuck herself. Brendan's phone vibrated in his pocket. He pulled it out. It was from Louise.

I'm holding a meeting with the team this evening. The topic of discussion will be to get them out to Greystone's house. You're welcome to join us. Any luck talking to that hot piece of tattooed ass?

Brendan laughed and half-way through the text, that hot piece of tattooed ass Louise was referring to spoke from directly behind him.

'He's away now, you can stop hiding.'

Brendan looked over his shoulder, and there she was stood over him, craning her neck a little to see if she could read his text. He locked the phone screen and set the device down on the table. 'Who am I hiding from?'

She smirked, then stepped around the table, sitting down at the table, holding his gaze, flirtatiously licking her lips. 'The rather hard looking guy that caught you eyeing me up at the rally today.'

'I believe it was you that was eyeing me up.'

She didn't bother to reply. 'I've got to admit, there's something interesting about you. And it's not just because you come from the same country as my soon to be ex-boyfriend.'

'Why do you say ex?'

'His Irish charm has worn off,' she sighed, looking across the shop towards where her brother was working. 'And you witnessed the way him and his meathead friends acted today. They're all going to get into a lot of trouble over that.'

'I got talking to your brother earlier,' Brendan looked around, as Mark was cleaning the display window. 'He's a nice guy.' He looked down at her tattoos. 'I guess he's the one who drew those?'

She looked down at her arm. The tats ran all the way down her slender limbs, spreading across the wrists and onto her hands. 'He's a great artist, his business is just starting out, so I've got to be showing support.'

Brendan admired the tribal style design that went down her arm. 'No Nazi designs or items to support the cause?'

She didn't laugh. She kind of narrowed her eyes and sucked her teeth at him. 'I have no love or loyalty to their bullshit.'

'Could have fooled me.'

'You don't know anything about me, so don't act as if you do.'

'You sat down at my table, not the other way.'

She smirked.

'I heard you and him arguing. Trouble in paradise?' Brendan was testing the waters, at least to see how well she'd respond. 'Actually, it's none of my business. I wouldn't want people knowing mine and my girlfriend's business.'

'You mean the blond you were with at the rally?'

He just nodded his head. 'Your brother tells me you've been going to Belfast on a holiday. I like that you think it's worthy of a holiday,' he laughed, 'to me it's just plain old Belfast.' He watched her reaction. Her facial expression changed, the cortisol was now coursing through her veins, and Brendan could tell she was uncomfortable.

She cleared her throat and shuffled in her seat, momentarily glancing down at the table then back up at him. Perhaps just enough time for her to think of an idea, perhaps a lie to give for the real reason she was in Belfast. 'He's got a lot of family over there, and he wanted me to meet them,' she lied, and Brendan knew it was lie. 'They're all nice, very welcoming. They do a lot of work in the community, and lot of cross-community relationship building.' She said broke her gaze from him.

Brendan knew it was a lie. Moore's entire family was put out of Belfast, and if they were ever to return, they'd all be shot. He didn't want to press her anymore. More questions would make her suspicious, and suspicion was something likely to scare her off. He offered her his hand. 'Simon.'

She accepted, softly holding his hand. 'Vanessa.'

Brendan paused for a second, now he felt as if he has a ball in his throat.

She looked at him. 'What?'

He shook his head. 'Nothing, just my mother's name.'

'Having the same name as your mother is upsetting to you?' She sniggered, 'it's a pretty common name.'

'Only because she's dead.'

Her smirk dropped. 'I'm sorry.'

'Don't be, you didn't kill her. Drinking did.'

'She was an alcoholic?'

Brendan looked around. A couple of guys walked in, their rowdy presence resounding around the entire shop. He looked back at her. 'I've got to go, but here, give me your phone, I'll give you my number.'

Her eyebrows narrowed, her eyes tiny slits. 'What makes you so sure I want to give you my number?'

'The same reason you've been sitting here chatting to me for the past five minutes.'

She smirked and pulled out her Samsung. 'You're confident, I'll give you that.' She unlocked the screen and handed it to him. He went into her contacts and thumbed in his number, then called the number. His phone vibrated. He handed her the phone back and smiled.

It was good chatting to you,' he said as he stood up. 'Chat to you soon.'

'Yeah,' she followed him with her eyes. 'See you soon.'

He pocketed the phone and headed through the shop, waving at Mark. 'See you later.'

'All the best, Simon, pal.'

Brendan stepped outside the café and called Louise.

She picked up almost immediately. 'You got my message?'

'I did, I'm just finished chatting to our hot piece of tattooed ass.'

'And?'

'Think I might need to fly back to Belfast to have a look around. But what time is the meeting tonight?'

'Eight, we're having it the place we're holding English. Just in case he's got something to add.'

'Okay, great. I'm going back to see Lorna.'
'Okay, I'm staying in the city. See you later.'

Chapter Twenty-Eight

ARRIVING BACK AT THE house, Brendan was glad to find Lorna up and awake, the colour had returned to her cheeks. She looked at him and smiled. 'You're on your own?'

'Yeah, Louise is staying in the city.'

'Best place for her if you ask me.' She mumbled.

'Are we jealous?'

'What?'

'It sounds to me like you're jealous,' he poked her playfully with his index finger.

'Me? Jealous of her?' Lorna sniggered.

'Glad you're feeling better,' he moved in, kissing her on the lips. He looked into her eyes. 'I think I may have to go to Belfast.'

She looked at him, her eyes gazing deeply into his. 'Why?'

Moore Jnr has been going back and forward a lot, I think they're either recruiting back home, or else trying to get their hands on some serious weapons.

'If any of them get seen in Belfast, they'll be shot. His old comrades are not going to give him any weapons.'

'I know, but Moore is smart, and I wouldn't be surprised if he's got a stash of his own somewhere. I've had a chance to talk to Moore Jnr's girlfriend, she's less than happy with what her boyfriend's been getting up, and after seeing what happened to those Muslims at the rally in Nottingham...'

'What happened in Nottingham?'

'A petrol bomb was launched into the crowd protesting against the rally. Some were set on fire.'

Lorna looked down. 'Shit.'

'Louise is in tight with a local community leader on the Muslim side. He seems a nasty piece of work and after what happened today, these guys are arming themselves to the teeth, and can you blame them?'

'Moore's very smart. This was planned, and it's no doubt than when the Muslim community reacts to what's happened today, it'll be a great way for bringing out a bunch of violent extremists, and then: the white skin heads will have more support. It's a smart tactic, and once again Moore will be seen by his small minded followers as a god, a fearless leader who once had the balls to face off against the Provisional IRA and is now conducting a new war, a war against Islamic radicals, radicals that they've created, turning them into human fireballs in the middle of the street.'

'Makes a good story.'

Lorna rubbed her head, appearing dizzy.

'Are you okay? Do you want me to go and make you something to eat?'

'Not sure if your cooking will help me or make me even more sick.'

'Piss off,' Brendan said, playfully pushing her back down on the bed.

She laughed as she pulled him in for another kiss. Her phone rang. She pulled herself away from him and grabbed it from the bedside cabinet. Brendan watched her act suspiciously, as if she were hiding something. She looked at the screen, then looked at him. She pressed the button to end the call, leaving an awkward silence in the room.

'What's wrong with you?' He looked at her, then looked at the phone. She didn't answer. 'What are you being weird for?'

'Nothing. I'm just a bit on edge.'

Brendan tilted his head to the side, looking at her. 'Lorna, come on, it's me. You're probably the most self-assured person I've ever met, not someone that suffers from *anxiety*.'

'It's my sister.'

Brendan's eyes widened. 'You've reached out to her?'

'I'm sorry, I know the risks involved. I just miss her so much, Brendan. And after taking sick, I just had to hear from her.'

'Okay, so we'll pay her a visit. But first, I've got to go to Belfast.'

'You're going straight away?'

'Louise is having a meeting with her team this evening, English is going to be there, too. We're going to inform her crew about Greystone. Have some of our Muslim friends watch Greystone's house. If we find out that Greystone then leaves his house, we'll know someone within her group are traitors and will suffer the consequences.'

'Which would perhaps be the one who's fed me whatever I've been fed.'

'I'll personally chop their balls off if I find out it was one of them.'

Lorna stroked Brendan's face. 'As sweet as that is, I'd rather deal with them myself.' She kissed him and stood up off the bed. 'This is a nice place.' She walked across the room, looking out the window. 'This would be the perfect place to live.' She looked over her shoulder at Brendan. 'For us,' she smiled at him and turned back to the window.

He joined her, both looked over the secluded gardens. 'She's very lucky. But I get the impression it means nothing to her without her father.'

'You really want to help her, don't you?' Lorna said, taking his hand softly in her grasp. 'It's nice.'

'Let's just say I know what she's going through. And a chance to take out a bunch of trouble making scumbags,' he put his arm around her, 'well that's exactly what my father would want me to do.'

She leaned against him, resting her head against his. 'You're a good man, Brendan Cleary.'

They both watched as the rain came on, the gardens appearing more green with the wet.

'You want to come to Belfast with me?'

'I'll buy us two tickets this evening.'

'Okay, I'm going to have a shower then I'll make us some dinner.'

'The last time you made us dinner was in your uncle Bobby's house just outside Belfast.'

'It means we've been eating out too much.' Brendan headed towards the wardrobe and grabbed a towel. 'You want to join me?'

She smiled and bit her lip.

Chapter Twenty-Nine

AFTER THEY ATE, BRENDAN made his way back into Leicester. Lorna, although feeling better, decided it would be better to stay away, at least for now. Whoever it was that drugged her, would be better to think she was still sick, at least that way, if things went wrong, all eggs weren't in the same basket. The time was seven thirty, and Leicester's inner-city traffic was starting to thin out after the usual evening rush hour. The rain was still thumping down, reminding Brendan even more of the beautiful city that he called home. The only difference between Belfast and the current city he found himself in, was Belfast had the sea spray coming in off the coast as an addition to what came down from above.

Brendan's phone had buzzed numerous times since he'd left. A text message or an email. Not something urgent. If it was, whoever it was would have called. He put the car in park and lifted the phone.

Just booked two flights to Belfast tomorrow. See you later. Lorna xxx

'One day I'll turn my back on that place.' He sighed, as he flung the car door open. He closed the door and made his way to the pub. Passing a tattoo shop, reminded him of the new friends he'd made earlier. Pulling out Mark Berry's business card, he thumbed the number into his phone, and sent a text.

Hey, mate. It was nice to meet you today. I'll come by some time and have a look around your shop, not promising I'm going to get a tattoo done, but I always appreciate good artwork. See you soon. Simon.

He dropped his phone in his pocket and pulled the front door open, entering the pub to be hit by the overpowering stench of fried chips and vinegar. Louise was stood behind the bar, serving a couple, a man and a woman that looked to be on a date, both of them glaring at each other, nervous smiles on their faces, both well dressed, clearly having made an effort for the other. As he approached the bar, he smirked, just as she caught his eye.

'What are you smirking at?' She said. She handed the lady of the couple her change and slammed the till drawer closed, walking closer to where Brendan stood. 'Well?'

'It's just funny watching the little empire princess rolling her sleeves up and acting just like anybody else.' He looked passed her. 'Can I have a glass of water?'

She smirked. 'My father always taught me never to get lazy.' She turned around and reached into the fridge, grabbing two bottles of water. She opened them both then handed one to Brendan. 'It's better for business if the owners are on the ground, then they know what exactly is happening.'

Brendan took a drink of the water. 'What about the manager you've employed.'

'The topics of our discussion earlier and later, were all employed by him. I'm not sure if he's up to the job, or if he needs to go into the meat cutter as well.' She took a drink of water and gasped as if she'd just quenched her thirst.

'We're going to Belfast tomorrow.'

'Who's we?' She looked on the spot.

'Me and Lorna.'

'Oh, I thought you meant you and I,' she smiled, 'how is she?'

'Feeling a bit better. But it's better she stays away, floats around in the background.'

'If whoever spiked her thinks she's still sick, she's one less threat to them...' she took another drink. 'Very smart.' Her eyes fixed on something behind Brendan. Brendan looked over his shoulder. The plasma screen was showing news report coming from Nottingham. At the local A&E. 'This isn't good.' She pulled a control out from under the counter and turned the volume up. They both watched as the reporter spoke with a police spokesman and local MP about the attack. They were now investigating two murders and attempted murder. When asked by the reporter, the police spokesman said they were following up a few leads but had not yet gathered any suspects. When asked how this was going to affect community relations in the area, the MP said she was confident that relationships with the Asian community would not suffer from this one-off attack. She did say that the Asian community should not take this as a direct attack from the wider community in Nottingham and that they shouldn't feel alienated.

Brendan sniggered. 'Yeah, right. Tell that to Omar.'

Louise was glued to the screen. Her eyes had glazed over.

'Hey.' Brendan waved his hand in front of her, trying to snatch her attention away, to no success. 'Louise...'

She slowly dragged her attention away from the screen. 'I'm sorry, I just can't wait to burn that scum.'

Brendan forced a smile, understanding her feelings towards the people responsible for her father's murder. 'We've got to be smart about this. Your father taught you how to use your head, didn't he?'

'Of course, he did.' She downed the rest of the water. 'Let's go.' She grabbed her coat from the hanger on the office door and joined Brendan on the customer side of the bar. She looked back at the barman who'd appeared from the office. 'I'll be back before closing.'

He waved them away as they exited the pub.

'I'll drive,' Louise said, pointing a key at the black Range Rover parked directly across the street.

Brendan zipped his coat up as they crossed the road. He pulled the passenger door open. 'Heavy door. Reinforced?' He got in.

She shook her head. 'If people acting as our friends try to snipe us out, they'll not get very far if we're in this. And if that car I've just spotted is what I think it is, we very well might be fired upon before we get to where we're going.' She climbed up into the driver's seat and dropped her handbag on Brendan's lap.

'Who?'

'Three cars behind us. Two men in the back and one in the front. They all looked a bit livelier when we both exited the bar. And the driver's just started the engine, and had just turned off his headlights the second they came on.'

Brendan looked behind but their view was limited on account of the rear window tints.

'It's a silver Mercedes, S class.'

'Moore's men?'

Louise nodded her head and started the engine. 'Guess they've known we were here.'

'They'll probably know we're on our way to the meeting with English.' Brendan pulled his father's pistol out. He checked it was loaded. 'Sounds like our little rat is going to the meeting. It's just a matter of finding out who it is.'

She put the car in gear and took off. 'We'll let them follow us for a while.' She looked at Brendan. 'Reach below your seat. You should find something quite useful.'

Brendan done so and pulled out a black Uzi sub-machine gun along with a box of ammunition. Holding the military grade weapon in his hand, he looked across at Louise. 'Looks like Moore isn't the only one to get his hands on some serious weapons.'

'Our Asian friends are quite resourceful.'

'Don't take this the wrong way, but you do realise that your entire team could be setting you up for the fall?'

She glanced over at him. 'What do you mean?'

'I've seen the way they look at you, I can smell contempt a mile away, even the guy you've left in charge back at the bar.'

She didn't say anything.

'Don't let your anger cloud your judgement.'

'The infamous Brendan Cleary is giving me advise on how to keep my cool?'

'Let's just say I've had to learn from past mistakes.'

'Now Mr Cleary is becoming philosophical in his old age.'

He checked the magazine. It was fully loaded. 'So, what's the plan here, boss lady? You want to go Arnold Schwarzenegger on this Merc?'

'That's why we're not sticking to the city roads, we're going to take the country road to Nottingham and then we can take their car off road, then if they want to talk, great, if they don't, their bodies will be left on the side of the road.'

Brendan set the gun back down again. 'You know if we leave a bunch of dead bodies on the side of a country lane, it won't be hard for the police to trace it back to us.'

'What do you suggest?'

'We get them talking. The fact we know they're following us, gives us the upper hand.' His phone sounded. It was Lorna. 'Are you okay?'

'Yes, I'm just checking up on you, how's everything going?'

'A car's following us from the Leicester Arms to the meet in Nottingham.'

'Do you know who it is?'

'Couple of Moore's men.' Brendan cleared his throat, knowing what was coming next, he said it first. 'I'll be careful.'

'I'm coming,' Lorna said. 'I'm not sitting here doing nothing. Ask Louise where the car keys are.'

Brendan looked at Louise. 'Where are the keys for the car at the house? Lorna wants to get more involved.

'Tell her there's a drawer next to the fridge it the kitchen. The keys to all the cars are in there. I'd recommend she use the Land Rover.'

Brendan repeated the instructions to Lorna.

'Okay, I'm on my way. You're going to the warehouse for English?'

'Yes, we think the one's following us are coming for English.'

'So there definitely is a rat in Louise's crew.'

'Her entire crew stinks to high heaven,' Brendan said, as he looked across at Louise, she was sill unusually quiet. 'We'll find the bastards.'

'See you soon.' Lorna ended the call.

'She's feeling better then?' Louise said, 'that's good.'

'She's tough. And trust me, when she get's her hands on the one who spiked her drink, you'll see, I'm the tame one out of us two.' He turned and looked out through the rear-view mirror. The car was still following them. He looked at Louise. 'You got anywhere in particular you'd like to make contact with the car behind?'

'I've a place in mind.'

Chapter Thirty

THE LEICESTER/NOTTINGHAM country road was a long, winding tree and field lined lane, seven foot tall hedges drew the outline of the road, sporadically breaking up by access gates to various different fields. The trees gave a feeling that it was later than it actually was, shutting out the sun. Quiet roads were a good idea for what they were planning, but equally as dangerous. The way Louise negotiated the turns and dog legs, it was clear she'd taken the roads quite often and was confident she wasn't going to put the chunky SUV on it's side.

On the other side on a sharp bend, she looked in the rear-view, then looked at Brendan. 'Is your seatbelt fastened?'

Brendan grabbed the Uzi. 'You're going wreck the rear bumper of this beautiful car,' he said sarcastically. 'Ready when you are.'

'This next bend is very sharp, they'll have no idea what's about to happen.' She flew up the gears, creating a little bit of distance from the Merc. As hoped, the Merc sped up, too. The corner approached, she took it, the moment the car behind was out of view, she slammed on the breaks, performing an emergency stop.

'Well done, you passed your test, here's...' Brendan didn't have time to finish his sentence when the sound of tyres screeching lasted a split second before it was taken over by the sound of a great metallic clunk and the feeling of them being shot forward in the seat. The rear window shattered and a body came through head first onto the back seat. Louise looked around, grabbing her pistol from her handbag she pointed at the body. It wasn't needed, whoever it was, were dead before they entered the car. 'That's why you should always wear your seatbelt.'

Brendan jumped out, Uzi pointed at the wrecked Merc. 'That was a good idea,' he shouted back at Louise, caressing his neck. 'Only problem,' he slowly approached the Mercedes, 'think they're all dead.' As he approached the passenger side of the car, the sheer damage of the impact became evident. The front bumper was caved in, almost reaching the windscreen, and the S class had quite a lengthy bonnet. The windscreen had a two-foot perimeter hole on the passenger's side. He looked in the rear passenger side window. The driver and front passengers were still in their seats, both slumped forward against the airbags. 'I'm guessing the guy in the back didn't think he needed a seat belt.' He pulled the front passenger door open. A gun was lying at the foot of the front passenger. He picked it up.

Louise approached the driver's side. She pulled the driver's door open and unbuckled the driver from his seat. He was fit for nothing but a few groans. She dragged him out.

Brendan dragged the passenger out. 'We can't be here for too long, if someone comes.' He dropped the guy on the ground. 'Reach below the steering wheel and open the boot. I want to see what's here.'

The boot released with a pop. 'Done,' She said.

Brendan ran to the back of the car and opened the boot. Inside were a collection of weapons more suitable to torture than a simple hit. 'I don't think this was going to be an assassination attempt,' Brendan shouted. He grabbed a green fuel cannister, hoping it was full. It was. 'Right, Louise, get back in the car, I'm setting this on fire. But we can take our friends with us. Hurry up.' He slammed the boot closed, and ran around the car, dousing it in fuel. He grabbed the passenger, they groaned in agony. Brendan lifted him, flung him over his shoulder like a dummy and marched him to the rear passenger door of the Range Rover. Pulling the door open with his left hand, he dumped the guy on the back seat. 'Don't move or I'll end your life and leave you on the side of the road. You might still live after this.' He slammed the door closed.

Louise was checking the rear of the Merc. She pulled out a bag, then lifted an Iphone off the seat. She looked at Brendan. 'Can you lift him? I'll light the car up.'

Brendan grabbed the driver. Doing the same as he'd done with the passenger, he took him to the driver's side of the Range Rover and dumped him in the back next to his mate. 'Have you anything to tie this pair down with?'

'Check the pocket of the driver's door, there should be cable ties.' Louise grabbed a can of hair spray from her handbag and struck the lighter, creating a flame blower, scorching the inner roof of the Merc, the flames spread instantly, covering the entire car. She tossed the can into the inferno, a hissing was quickly followed by a pop then a bang. She ran back to the SUV and jumped in.

Brendan finished tying the two in the rear, then jumped into the front passenger seat. As he pulled the door closed, Louise had stomped on the accelerator and the car took off, sending them both into their passenger seats. She quickly flew up through the gears. The road was long and straight with few hidden dips, so a perfect place for them to gain some distance from the wreckage. Brendan put the window down, letting some fresh air in. He looked over at Louise. She was again quieter than usual. Her focus was on the road and nothing else.

'It's about to get a lot warmer,' Brendan grasped the Uzi. Looking into the back, the driver was conscious; dazed, but conscious. 'Where do I know your face from?'

'Judging from your accent, I'd say back home.' The driver spat. 'Whoever you are, you're on the wrong side. You're a disgrace to the cause, and your people. Just you wait. We'll find out who you are, and you, and your whole fucking family will die because of this. Mark my words.'

'Fair enough,' Brendan said. He glanced at the other passenger, still unconscious. He turned back to the front. Louise was still bombing it up the country road. 'How far are we away?'

'About ten minutes,' Louise said. She glared in the rearview mirror then tore her eyes back to the road again.

'Hey, remember what I said? Calm'

She cast a quick glance at Brendan, offering a fraction of a smile.

'Louise, you're going to die the same way your da did,' the driver sniggered at the back.

'You remember knee capping the Provos and the UDA used to dish out back home?' Brendan took his pistol and shot the driver in the calf. The guy screamed. Gritting his teeth like and angry dog wanting to tear into someone. Brendan looked at Louise, she was smirking. 'Don't worry, I'll leave the rest of him for you.'

'You're very kind.' Louise laughed.

Brendan holstered the weapon. He pulled his phone out and called Lorna.

'Brendan, I'm on my way to the warehouse now. Should be there within the hour, according to sat nav.'

'Great, we've just bagged ourselves two more bargaining chips, the Merc is now a blazing inferno, one of the passengers shot through the windscreen straight into our back seat like a human cannonball.'

'Should have been wearing a seatbelt,' Lorna joked.

Brendan smirked. 'We're almost there. Call me when you get here.'

'Love you.'

'I love you, too.' Brendan ended the call and put the phone back in his pocket.

'We're here,' Louise said, as the country road finally came to an end. The car gradually slowed on approach to a roundabout. She indicated right, and took the third exit, leading them into a concrete city. Steel fenced warehouses and factories, manufacturers, mechanics, car dealers, and car washes, all had their own little plot, doing business. But at this time of night, most, if not all were closed.

'I don't recognise this,' Brendan said.

'We've just came in the back entrance. The meat processor's is just around the corner.'

Someone's phone started to ring. It wasn't Brendan's. He looked at Louise. 'Is that yours?' She shook her head. He looked behind him. One of the guy's phone. He snatched it up. BM JR flashed across the screen. 'He looked at Louise. 'Who do you guess BM JR is?'

Louise smirked at him. 'You want to answer it?'

'No, we'll let it ring. It's better he doesn't know what's happening. It gives us the upper hand.' He tossed the phone back down onto the rear seat. It rang for quite a while before eventually stopping. Then the sound of a text message came. 'Do we have any medical supplies for our friends wound in here?'

'You're worried about him dying?' Louise said.

'Not at all, but we should at least keep him alive until he becomes useless to us.' He reached in behind again and grabbed the phone. 'Make yourself useful, mate, we need the digits to unlock your phone.'

'Fuck you.'

Brendan looked at Louise. 'He's no use to us, we'll just kill him.'

'I'm putting him into the meat processor.'

'The digits are 1690.'

Brendan sniggered, shaking his head. 'Should have known.'

'What's 1690?'

'You know the 12th July Orange parades?'

'I've heard of them.'

'Well the year 1690 was the year William of Orange led his army to victory against the Irish Catholics.'

'Lovely little history lesson.' Louise joked.

Brendan punched in the digits and opened the phone. He opened the message. It read: *Pick up the phone. We need confirmation that you have her and whoever the soon to be living the rest of his life in agonising pain is. My da's sending a few guys back to Belfast with Greystone. Nothing can go wrong. Ramadan is going to be a day to remember in England. Those Muslim cunts want a war, we'll fucking show them.*

'Looks like Greystone is in Belfast now, probably preparing the bombs. Or at least getting the materials.' Brendan closed the message. The list of text messages flooding the inbox were all from JM and JM JR. He scrolled down the list of texts, coming across a name that popped out at him. 'What's the guy called who I thought was your boyfriend?' He looked at Louise.

She indicated right into the grounds of the location. 'Steve.'

'Well, it looks like Steve's the one that's been feeding information back to Billy Moore.'

'Fuck Brendan, he knows your name.' She guided the car around the side of the warehouse, approaching the rear.

'This could be a big problem.' He looked out through the window, trying to think. 'We'll figure it out tonight.' He closed the phone and put it in his pocket alongside his own. 'Nobody else here yet.'

'I thought it better to get here early. Have a chat with Davy English while he can still talk.'

Brendan looked over his shoulder into the back. 'If you pair want to live, you both need to cooperate. Is that understood?'

Neither of them spoke. The one with the bullet wound was now sweating as if he'd just stepped out of a sauna. The other was now conscious, but obviously not in the mood to talk.

Brendan clasped the Uzi tightly in his hand. His own pistol holstered. As Louise pulled the van up to the back door, he quickly opened the door and jumped out. 'I don't like sitting in a stationary target too long.' He pulled the rear door open and dragged the first hostage out. He stumbled on his feet, Brendan held him by the scruff of his shirt, making sure he stayed on his feet.

Louise grabbed the wounded out from the other side and marched him around to the passenger side of the car. She pulled the keys out and led the way towards the red door, looking as if it started to rot before Brendan was born. She unlocked the door and gave it a heavy shove before it budged. When it opened, she was about to step inside.

Brendan pulled her back. 'Never enter a dark room.' He reached his arm around inside and hit a switch. The light came on, revealing a derelict old staff room. He stepped inside first. The room was empty. The only sign of life was the naked posters on the wall and the world cup 2010 calendar pinned to the flaking paint above the sink. The smell was almost enough to drive them back out the door again.

'They've left English in the office,' Louise said.

'Lead the way,' Brendan said.

She crossed the room, noting her shoes sticking to whatever was on the concrete floor. She pulled the door open and exited the room, into the hallway.

'How long have you had control of this place?' Brendan said. 'You could have hired some cleaners to take some disinfectant to it.'

'Toughen up,' Louise joked.

'Nothing to do with being tough, I just have more respect for my sense of smell.'

'You're right, actually. Louise stopped at the manager's office. 'It stinks of piss and shite.' He opened the door and stepped inside. 'English was on the ground, handcuffed to the radiator. He wasn't asleep, but he was barely conscious. His face was swollen, it had ballooned up in a purple ball that looked like it was ready to pop, his right eye was swollen closed.

'Well, we now know where the smell's coming from,' Brendan walked closer to English, seeing from the dampness on the front of his jeans that he'd urinated inside them, and from the brown stains on the rear, he'd also gone number two. 'Jesus fucking Christ.' He lifted a half empty bottle of water off the ground, opened it and squirted some on English's face.

'Just kill me, please,' English pleaded.

Brendan looked closer at him. English's right earlobe had been cut off and the wound burned closed to stop the bleeding, deep lacerations carved into his face, extending out from the sides of his lips in a smile. Brendan stood up and looked at Louise. 'This is too much. Suhag, Omar – they've gone too far with this.'

She just looked at English, lying there helpless. 'What use will he be now.'

'Do we have any more cuffs for this pair?' Brendan gestured at the two they'd brought in with him. 'I'm going to try something.'

'What?' Louise asked.

'You want to scare the bollocks out of your team when they arrive?'

She looked at him, her eyebrows meeting in the middle, 'of course.'

Brendan looked at English, 'well, look at the fucking state of him, that's horrific, that will scare the shite out of anyone that sees it. We take him and those two out into the warehouse, and we crucify them.'

Louise looked at him

'We make it look like they're dead,' Brendan walked over to the two from the car, 'and if you two want any chance at survival, you'll both play along.'

They both looked at him, their expressions were more of a screw you than and yes sir.

'Do you have anything here to stop his leg from bleeding?' Brendan said, 'we don't want him bleeding out, until we can get the best out of him.

Louise grunted to agree. 'I've got stuff.' She walked back out of the room.

Brendan looked at the guy's phone again, thumbed in the 1690 and opened the contact list. All the key players were there. Billy Moore, Billy Moore Jnr, Greystone, Davy English, and a lot others Brendan was aware of, but he was sure he'd soon get to know the rest of them. As he flicked through it, the phone rang again. This time is was the member of Louise's crew. His anger caused him to grip to phone tightly, as if his grip was around the neck of the caller. He was tempted to answer but he pulled back. He just watched as it continued to ring, for quite a while.

Louise came back into the room. 'Who's that?'

Brendan held the phone out in front of her.

Gritting her teeth, she said, 'The piece of shit. I'll chop his balls off and feed them to him.' The two hostages, obviously aware of what was pissing her off started to snigger. She turned around and sent the toe of her right foot into the first's face, then followed up with one for the other. The laughter stopped. She threw the pack of bandages down on her ground. Pulling a knife out she crouched down and cut the cable ties off the one who wasn't injured. 'Here, make yourself useful, stop your mate's bleeding before he dies.' She pulled her pistol out of her handbag. 'And if your even think of doing anything else, your brains will be all over the floor.' She forced the pistol into the back of his head. 'Please, just test me, and see.'

Chapter Thirty-One

THE TIME WAS NINE TWENTY-five when Lorna arrived. Following Brendan's directions, she parked the car alongside the Ranger Rover and entered through the red door, as instructed. She produced her pistol, hearing muffled voices coming from the office. She didn't go any further. Pulling her phone out, she called Brendan. Before he answered, she could hear his phone ring and the voices coming from the office stop.

'Lorna, where are you now?'

'I'm just outside the office.'

Brendan stepped outside. He hung up the call and called her over.

'You better have a strong stomach, it stinks in here.'

Her expression was evident that she'd already picked up the smell. Stepping into the office, she seen the three hostages.

'The meeting with Louise's team is at ten thirty,' Brendan said, 'we're going to put on a little show, prove we're not messing about, scare them all a bit.'

'How?' Lorna said, as she strolled further into the room. Looking down at the state of English, she shook her head. 'I don't want to see this. This is horrific.'

'Agreed,' Louise said. She stood up and went to the cabinet in the corner of the room. She unlocked it and pulled out a roll of tape. 'This'll keep their mouths shut.'

'Do you have any hoists?' Brendan said.

'Should have, out on the warehouse floor.'

'I might also have something to put them to sleep with, too, make sure they don't decide to shout out,' Louise said. She stepped around the office desk and crouched down in front of the safe. Inserting the key inside, she opened the door, pulling out a plastic box, she removed a bunch of needles and a bottle.

'Tranquillisers,' Lorna said.

Louise stood up and tossed them to Lorna. She looked at them, nodding her head.

Brendan grabbed English, dragging him to his feet. 'Let's go.' He lifted English and put him over his shoulder. 'Don't worry, English, you're not really getting crucified, you're just going to look like it.' He headed towards the door. Pulling the door open he made his way down the corridor towards the meat processing part of the warehouse.

As he stepped out into the airy open space, he looked around, planning the scene for the meeting. A row of ten operating tables drew a straight line from one end of the warehouse to the other, all the way down to the large roller door where the lorry loads would be dropped off and picked up. He dumped English down on the table closest as the hostage's phone rang. It was Moore Jnr again. Again a few seconds after a text message came through. He opened the text.

Tell me you three dumb fucks haven't taken them drugs and fallen asleep. If you have, don't bother waking up.

'What's got your attention?' Lorna said, as she and Louise brought the other two out.

Brendan turned and looked at the one he'd shot in the leg. He grabbed him from Lorna side kicked him in the shin, dropping his to his knees. He pulled his pistol out and put it to the guy's temple. 'What drugs were you to give us?'

'Don't know what you're talking about, pal. We were sent to follow Louise and...'

Brendan cracked him on the side of the face with the pistol. 'Don't waste your time, a message had just came through from Moore Jr. He said if you clowns have taken the drugs and fallen asleep don't bother waking up.'

'There's a new kind of drug floating around,' Louise said, 'it's came in from Germany. Apparently it leaves you feeling like an outer body experience. But the after-effects leave your like crap for days,' she looked at Lorna. 'Bastards, our little rat must have gotten his hands on some and slipped it into your drink.'

'I look forward to getting my hands on him,' Brendan said.

'No, Brendan. I'll deal with him,' Lorna said.

Brendan pulled the hostage back to his feet again. He was about to dump him down on the operating table again, when he spotted the operating console of a hoist, dangling down along the edge of the table. His eyes scanned the area above the table, a steel hook dangled in mid-air, coming down from the rafters. He looked at Louise. 'Where are these hoists?'

'We have some construction workers doing work down in the manholes around the building,' Louise said, smirking at him. 'You're very creative. I'll go and check if they've anything we can hook these guys up to.' She made her way back towards the offices. Lorna followed her.

Brendan looked at the three. Then pulled his phone out of his pocket. He had a message from Moore Jnr's girlfriend. It read.

He's going to Belfast tomorrow. It's for something very important and he'll be away for a few days, if you'd like to get to know me a bit more, that would be great.

'That's interesting,' he said to himself. 'Be funny if we're on the same flight.' He replied to her.

I'd love to. I've just a few meetings to go to first. I'll be in touch very soon. But I definitely want to meet up with you.

He shoved the phone into his pocket and grabbed one of the hostages, moving him down to the next table, and the other to the next.

Louise and Lorna came back. Orange construction worker's straps were about to used for something a little more sinister than lowering someone down into a manhole.

'Okay, I'm going to go and make myself invisible,' Lorna said. 'But you'll both be in my view and if something escalates, I'll be there.'

Louise handed the straps to Brendan. He fitted the first one to English. Louise injected him, knocking him out. Brendan grabbed the console and lowered the hook. Clipping the back of the belt, English began to raise up into the air. Once English was suspended a good fifteen feet above the operating table. He moved onto the next one. They both put up a bit more of a struggle, but the injection from the drug worked quickly, and Brendan eventually got both suspended to the same height as English.

Standing back looking at their handy work, both Brendan and Louise appeared impressed with the job.

'Don't let this change you,' Brendan said to Louise. 'Avenge your father's murder and once that score is settled, move on with the rest of your life. Don't be ruled by it.'

'You're very wise for a guy of your age,' Louise said. 'But why are you still mixing with this type of people, then? Why don't you take your own advice?'

'I'm starting to think you're right. But as my father bled out in my arms, the last thing he told me was to use everything he'd taught me to continue the work that he'd been doing.'

'Which is to go around fucking up criminal empires built at the expense of those less fortunate.'

'Pretty sick, isn't it?'

Louise shook her head, looking up at the three men hoisted high in the air in front of them. 'What? Punishing people like those? Not at all, they deserve everything they get.'

'With all due respect, Louise, and forgive me but...'

'Isn't that how my father built his empire?' Louise was quick to the finish for him. 'Yes, you're right, but it's never too late to see the error in one's ways and make a few changes. Even my father had started trying to distance himself from it. He moved away from drugs and used the money he'd made to open up legitimate businesses.'

'But it's like being in the mafia, once you're in, it's very difficult, to get out of.'

Louise nodded her head, pulling her phone out as it started to sound. 'It's them,' she said, as she answered. 'Hello, are you here?' She looked at Brendan, her eyes glazing over in a child-like excitement as if she were getting a kick from the entire thing. 'Okay. We're in the warehouse, come around the back, I'll open the big door.' She hung up and dropped her phone in her pocket. 'It's about to get started.' She pulled her pistol out of her handbag that was sat on the ground by her foot and marched across the factory floor towards the large door.

Chapter Thirty-two

THREE CARS PULLED UP. A black BMW 6 Series, a silver Jaguar XKS, and a blue C Class Mercedes. The rain was heavy, the window wipers frantically waving side to side looked as if the vehicles were anxiously trying to get the water off. Louise waved them to come in. The three vehicles positioned themselves in curved line, almost a semi-circle. Brendan hopped up on one of the operating tables, casually twirling his pistol in his left index finger, Davy English suspended a few feet above him.

Steve got out of the BMW. His smug grinning disappearing upon seeing the three suspended in the air. Richard got out of the Jag, with four of the youngsters Brendan remembered from the party in Quorn. And whoever was in the Mercedes stayed in the vehicle, with the engine idling for what seemed not too long, but long enough for both Brendan and Louise to wonder what he was doing, was he spooked? Perhaps he was trying to make a call to Billy Moore Jnr.

Growing impatient, Brendan hopped down off the table, and strolled towards the car. He pulled the driver's door open and snatched the guys phone from his hand, with every ounce on force in his arm, he chucked it into the ground, smashing it into the concrete ground, shattering it into pieces.

'What the hell are you doing? Do you know who the fuck...'

Brendan raised his pistol. 'I don't give a shit who you are or who was on the other end of that call, we've got a meeting, and you're sitting on your fat ass acting like you're above it all.' Brendan put a bullet in the bonnet. 'Now get out before you're the next to be crucified.'

The guy got out of the car, he stood up, towering over Brendan. He was easily six inches taller, and fifty pounds heavier. His greying beard that hung down off his chain gave him a slight hint of Santa Clause, but the appearance was the only similarity to the festive figure. The scar that ran a sharp line down through his left eye made him more suitable for what he was: involved with the wrong people.

'Okay. I called this meeting because we've had some very unsettling news. Someone, or persons, have been feeding information to Billy Moore and his racist gang of inbred scum,' Louise said, the men forming a circle around her. She took centre stage as confidently as a veteran performer. Pointing with her pistol at the three suspended bodies, still dangling lifelessly. 'Does anyone here know anything about this?'

The group all looked at each other. Brendan paid particular attention to Steve. He had to give credit where credit was due. The guy was as cool as a cucumber. Which bugged him. Either he was very confident, a great actor, or worse: his confidence came from something else up his sleeve, something that they weren't aware of. Brendan was in deep. He couldn't just walk away from this. He remembered joking with his mates as a teenager how much they'd love to be the ones to pull the trigger and take out someone that was responsible for so many innocent lives in Belfast. Another reason, he looked at Louise and knew exactly what she was going through. He'd went through it for the entire six months that he waited to avenge his father's murder. And now Lorna – violating someone with the use of drugs was an offence that brought the death penalty, and Lorna herself would want to be judge, jury and executioner.

'Nobody knows anything about what I'm talking about?' Louise shouted. 'Whoever it was, we will find out, and it'll be a slow and painful death. If you own up to it, it'll be much better on you, trust me.' She turned, pointing up to the three bodies above again. 'Those three did not have a good end. They were in a lot of pain. And their deaths were at their own request. They begged for it. And now they're about to go into the meat grinder.'

'I don't know who it was, but when we find out, I'll help you put the scum in the meat processer,' Richard said. 'I've worked for your father for many years, he was like a brother to me. And you, a daughter. If I apologise for anything, there's always a likely chance I brought them in, and for that, Louise, I'm sorry. Let me make it better for you.'

'How do you plan on doing that?'

Brendan's phone vibrated. He pulled his out of his pocket. He didn't recognise the number. It wasn't Lorna, so whoever it was, would have to wait.

Richard walked over to his three heavies. 'I, along with this three will get to the bottom of this, Louise.' He looked at Brendan. 'Where is your beautiful lady friend? Is she okay?'

Brendan's eyebrows met in the middle. 'Why would you ask is she okay?'

'I haven't seen her. I wondered maybe you two have fall-en out, if you have, could she be perhaps be the person who's feeding information...'

Brendan pointed his gun at Richard. 'Be very careful about what you choose to say next.' He walked towards him, gun still pointed. The others raised their guns, Brendan was now outnumbered, if it weren't for Lorna's nearby eyes.

'Brendan. Don't go too far,' Louise said. 'Now all of you drop your weapons, now!' She shouted. Slowly, they all low-ered their weapons. 'That goes for you, too, Brendan.' She ap-proached him from the side.

He was stood right in front of Richard. Glaring into his eyes.

'Brendan,' Louise repeated.

Brendan lowered his weapon. Richard's smugness re-mained on his face. Brendan swung the back end of the pistol, clocking the him on the temple, sending him stum-bling back into his three associates. One of them went for Brendan, throwing a punch, Brendan side stepped the blow, the guy's momentum send him stumbling forward, Brendan added a bit extra force, sending him to the ground, another one swung a kick at Brendan, Brendan dropped to one knee, caught the guy's foot in mid-air and punched him between the legs, a full force blow that caused a glass-shattering yell to resound around the factory.

The driver mumbled to the guy next to him. 'Guess Louise has found herself her new protection.'

Louise turned to him. 'Brendan's part of our team now,' she lied. 'Now you're all going to have to get along. Because someone working within our organisation is feeding info to those bastards. And if they're feeding info to Moore, they could just as easily be giving intel to the fucking police, too. So, it's in everyone's best interest that whoever it is gets caught and stopped.'

'Why'd you choose here to have the meeting?' Steve said. 'You had us believing we were walking into an execution.'

'There's still time,' Brendan said, 'does Louise have a reason to make room for you up on the hoist beside those three.'

'Who the hell has put you at the head of this organisation?' Steve shouted.

Brendan smirked.

'He's right, Brendan,' Louise said, 'I'm in charge and I make the decisions. And if I find out anyone else in here has been bringing us trouble, they'll be praying for death.' She turned and looked Richard. 'Go and crack some heads. I want to know who's been talking. And when you find out, keep them alive.' She paused and looked around the room. 'Now all of you fuck off, and don't come near me unless you've got something for me.'

They all quickly dispersed, leaving Louise there with Brendan. He was smirking at her.

'What?' she said.

'The big bad boss lady.'

'Piss off.' She smirked. 'Don't you have a flight to catch?'

'Not until tomorrow morning.'

'Let me buy you and Lorna dinner then. I know a nice Asian restaurant on the outskirts of Nottingham.'

Chapter Thirty-Three

THE NEXT MORNING, BRENDAN'S alarm went off at five thirty. His eyes shot open. He hadn't slept much through the night. The thought of going back to Belfast wasn't very appealing to him, especially after the last time. He lay there for a few minutes, his hands joined, resting behind his head. Looking at the shadows on ceiling, elongated lines stretching from the window the entire length the white canvas above. The window outside was making the branches dance in harmony with the weather that he'd hoped wouldn't be his excuse to not board the plane. But given the fact it was summer, and no weather alerts had been broadcast, he'd put the thought to the back of his mind and rolled over, kissing Lorna on the cheek. She groaned and turned into him. They kissed for a short while, but before it got too intense, Lorna, being the one more in control of her bodily urges, reminded Brendan they had a flight to catch and perhaps it would be better to leave the sex until at least they'd made it to Belfast.

'What time is not now?' She said.

'Twenty to six,' Brendan said, getting off the bed. He put the light on, almost blinding the two of them. Both could barely open their eyes, waiting for them to adjust. 'I'll let you have the shower first.'

She pecked him on the cheek. 'You're a gentleman.'

'Not a gentleman, you take all day getting ready, so it's best you start getting ready first.'

She laughed and blew him a kiss as she walked into the bathroom. Nothing but a pair of black panties on, her slender body glistening under the fluorescent lights.

Brendan sat down on the edge of the bed and checked his phone. A text message from a number he recognised. It was his aunt Mary. He opened the text in record time. The text message had come though only an hour prior. Mary didn't sit up late at night, she went to bed early and got up at six thirty every morning, without fail, ever since he was a young boy. She wouldn't be sending a text at this time unless it was urgent. He didn't bother reading the text, he clicked on the mobile number and hit the call button.

Within seconds, she'd answered it. 'Brendan, where are you, love?'

'Probably safer you don't know that, Mary,' he said, looking towards the en-suite, Lorna singing from the shower. 'What's up?'

'You've been spotted in England. There's been a hit put out on you, love.'

Brendan kept his stare on the shower door, then a knock came on the door. Louise stepped in. 'By who?'

'The government, son.'

'The government are issuing contracts on people's lives?' Brendan sniggered.

'Someone on the UDA side in Belfast has heard word you're in England has tipped off their old UDA buddies from Belfast, asking for an updated photo. They know you've changed your appearance.'

'I'll see you this morning, Mary. We're just making our way to the airport in an hour.' He looked up at Louise, she stood with a tray of cups and a coffee pot.

'Maybe you shouldn't come here, love.' Mary sounded concerned.

'Where are you?' Brendan asked, dismissing her last statement.

'At the safe house in Donegal.'

'Glad you've stayed out of Belfast. Stay where you are, we'll come see you later.'

'Take care, son. See you soon.'

Brendan ended the call and stood up. 'Is that coffee?'

Louise opened the pot then closed it. 'It is, would you prefer tea?'

'Coffee's fine, thanks.'

'Was that an urgent call?'

'According to my aunt, the government has put out a contract on my life, under the table of course. They've also made my new appearance known to the old paramilitary's in Belfast.'

Louise looked at him, the humour in Brendan's words not evident on her face. 'Brendan, look – I appreciate you offering to help me get the ones who killed my father, but I don't want you getting killed in the process. Maybe you shouldn't go back there if it's dangerous.'

'It'll be fine, don't worry.'

'You sure?'

'Thanks for your concern. But I want to help you. And judging from the people you have working for you, you could do with having someone on your side.'

Louise set the tray down on the dressing table and made her way out of the room. 'I'll be downstairs.'

'Thanks for the coffee.' Brendan poured himself a cup then sat down on the edge of the bed. He opened his phone and checked the BBC News website. Clicking on the Northern Ireland section, he found the story of Brendan Cleary and ex British Intelligence agent Lorna Woodward at the top of the list. Wanted in connection with the recent discovery of bodies found on Belfast docks, in addition to events that took place at Stormont estate.

'Anything interesting?' Lorna said, as she stepped into the room, a towel wrapped around her. She sat down on the bed next to him. He handed her the phone.

'I'll go get a quick shower then we'll make our way to the airport.' He pecked her on the cheek. 'Glad you're feeling better.' He stood up and made his way into the bathroom

.

Arriving at East Midlands Airport, Brendan reached into the back of the car, and grabbed their bag. He looked at Louise, thanks for the lift. And don't be starting anything until I come back.'

She laughed. 'I'll try not to. Don't you both be getting caught in Belfast. I'm indebted to you both.' Louise looked back at Lorna in the back seat. She offered her hand. 'Take care.'

Lorna accepted. 'Thanks, you, too. We'll see you soon.'

They stood on the side of the road, watching as Louise took off. Brendan turned and looked at Lorna. 'Well, let's go and see Belfast again, then.'

They both looked at the sign above the terminal entrance: *East Midlands Airport*, then made for the automatic doors, passing two Kinch buses, one of them the Leicester route and one going to Nottingham. 'Hope Nottingham doesn't explode while we're away.' Brendan joked. 'It seems a nice city.'

Entering the airport, they were introduced to English chaos at it's best. Middle-aged men carrying nothing but brief cases, rushing as if they were about to miss their flight which they were perhaps too early for. A family of Asians, dressed in the traditional Islamic style dress code bundled together, the man and what looked like, two teenage sons carrying the suitcases. They were all headed in the same direction. A queue of at least thirty people waited to have their issue dealt with. He felt sorrier for the poor security officer who didn't look too experienced and was only there to do a job. They steadily advanced the through the crowd and joined one of three lines that waited patiently to go through.

Brendan removed his belt and jacket, the two items joining their bag and his loose belongings in one of the plastic containers. He untied his shoes and stepped into the metal detector. After being swiped up and down by the machine, he continued through, being pat down by a male security guard. While going through the process, he exchanged polite small talk with the guard, watching as other guards were being looked at by their subjects as if they were simple villains who wanted to ruin their day. Brendan moved on through, then Lorna was next. She thanked the guard who wished her a safe flight.

Strolling through the departures lounge, they stopped for coffee. Lorna took a seat. Brendan queued up for the order. In the queue, he stood reading the news on his phone. Halfway down the BBC's home page that consisted of an arrest of a group of three Asian men, he received a message from Louise. She again thanked him for his help and asked him to check the BBC news. As he continued on the news page, he understood why she'd text him: the bodies of two men from the Leicester area were found dead in a car around the corner from a newly opened nightclub that had been linked to the increase in Britain First and Combat 18 activity in the city. At the bottom of the story, he clicked on a report from Number Ten Downing Street.

He opened the report. British Prime Minister was holding meetings with newly appointed first and deputy first ministers of Northern Ireland. He was also inviting his Irish counterpart to the discussion to discuss local issues that have caused Northern Ireland's local assembly to collapse. Brendan closed the story. Having read enough, he waited patiently, carelessly watching others pass by, going about their normal live

Chapter Thirty-Three

TOUCHING DOWN IN BELFAST, Lorna woke on impact with the runway. She'd slept the entire journey. Brendan wasn't surprised she'd slept. She was as comfortable on an aircraft as she would be on a recliner in her house.

As he looked out the window, he seen the sky was grey. Not a spot of blue anywhere. But this was Ireland. Nothing new to him. The seatbelt light went out and they stood up. Lorna stretched, then ran her fingers through her hair. Brendan opened the overhead compartment and handed Lorna her jacket, then took his. Pulling his jacket on, he grabbed the bag and led the group of passengers disembarking through the rear entrance.

'Good morning,' he said to the air hostess who stood at the door, her smile as refreshing as the cool Irish air.

As he descended the steps and approached the terminal, he pulled his phone out and deactivated flight mode. Three messages came through instantly. Two from Louise who'd wanted to wish him good luck and thank him again. The other was from Omar, highlighting the importance of "mums the word" with regards to his visit to Belfast. He dropped the phone back into his jacket pocket and took Lorna by the hand. Brendan first questioned how the hell did Omar know he was going to Belfast, then assumed Louise had told him. Omar could prove very handy with his resources. Brendan quickly replied to them then pocketed the device again.

As they walked through the terminal, they spotted two men, looking as conspicuous as a pair of naked guys, dancing a jig. One was short and round with long wavy hair that looked about as in order as a writer's bureau. The other was about half the other's age, tall and just as round. He had black cropped hair, receding almost to the crown of his head. Both wore suits that looked like they came from the top end shops on London's Saville Row.

'I know government when I see it,' Lorna whispered. Her suspicions were proven when they reached the security check. The rest of the passengers stood waiting impatiently. But these two looked more flustered and stressed than just momentarily inconvenienced. If they were government, why were they there? If they were on the flight to keep an eye on Brendan and Lorna, the tables had turned slightly.

'Okay,' Lorna whispered in Brendan's ear. 'They're definitely government. I don't think it's a coincidence they're on the same flight as us.'

'Looks like we've been fingered by someone.'

'But who else knew we were going to Belfast?'

'Nobody.'

'Fuck.'

'We can't make a run for it,' Brendan said. 'But what we can do is, we can become the predators.'

She smiled.

'I guess it was just their bad luck, a royal operational fuck up to get off the plain first.'

'What's the plan then, big chief?'

'We act as normal, but now we follow them. They don't know we're on to them. Perhaps they're hoping we haven't caught on. It would make sense for why they seem so nervous at present. So, we let them believe we haven't. Let them carry on.'

'Usually they will have a rental waiting for them. Something big and quite fast. Probably a Merc. They'll play the whole tourist thing for a while.' Lorna said. 'They'll meet with their contacts in Belfast, confirm we've landed and will have eyes on the obvious places that we could go.'

'Look,' Brendan gestured towards one of them. The taller of the two had just answered the phone and turned his back to them. 'How much do you want to bet that's a confirmation call.' He grabbed Lorna by the hand and walked with her. 'Let's go grab a coffee.' He led them towards the Costa. 'Grab a seat, keep your eye on them.' Brendan joined the queue or three. His back was to the agents, but he could see them in the reflection of the stainless-steel lining of the counter fridge that sold sandwiches and other ready to eat smacks. The one on the phone had finished his call and was now talking to his partner. They both made their way towards the car rental desk. Brendan quickly ordered his two white coffees to go and returned to Lorna.

She stood up before he got to the table. 'Let's go, I don't want to lose them.'

Brendan handed her a coffee, turning on his heel and rushing through the terminal towards the exit. As they stepped outside, the wind was heavy and the rain had come on, light rain, but heavy enough to give them an excuse to put their hoods up. 'I love the Irish drizzle sometimes,' Brendan joked. They turned left on the terminal exit, the two agents were both walking at a fast pace, fifty yards from them.

The rental carpark was five minutes-walk from the terminal, and by the time Brendan and Lorna got there, they were both in desperate need of a hot shower and a change of clothes. As they rounded the row of rental cabins, they seen a lady wearing a hi-vis jacket, holding her hood over her head while clasping a clip folder with her other, escorting the agents to their car.

As they approached the rental cabin, Brendan looked in the window, it was empty. A one-man operation and the only man, or woman in this instance was busy with the two customers. 'Wait here a second.' Brendan run inside the cabin, around the back of the service desk and grabbed himself a clipboard and two high-vis jackets. He rushed back out of the cabin and handed Lorna a jacket. 'Here, congratulations. You've just been employed.'

She smirked and put it on. He handed her the clipboard. 'What's your plan Jason Bourne?'

'Jason Bourne wishes he was me.' Brendan put the hi-vis on and made his way back towards the entrance to the carpark. 'Here, give me the clipboard, it's better if I do the talking, your accent will blend in better over here.'

'You're the boss.' She gave him a mock salute.

They both stood on either side of the access gate, the only exit. Brendan stood on the driver's side. A moment later, the sound of a car engine broke through the morning air. Then came the sound of gears changing and finally the sound the tyres crunching over the gravel of the carpark. The car approached, and Brendan had never felt so grateful for the rain. The car approached and Brendan stepped off the pavement and waved the car down. He looked at the registration plate then pretended to mark something down on the clipboard. He walked around the car, approaching the driver's door, circling with his index finger to signal he wanted the window lowered.

'Stinking weather isn't it?' He said. 'Can I just have your Id please mate.'

The guy reached into his jacket pocket and before he or the passenger knew what happened, Brendan threw his left hand in through the window, chopping into the driver's throat, caving in his windpipe, the driver chocked, instinctively reaching his two hands up to his throat. Brendan, seeing the bulge under the driver's left arm, reached inside his jacket, pulling out his pistol, pointing it at the guy in the passenger seat. 'Slowly remove your weapon and set it on the dashboard.'

Lorna pulled the passenger's door open. 'Better still, give me the weapon and while you're at it, I'll have your hand cuffs, too.'

'You won't get away with this, you know.' The agent in the passenger seat said.

'I don't think you want to test me on how far I'm willing to go to get what I need,' Brendan said. 'Now do as she says.'

The agent passed Lorna his gun, then produced a pair of handcuffs. Lorna ordered him to handcuff himself to the handle of the seat. She got in the back. Brendan got in the behind the driver's seat.

'Okay, let's go for a wee drive somewhere a bit quieter,' Brendan said. 'And don't worry, we're not going to kill you, we just want to know who sent you after us.'

Brendan snatched the driver's Id from inside his jacket pocket. 'James Blackwood – do you know where the Newtownards airfield is? Take us there.'

The agent didn't say a word. He just put the car in gear and took off.

Brendan studied Blackwood's Id. He was thirty-four. London born. He looked much younger and thinner in his photograph than he did in person. His hair was fair and trimmed short around the sides. Very neat. Almost military. His build made him look athletic, and his chiselled face had puffed out a little, perhaps by spending too much time sitting at a desk and not going to the gym.

The journey was quiet, none of them spoke. Not even a whisper of small talk. The two agents knew they were caught and clearly didn't feel the need to talk For them it was perhaps more a case of what Brendan and Lorna were going to do with them, maybe in silent prayer or hope from above that somehow their corpses wouldn't be the only things left on the airbase.

As they arrived at the old airbase, the driver was ordered to drive the car to the far end, usually used by supercar enthusiasts, who wanted to test drive their favourite Lamborghini or Ferrari.

'Park it over there,' Brendan said, pointing towards a portable cabin tucked away nicely, giving them some privacy. The driver reversed alongside the cabin. 'Good. Now shut the engine off and pass me the key.' Blackwood did as he was told. 'Now, if you both want to live, you'll tell us who sent you after us.'

'Does it really matter?' The passenger said. 'You're going to kill us anyway.'

'Not necessarily,' Brendan said. 'You see, unlike you guys, I don't just kill people to make my own life easier.'

'We've been sent by the powers that be. The very government that you, Agent Woodward used to work for.'

'So, you were sent to take us out?' Lorna said.

'No, just to watch what you got up to.'

'Don't give me that.' Lorna pressed her pistol into the back of his head. 'I know the drill. I practically wrote the fucking book on it. That training manual you little dipshits had to study when coming into your training, I tried and tested it in the field, making sure what was the best method to get things done.'

'The Prime Minister has got wind the both of you have resurfaced and sent us to take you out.' Blackwood smirked, looking at Brendan in the rear view. 'Well done for taking out Agent Short. It's a pity you weren't interested in coming to work for us.'

'That's actually why we were sent.' The other added. 'We weren't sent to take you out, well, only if you didn't agree to come in and accept the Prime Minister's offer.'

'And what offer would that be?' Brendan said.

'The British government always wanted you to take over after Hughes retired, Lorna. You're brilliant, and whether you'll admit it or not, you know you're one of the best in the world at the intelligence game. And, the Prime Minister thought with the son of The Ghost working alongside you,

you both would be more valuable than any other agent that has gone before you.'

'You definitely tell a good yarn,' Brendan said, 'I'm not sure if I buy it or not.'

Lorna nodded and looked at Brendan. 'They've been told to say this, in the event this were to happen.'

Brendan smirked. 'They had more faith in this happening than this pair of clowns did then.' He leaned forward. 'Well, we don't need you alive. So, we can kill you both and leave you here if that's what you want. Give me your phones.'

Blackwood reached into his jacket pocket and pulled his phone out, handing it back to Brendan. Lorna reached over into the front passenger side pulled the passengers out of his pocket.

'Is your pistol fitted with a silencer?' Brendan looked at Lorna.

She pulled a silencer out of her bag and fitted to her weapon.

'Okay, this pair are proving useless, we'll need to dispose of them, if other's find out we're here, it's just going to make our lives a bit more difficult.' He flung the door open and got out. 'We can leave them here, by the time their bodies are found we'll be out of the country, anyway.'

'Alright, alright,' Blackwood shouted. 'Alright. We'll tell you what you really want to hear. Just, please don't kill us.'

Brendan got back in the rear driver's side. 'Talk.'

'We know you're here because of Billy Moore and his son. The government is aware of him leading the newly formed amalgamation of C18 and Britain First.'

'Do you know their planning something very big,' Lorna said. 'More like explosive. And is set to take off on Ramadan?'

'We know.'

'And what are you doing to stop it?' She said.

Neither said a word.

'Tell me you're not doing what I think you're doing?' Brendan spoke through a sigh. He looked at Lorna. 'The government are doing what they did in Belfast to fight the IRA, aren't they?'

'It's the only way to stop the dirty bastards.' Blackwood said.

'Collusion,' Lorna said.

Brendan nodded.

'So...' Brendan paused for a moment. 'The former leading loyalist, who is now leading the new improved Britain First, is taking his experience from working with the British government and using it to combat Islamic extremists throughout England. They're starting another dirty war on English streets this time.' He shook his head. 'I didn't work against the Provisional IRA, what makes them think it's going to make the streets of England safer?'

'Maybe we should talk to the powers that be instead of this pair of clowns,' Lorna said. 'They could be feeding us anything...' she paused for a second.

Brendan looked at her. 'What?'

'You, you're Andrew Dobson, aren't you?' She pressed her pistol into the back of the passenger's head. He nodded. 'I remember you in recruitment. I never liked you. Thought you were a little rat.' He didn't reply. She reached around and took his phone. 'What's the passcode?'

'2020.'

'She accessed his phone and looked through his emails.

'Are you reading anything classified?' Brendan said. 'They wouldn't be stupid enough to keep classified stuff on their phone, would they?'

Lorna looked at Brendan briefly, smirking. 'You'd be very surprised.' She pressed a few buttons.

'What are you doing?'

'Emailing these to myself. We can have a proper look through them on our way to the next place.'

'Okay, let's go,' Brendan said. 'Let's dump them here, you guys don't mind if we borrow the car do you?'

'Don't worry, we're not going to kill you, but we are leaving you here.' Lorna pocketed Dobson's phone. 'I'm actually going to keep this, too. Just in case someone wants to have a little chat.' She flung open the rear door and got out. Opening the front passenger door, she dragged Dobson out. He stumbled, she helped him to his feet. 'Get over there, to those railings.'

Both agents got handcuffed to the railings of the steps that led into the old disused office.

'You want to drive?' Brendan said.

'No, you drive. I'll skim through these emails, see if I can find anything.' She jumped into the front passenger seat. Brendan got behind the steering wheel and took off.

As he guided the vehicle across the airfield, he looked at the fuel gauge. 'We've enough to get us over to the west coast to see Mary.'

'Let's grab something to eat on the way over. I'm starving.'

Brendan glanced across at Lorna. 'You need a good Irish breakfast.'

Chapter Thirty-Four

SEATED IN A WINDOW booth just twenty minutes out-side Derry city centre, Brendan sat people watching, part paranoia and part interest. Watching normal people go on about their daily lives. He found himself particularly inter-ested in a young couple who'd just walked into the pub. The guy was wearing a County Antrim football top, meaning they weren't from the area. The lady was dressed in a pair of slim fit jeans than clung to her athletic figure and given the face of the baby in her arms, it looked no more than a month old. The lady took the booth next to Brendan and Lorna. Brendan watched as the guy didn't take his eyes off the child.

Lorna nudged him with her elbow.

Brendan looked at her. 'Mabey one day we'll have a nor-mal life like that.' He took Lorna by the hand. 'Sooner rather than later.

Lorna looked at him. 'You're growing tired of the life we're living?'

He nodded his head. 'Are you not?'

'God yes.'

'We can't save the world,' Brendan said. 'But we can help some people out before we sail off into the sun.'

Lorna kissed him. 'Even after your father's last words?'

'His last words were that I use everything he taught me to help those that need it.' Brendan pulled out his phone.

Pressing the power button, a photo of young Brendan and his father together was the screen saver. 'I think more than anything else, he'd want me to be happy, live the life he never could, with a family.'

'As lovely as it is to hear you speak like that, Brendan, don't start thinking like that until we're finished this.' Lorna reached over and gave him another kiss. 'Trust me, Brendan Cleary: the father, perhaps husband would be the best gift I could ever ask for, but until we're finished, Brendan Cleary needs to remain the fucking badass that the late Damien Cleary moulded him into.'

The waiter came over with their food, a steaming hot plate in each hand. She set one plate down in front of Lorna, then the second on Brendan's side.

'Thanks,' Lorna said.

'Do you need anything else?' She spoke in a local accent, a world of difference between hers and Brendan's, even though Belfast and Derry were no more than eighty miles from each other.

'Another pot of tea, please?' Brendan said.

'Of course,' the lady turned and approached the young family in the next booth. Handing them a menu each, she turned and went back to the bar.

Brendan looked at the plate and smiled. 'It's the small things in life that's the most important.' He gestured at the food, 'and a good Irish breakfast is one of the most special small things you can get.'

Lorna sniggered as she grabbed the bottle of red sauce. 'Men... you're always so easily pleased.' She shook the bottle then tipped some sauced on the side of the plate. She offered it to Brendan, but he was too busy dipping the sausage into the egg yolk.

The waitress brought over their tea and told them to enjoy their food. Lorna asked if she could put the tv on.

The large plasma mounted to the supporting pillar ten feet away from them was default set to Sky News. The news was showing the weather, which gave it to be warm for the following week or so. The poor weather was gone and the summer was about to begin. The news updates ran along the bottom of the screen that coursed along on a black belt, that, if you were slow at reading, you'd have to wait until it came back around again. No mention of Blackwood and Dobson being found.

'Guess no news is good news,' Brendan said, smearing some of his soda bread in egg yolk.

Lorna looked at him. 'How are you feeling?'

Keeping his eyes on his food, Brendan smirked. 'I'm with you, I couldn't be happier.'

Lorna laughed. 'Could you be any cheesier?'

He looked up her. 'I could be if you wanted me to be.' He blew her kiss with a mouthful of bread and egg. Then his line of sight fell back to the plate again, 'but more importantly, how are you? No more sickness?'

'I'll be happier when we I get my hands of Steve.'

'What do you think about Blackwood and Dobson?' Brendan set his knife and fork down, resting his arms on the table and leaning forward on the desk. 'Was that too easy us getting our hands on them, it seems far too easy. I mean come on. British Intelligence wanted us to find them.'

She paused momentarily, looking across the room as if searching for the answer. 'It does seem like we've gotten our hands on them, too easily. Or maybe we just count our lucky stars and...' She trailed off.

'You're the one who's worked for them. And from what I've heard, you were one of the best.' He picked up his knife and fork again. 'Or should I say the best, given the level of clearance you had. You have to be quite high up to have been those kinds of privileges.'

'Stop, you're making me blush.' She joked. 'And yes, I think we need to be very careful about who we come into contact with. The government was very foolish the last time in letting us get away. They won't be so silly the next time.'

'Agreed. And if we are going to going around loyalist parts of Belfast, we'll need to stay away from anyone that can recognise us.'

'What about your uncle?' Lorna said.

'Ivan?' Brendan's eyebrows met in the middle.

'You think maybe he'd be willing to help?'

'I don't know.' His tone had changed.

'You saved his life, I guess you owe him one. Maybe you should cash it in.'

I've got an idea on how to navigate the place. And I think Moore Jnr's unhappy girlfriend is going to prove very helpful. She said he's coming back to Belfast. And it's for an important meeting.'

'The kind of importance that would involve explosives and a daring plan to start blowing up a load of mosques across England?'

Brendan nodded his head then smiled. 'I'm actually more excited to see my aunt Mary more than anything else. I love that old doll.'

Lorna smirked then laughed. 'Don't call her that or she'll be the one that want's you dead next.'

The news snatched their attention away from their meal. It was a live news report from Nottingham. The night before there'd been a lot of trouble in various different parts of the city. But the violence in Nottingham according to the reporter was on a tiny scale in comparison to what happened in Leicester.

'Leicester's burning.' Brendan spoke humorously, until the report changed to a live feed of a burning building on one of Leicester's central business areas.

The reporter said. 'This tattoo shop was the scene of a horrific attack this afternoon. One man was badly assaulted. He remains in a critical condition in Leicester hospital. We're speaking to the man's sister who was one of the first at the scene.' The camera turned from the devastation, to the tattoo artists sister, and more importantly Billy Moore Jnr's girlfriend.

Realising the significance of the attack, Brendan said. 'Well, this is the start of it. A tit for tat string of attacks that'll just grow more intense.'

'Who's that?' Lorna looked up at the screen then back at Brendan.

'That's Jnr's girlfriend,' Brendan said. 'I spoke to her brother today. He's a tattoo artist, lovely guy.' They both went silent to listen to what she said.

'I came into the shop,' her voice was trembling, her nose running, her eyes water watering. 'They'd held him down and tattooed his face, and other parts of his body that nobody should ever...' she exploded into fits of hysterical tears, 'the bastards tortured him by using the one passion he had.'

Brendan winced, feeling his muscles cease up. He looked at Lorna. 'I met the guy yesterday. Not involved with Moore and his clan of scum.'

'The ones that done this didn't know that.' Lorna kept her gaze on the screen. 'My guess is they know she's with Moore and couldn't get their hands on her so decide to make an example of him instead.'

The camera then turned to a police officer. When asked what he knew about scene, he said. 'An attempted murder investigation is now underway. It's clear that this was not only an assault. The culprits had left this young man to burn to death in his premises. And if it were not for the man's sister here, we have no doubt we would have been dealing a murder investigation.'

The reporter asked. 'There is a growing speculation that this attack is in retaliation to the anti-Islam protest and petrol bomb attack on a crowd of Muslim community leaders in Nottingham yesterday. An attacks people have died because of their injuries. Can you confirm that there is a connection between the two?'

'This investigation is still at the early stages and...'

'Of course, it was,' Vanessa yelled. 'And instead of getting the person they were after, they got someone who's completely innocent.'

Brendan looked at Lorna. 'I think we may have lost our inside man to Moore's dealings.'

'Let's wait and see.'

Chapter Thirty-Five

THE SAFE-HOUSE IN DONEGAL was open to the world, the gate left open. Mary was outside brushing the driveway. With her brush in hand she turned on her heel almost fast enough to give herself a whiplash. Her facial expression serious and defensive, strands of her dark, greying hair blowing in the seaside wind. Brushing a strand out of her eyes, her expression lifted when she seen who it was.

'Brendan, thank god you're okay, love.' She stepped out of the way for them to drive the car on through the gate. 'Go on up to the house, put the kettle on. I'll be up in a minute, I'm nearly finished.'

'Glad to see you're making yourself at home, Mary,' Brendan said out the window, as he guided the vehicle passed her, up the drive and through the gate. 'God, she'll have this place ready for a presidential visit in two days, guaranteed.' He smirked, looking in the rear-view as Mary collected the pile of rubbish and shovelled it into the black bin liner that blew carelessly in the wind.

'She takes good pride in her home,' Lorna said. 'God, I love this place. If it didn't have some many bad memories for you, I'd sooner stay here than go anywhere else.'

'Maybe one day we can come back.' He put the car in neutral and activated the parking brake. 'When we're old and grey.'

Lorna looked at him, 'hopefully we'll get to that stage in life.'

He looked at her. 'We will.' He threw the door open and stepped out. 'I'm just not sure it'll be here.'

Lorna jumped out of her side and slammed the door shut. 'I don't really care where, as long as we're together, Brendan. That's all I care about.' She walked around the front of the car, looking across the garden. 'But this place is really tranquil.' She closed her eyes and inhaled deeply. 'So peaceful. I can see why your father was so drawn to it.'

'I know.' Brendan joined her at the front of the car, putting his arm around her. His phone buzzed in his pocket. Pulling it out of his pocket, he looked at it, then looked at Lorna. 'Maybe we haven't lost our inside man, or woman yet.' He answered the call. 'Vanessa, you okay?'

'I'm fucking pissed off. Something terrible had happened to my brother, and it's the last straw. That piece of shit boyfriend of mine and his even bigger bastard of a father are directly to blame for what's happened.'

'I'm sorry but...'

'Don't give me that sorry bullshit, why do I get the impression that it's not just a coincidence that you – a guy from the same neighbourhood who's about the same age as my boyfriend – just happened to come into my life at the same time Billy's planning something very big?'

Brendan looked at Lorna, instantly caught off-guard.

'Are you investigating him?' Vanessa said.

His mind reeled. If he gave her the right answer, he could lose her as an ally.

'If you are investigating him, then you've just become very lucky. Because I know everything he's planning. And trust me it's very big. Explosive, actually.'

'What's he planning?'

'It's not that easy. I know you've given my brother and me bullshit name. I'm not stupid so who are you?'

Brendan looked at Lorna, then down the driveway as Mary approached them with her brush, shovel and bag in hand, the estate's gate closing behind her. 'Okay.' He sighed. 'Screw it. Search Brendan Cleary from Belfast. If you still want to talk, call me back. I've got to go.' He hung up the phone.

'So, she knows who we are now?' Lorna said. 'You think that was wise?'

'She knows I'm not who I said I am anyway. For all we know, she already knows and is just testing me to see if she can trust me.'

Mary approached them. It's good to see you again, love.' She dropped the bag at her feet and pulled Brendan in for a hug.

'Lovely to see you, too, Mary.' Brendan hugged her, giving her a kiss on the cheek during the embrace.

Mary looked at Lorna, offering her hand to over. Lorna accepted. 'I'm glad someone's been able to straighten him out.' She pulled Lorna in for a kiss on the cheek.

'I wouldn't say I've straightened him out, he's probably been as good for me as I have for him.'

'As lovely as this is, can get inside?' Brendan said, lifting the bin bag. He led the way towards the front door. Turning towards his aunt, 'how've you been, Mary? And what about the rest of the family?'

'I'm fine, love. You don't need to keep asking that. Your father used to do the same, but he forgets I wiped both of your bums at one point in time.'

Lorna laughed. 'That's cute. Little Brendan getting his ass wiped,' she poked Brendan with her index finger, following him inside.

'All babies get their asses wiped,' Brendan protested, making his way across the hallway towards the living room. He looked around. The black piano was gleaming in the sunlight, the walls looked whiter, brighter than the last time they'd been there. The house had never smelled cleaner. 'You've given the place a sprucing up?'

'Not me, love.' Mary shut the front door. 'I've only arrived today. The house was spotless when I got here.'

'Must have been Diana and the other girls,' Lorna said. 'We did tell them to make themselves at home.' She took her jacket off and lay it down along the back of the white sofa that ran along one of the walls of the living room. She sat down, crossing her right leg over her left.

Mary sat down beside her. 'Diana, who's that?'

'Remember the Romanian ladies we'd dragged out of Belfast?' Lorna said.

'They stayed here?'

'We'd nowhere else to put them, aunty Mary,' Brendan opened the window then sat down on the single recliner to their right. 'There was nowhere else to go and it was here or ship them all back to Romania and probably into the hands of more scumbag traffickers.'

'Well, you know saving your uncle Ivan's life in that little episode is going to benefit you,' Mary said.

'Why?'

'We both know Ivan was a true Ulster loyalist. Nothing more or less. But he knows the war's over, and he doesn't agree with the gangster lifestyle a lot of the younger ones seem to be more attracted to. And he's the one that told me about the hit that's been put out on you. It's got nothing to do with your father or anything Loyalist/Republican. It's all been a nicely cooked up story that gives the government a reason for your body turning up dead. Blame it on the loyalists. The loyalist that pulls the trigger will be recognised as the person who puts down the son of the infamous Damien Cleary and the heads of the government can sleep easy knowing that the two people,' she looked at Lorna then back at Brendan, 'with so much dirt that it could start a third world war, are dead.'

'Ivan told you this?' Brendan said.

Mary nodded. 'Said he sat in on the meetings with the other heads of the UDA. He was asked which side he was taking. Obviously for his own life he had to say he was for it. But you saving his life at the docks left him with a dept to you and this is his way of telling you to stay away, without him actually having to get involved.'

'That way he gets to look like he's still supportive of his old UDA comrades while at the same time gets wind to you to stay away.' Brendan looked at Lorna then Mary. He sat forward in his seat, resting his forearms on his knees. He joined his hands, interlocking his fingers as if in silent prayer. 'We can't walk away yet, Mary. They're about to slaughter people in England.'

'Who are?' Mary sat forward, imitating Brendan.

'You know Billy Moore and his son have been elected to lead the revived Combat 18 in England?'

Mary nodded. 'They've been all over the news here, too.'

'Well they're planning a series of attacks on Muslims celebrating their most precious day of the year,' Lorna said.

Mary looked at Lorna, then back at Brendan. 'You're not serious?'

'As serious as a bomb in a mosque on Ramadan, Aunty Mary,' Brendan said, sitting back in his chair. 'And the government know all about it.'

'How do you know the government's in on it?'

'Because we were followed by two agents on the plane from East Midlands and they coughed up what exactly is going on.' Brendan's phone rang. He pulled it out of his pocket and looked at the screen. He looked up at Mary then Lorna. 'It's her again.' He answered and put it to his ear. 'So, you looked me up I'm guessing?'

'You're quite the famous guy, Brendan Cleary.' She spoke sarcastically. 'Or should I say infamous?'

'That's probably a better word to describe me, yes,' Brendan said.

'So why don't I just hand you over to the police and probably received a healthy reward for it?'

'You might have already done that,' Brendan said. 'But judging from the personal rage that came from your voice earlier, I'd sooner say you're more interested in making someone pay for what happened to your brother than earning a quick few quid.'

'So, what are you planning on doing?'

'Stopping the massacre that your boyfriend and his father are about to cause.' He looked at the photo of him and the late Damien Cleary on the mantel. 'It looks like they want to write themselves into the history books of not only Irish politics, but also British politics.'

'And how do you plan on stopping them?'

'With your help, of course.'

She didn't say anything. There was a momentary silence.

'How's your brother?'

'He's alive,' she said bluntly, then cleared her throat. 'Okay, well the reason they're in Belfast is not only to recruit into the ranks of the new and improved Combat 18 and Britain First, but their number one bomb maker is a bit strange and will only prepare the bombs in Belfast. He's weird.'

Brendan smirked. 'Yes, Greystone is a very strange man, but brilliant. Don't let his strangeness fool you, if you do that, you could be in a lot of trouble.'

'Well my ex-boyfriend and his father are currently in Belfast to meet with Greystone, making sure he sticks to the deadline.'

'Do you know where he's hiding out? Greystone?'

She sighed. 'A safehouse somewhere on the Shankill Road. I've never been to the house, but I remember Moore and his mates joking about how weapons that would be used to make Britain great again were built in the heart of Ulster loyalism.'

Brendan looked at Mary then Lorna. 'Okay, thanks for that. If you can think of anything else that might help, let me know.'

'I will.' She cleared her throat. 'I can also tell you where exactly they're targeting.'

Brendan's eyes lit up. 'Where?'

'I'll tell you, but only when you tell me the whereabouts of the bastards that did that to my brother.' She paused for a moment. 'Once I know where they are, I will tell you exactly where the bombs are going to go off.'

Brendan looked at the ground. 'He was going to have to give someone else up to save more lives. But the person or people he'd be giving up were bad people anyway and with that, he was happy to agree. 'Okay. Send me the CCTV footage of what happened, and I'll make sure you get your hands on them before the police do.' He hung up and called Louise.

Louise answered the call almost immediately. 'Brendan, how's life in Belfast?'

'Great.' Brendan put the call on loudspeaker. 'I'll get straight to the point. Have you seen the news in Leicester?'

'Yes, horrible. That was Moore Jnr's girlfriend, balling on the news a little earlier, wasn't it?'

'It was. She's offered to help us stop what they're doing. She said she knows the exact locations of where the bombs are going to explode. But she'll only give us that if we can hand her the ones responsible for what happened to her brother.'

'I know who ordered that...'

'Our friend that gave us the ride in the car after the riot?'

'Omar runs the streets with a sadistic iron fist, Brendan. He's a mean bastard. But he's been conditioned by what the likes of Moore have done to his people.'

'Fair enough,' Brendan spoke with zero emotion. 'But he needs to go, if we're to stop these attacks. She may be the only person that can help us, and as she's just said a moment ago, time is running out.'

'I've got no problem handing him over to her,' Louise said, 'but it's getting to him, people like him are heavily protected. His people love him, they would stand in front of a bullet for him.'

'That's handy because I don't really mind having to blow a few of them away if need be.'

'I just want Moore's head,' Louise said. 'Whatever I can do to help.'

'Well, the thing about Moore Snr is, he's always seen himself as a commander from the front, which means he'll be personally delivering one of the bombs to it's intended target. So, if we can find out where he's going to be, he's all yours.'

'And you?'

Brendan looked at his aunt Mary, smirking. 'Billy Moore Jnr once said something about Damien Cleary that was unforgivable. He once spread news around Belfast about my dead mother which was a little upsetting...I'll be happy to get my hands on him. In fact, I'd almost pay to see the expression on his face when I reveal myself to him when it's only us two, one on one.'

'How's Lorna, is she okay?' Louise asked.

'I'm fine, thanks,' Lorna shouted at the phone. 'I think we all need to work together before this get's too messy.'

'I agree,' Louise said.

'We were followed by government agents on the plane. Our friend Moore has again got the government in his pocket, he'll be doing their dirty work, whatever their messed-up methods, much like the history of loyalist collusion in Belfast. You need to be careful who you talk to, and don't go too far without protecting yourself. When the two agents don't check in with their superior, the bosses back in London will know something's up and will look to find something or someone to use a ransom to stop us.'

'Okay, well, you're the one with the experience. Let me know what I can do.'

'Just sit tight until we get back to England,' Lorna said, 'we're not going to be in Belfast any more than a day. And, Louise, watch your back. The government may already be watching you. If you do have to go out, stay in public as much as you can.'

Brendan lifted the phone off the table and ended the call.

'You pair must be hungry.' Mary got up off the sofa. 'I'll make you something to eat and a cup of tea.' She stopped at the doorway and looked back at Brendan. 'You should pay your uncle Ivan a visit. If anyone knows where Greystone is on the Shankill, it'll be your uncle.'

Chapter Thirty-Six

LORNA STAYED IN DONEGAL with Mary as Brendan returned to Belfast to see his uncle Ivan. One of the top Ulster loyalists and ex-British soldier who'd helped form the UDA in the early seventies, Ivan hated Brendan as a kid. Which wasn't surprising, given the fact Brendan's father – Damien Cleary – was part of the Provisional IRA's army counsel, calling the shots and directing their operations from the Falls Road. Regardless of whether they liked it or not, they were both bonded. Brendan's mother, Vanessa, was Ivan's younger sister who'd fallen in love with and married Damien Cleary. It was like a story of Romeo and Juliet, but with a blood-stained Irish spin on it. Brendan had taken a chance to do the right thing by saving Ivan's life. Watching his uncle on the verge of execution, at the hands of a Romanian gangster was something he couldn't live with; perhaps doing it more for his late mother, than for himself. Either way, saving Ivan's life had now become a blessing in disguise, if Ivan were willing to help Brendan with what he needed to do.

The Shankill Road was a couple of miles long, a road that drew an adjoining line with the Falls Road, and still, it was lined with the infamous peace wall that separated the two. An eyesore to most. But a necessary part of Belfast, keeping the two communities separated. On the Shankill side, every lamppost had an oversized Union Jack flag, clearly marking the territory as being part of the Queen's country, whilst also sending an anxious shiver down the spine of many Catholics who'd dare go into the area. Kerbs lined the road in the red white and blue, and the upcoming twelfth of July parades only added to the spectacle of a tiny city like Belfast consumed by two opposing cultures trying to flex their sectarian muscles.

Arriving at the bottom of the Shankill, Brendan shut off the engine, not too keen on being in the area, but willing to go that extra mile to help someone a few hundred miles across the Irish sea. Louise needed someone's help and perhaps Brendan and Lorna were the only two that weren't interested in taking over her inherited empire.

He pulled his phone out and called his uncle. After a few rings, the phone was answered.

'Hello?' Ivan said.

'Ivan, it's Brendan.'

There was a momentary pause, then a sigh. 'Fuck sake, Brendan. I told Mary not to bring you back. I can't protect you.'

'I don't need you to protect me. I can look after myself. I need to know where Greystone is making the bombs. Then I'll do the rest.'

'You're too late, Brendan. The bombs are already gone.'

'What do you mean?'

'A few sprinter vans have left the Shankill, on their way to the docs.'

'What docs?'

Ivan paused, then cleared his throat. 'The...the Dublin docs.'

'Ivan, you're lying. Why?'

'Look, Brendan, son, if you want to stay alive, get away from Belfast, and don't show your face around here again. I'll get killed just for talking to you.'

'Too late. I'm on the Shankill Road now.'

'What?' Ivan sounded astonished. 'Where are you?'

'At the bottom of the road, near the Orange Hall.'

'Wait there, I'll be out in two minutes, Brendan, for God's sake, don't move.' Ivan hung up the phone.

Brendan set his phone down on the passenger seat and put the radio on. Belfast's Cool FM Radio playing some old dance music, bringing him back to his days as a teenager, doing the things every teenager did – partying, getting into fights. The thought of him and his mates brought a smile to his face. The trouble they'd all gotten into at times. Brendan found himself grateful for the strict upbringing from his father, giving him the common sense to walk away from that life before he'd ended up like most of the guys he ran with – either dead, in jail, or so strung out on drugs and alcohol that they may as well be dead.

The passenger door opened. Ivan dropped himself onto the seat, Brendan's fast hands managing to snatch his phone up before it got crushed.

'Get the hell out of here now, Brendan. Before you get the both of us shot.'

Brendan put the car in gear and took off. 'I thought you were still in charge of the Shankill Road UDA? Sure it was you that put Billy Moore and his buddies out of the city.'

'Aye but you still killed Burrows. He was one of the top
men in the organisation. I got some headache for that, just
because I was remotely linked to you.'

Brendan led the car off the Shankill and towards the city
centre where it was a little more mixed. No loyalist or republican markings, just a city full of people. Not culturally dis-
tinguished. He led the car down a narrow street next to the
city's old central library that stood next to the Belfast Tele-
graph.

'So, where are Greystone and the others?' Brendan said,
parking the car on the side of the street next to a small café.

'I wasn't lying about bombs having already been shipped
across to England. But he is making more bombs, a second
batch if you like.'

'You know what they're planning?'

Ivan nodded his head. 'A massacre. On Ramadan.'

'They'll start bloody mayhem over there,' Brendan said,
looking at the café. The shop had only two customers. With
five members of staff, it looked like they were crying for some
business. 'Come on, I'll buy you a cup of tea.' He got out just
as the rain came on.

They entered the shop. The smell of sausage and bacon
was a welcome one. 'Go and grab a seat, I'll go order the tea.
Do you want a sausage and bacon sandwich?'

Ivan nodded his head, his face serious, his expression trying to figure out could he trust Brendan or was he being led
into a trap.

'Christ, Ivan. You need to stop taking whatever drugs it
is you're taking now. Your paranoia can be seen a mile off.'

'You always were a cocky little bastard.' Ivan tried not to smirk but Brendan sensed it.

After ordering two sausage and bacon sandwiches, Brendan brought two cups of tea over. Ivan's was black, no milk or sugar. Brendan set the cups down and sat facing his uncle.

'I don't know how you drink that without milk.'

'From what I remember, your ma drunk her tea that way, too. God rest her.' He looked at Brendan. 'So, Brendan....' He lifted the cup, blowing on it, chasing steam out, looking directly into Brendan's eyes. 'What's the deal? Why are you running around getting yourself involved in all this?'

'I like to think of myself as Batman, or Robin Hood.'

Ivan smirked, then looked over Brendan's shoulder, his paranoia still not settled. 'You'll eventually get yourself killed, kid. From what I've heard your old man had collected quite a savings before he died. Why not take that and sail off into the sunset with British Agent Lorna Woodward.'

'Ex-agent.' Brendan was quick to correct him. 'And my father's dying words were for everything he taught me to be put to good use. He didn't want everything he'd learned to go to waste, so he passed it all on to me.'

Ivan took a sip of his tea. 'He always was someone that wanted to make a difference...'

Brendan cut Ivan off. 'Don't be blowing smoke up his arse now just because he's dead. You never like him, you certainly didn't like the fact my mother, your sister, married him and had me.'

'It was a war, Brendan.' Ivan kept his tone level and calm. 'Christ, if I had of been from the other side of the peace wall,

I would have been just as involved with the republicans as I am with this side.'

'Well, it's in the past. But, why haven't your people taken Moore and his son out since coming back.'

'God, Brendan. Moore's got some very influential backing. I mean backing from London.' Ivan took another drink of his tea. 'All the way from Number Ten Downing Street.'

'Why doesn't that surprise me.'

Ivan shook his head. 'Government is rotten to the core, son. It always has been. Always will be. Rich guys in fancy suits who can be very persuasive with their words. Things will never change.' He looked at Brendan. 'Why you? Why do you have to be the one that stops all this? Why not just go on with your life, son. I know that's what Vanessa would have wanted.'

Brendan took a drink of his tea then slowly set the cup down, leaning forward, resting his elbows on the table. 'My mother drank herself to death because the thought of my father lying in some unmarked grave was too much for her to bare. And when the *legendary Damien Cleary* finally re-surfaced and told me that the government, acting on it's own greedy agenda, made him disappear, then tried to kill me to cover it up, well...' He sat back in his seat and sighed. 'My father died in my arms. I watched the life drain from his face, felt his pulse speed up, then fade, finally stopping. He used his last breath, his final burst of energy to get one message to me.'

'What was the message?'

'Make the British government regret ever fucking with our family.' He swallowed. 'Now, tell where Greystone is, Ivan. Please.'

Ivan looked up at the ceiling, as if in silent prayer. 'Fuck.' He looked at Brendan, then leaned forward. 'They're bringing the final shipment of bombs to England tomorrow evening. Sailing from Belfast to Liverpool, then the bombs are being divided out into a number of vehicles, from there, they'll disperse to various different targets, ready for the Ramadan celebrations.'

'Thank you.' Brendan looked at his uncle. 'You realise this is the most civil conversation we've ever had.'

Ivan laughed. 'Just shows how messed up things have been for both of us.'

Chapter Thirty-Seven

AFTER LEAVING THE SHOP, Ivan shook Brendan's hand and again, wished him all the best, advising him that he should walk away from the entire life. Brendan smirked, first a smile of adolescent rebelliousness as Ivan's troubled nephew, then it softened into one of a man with his heart in the right place. He took off on his own, with the address for Greystone's safehouse. He called Louise.

'Brendan, are you okay?'

'I've got good news and bad news. The bad news: some of the bombs have already set sail and are already in England. The good news is: I know when the rest of the bombs are arriving, tomorrow night. And it'll be Billy Moore and his son bringing them over, along with some helpers.'

'Great, we can stop them when they arrive.'

'The only issue, this has got some very influential support, so we can't just go at them all gung ho.'

'What do you suggest?'

'We let them take the bombs to their locations, then, when they think it's all good to go, we stop them. If we stop them when they come over from Belfast tomorrow, then we'll frighten to other bombers off and we'll never find them.'

'Okay,' Louise said. 'I've picked something up from my end for you, too.'

'What?'

'Our friend from Nottingham who gave us a ride in his car is the one who ordered the attack on the tattoo artist in Leicester.'

'How do you feel about that?'

'What do you mean, how do I feel?'

'I know you've got a respect for him because he was friendly with your father.'

'If my father was alive, he'd probably cut the bastards balls off himself.'

'So, you won't have a problem giving Omar up to her?'

'Even if we weren't getting anything in return, I'd still hand him over. From the word in Leicester, what the bastards did to him was horrific. Like something from a sadistic horror movie.'

'Great. I will call her later, send me his details. She'll want proof that we're legit and not blowing smoke up her ass.'

'I'll send you everything this evening. I've been asked to meet with the man that I've trusted to run my father's pub. He said he'd got something I should here. He said it's very important.'

'Louise,' Brendan spoke calmly, but with a tone that ensured that it would open her ears. 'Do me a favour. Find a reason to not go to that meeting. It sounds a bit dodgy.'

'You think I'm in danger?'

'You tell me. Is Richard worried that he's going to be found out as the snake he is. Is he going to try and take you out before he loses his shot?'

'When are you and Lorna coming back to England?'

'Hopefully tomorrow night.'

'Okay, great. Let me know when you need picked up from the airport.'

'I will. Be very careful. The moment we caught those two agents on the plane, we realised very influential people are involved in this. And the government have got ways to make people disappear, forever.'

'This is dangerous, Brendan. Why don't you and Lorna just get away before either of you get killed.'

'Because my father would turn in his grave if it did,' Brendan said. His phone buzzed against his cheek. It was Lorna. 'I'll call you later.' He ended the call, then answered Lorna. 'I've just spoken to Louise. She's found out who was behind the attack in the tattoo shop in Leicester.'

'Let me guess, the top drug lord in the Muslim community in Nottingham?'

He hummed to agree.

'Brendan this is going to get out of control. And this guy, whether he ever agrees to it or not, does have contact to Muslim extremists in England. If he spreads the hate, a lot of people are going to suffer.'

'That's not going to happen.' Brendan started the engine. 'Because I'm going to serve him and Moore up to their makers, whether it's fucking God or Allah, they're going to meet them.'

'What about Ivan, did he come through?'

'He did. Reluctantly. I'm on my way back to Donegal. I'll see you in a couple of hours.'

'I'll book us a flight back to England.' Lorna hung up the phone.

Brendan looked out the window of the vehicle as the rain began to come down, the sun was blinding, but the rain was emptying out in bucket loads. Before Brendan took off, he just sat for a moment, wondering, thinking about what his uncle had said. It had taken the death of both parents, almost being killed on numerous occasions and saving Ivan's life before the two actually sat down and had a civil conversation. Ivan was bitter. But Brendan was his nephew. Ivan's little sister was Brendan's heart, and Brendan was the apple of the late Vanessa Cleary's eye. He looked up at the sky, thoughtful. He hadn't thought about her as much for ages. Not simply because his life had been in the fast lane for so long, but he'd buried the thought of her with the coffin. He blocked out the thoughts, a fear of breaking down, and appearing weak. In the world he'd found himself, having to make his own way in the dark world, he became somewhat robotic. But seeing his uncle and remembering why he'd saved Ivan's life was simply for the lady who'd loved him dearly. And in that moment as if a sign from somewhere up above, his mother's favourite song came on the radio. He closed his eye, his eyelids squeezing a tear out, slowly running down each cheek. After taking a few deep breaths and wiping the tears from his face, Brendan put the car in gear and took off.

Chapter Thirty-Eight

DONEGAL WAS IN COMPLETE darkness by the time Brendan had returned. He'd taken a detour, visiting his mother at Milltown Cemetery in West Belfast where the majority of Catholics in that part of the city were laid to rest. As he arrived at the gate, the unmovable looking chunky gate began to open before he'd even touched the remote control. Either Lorna or Mary must have been close to the CCTV monitors.

The garden was in darkness, apart from the blue night lighting that illuminated the white surrounding walls. As the car climbed the slight gradient, approaching the entrance, the porch light came on, and Lorna emerged from behind the front door. Leaning against the doorframe, her arms folded as if trying to conserve whatever heat she could.

Brendan got out of the car, slamming the door shut behind him, feeling drained.

'What took you so long? We were beginning to worry something had happened to you,' Lorna said. 'And you weren't answering your phone.'

Brendan felt like he was being nagged, and in his tired state, almost lost his temper and snapped, but he knew their worries were legit. 'I'm sorry,' he said, approaching the porch. 'I'm just really tired.'

'What's wrong?' Lorna took a few steps out onto the porch, meeting him at the steps. 'And don't say nothing. I can tell by the tone of your voice and that miserable fucking excuse for a walk. I've never seen such pathetic posture.'

He smiled, appreciating the humour covering her concern and stepped up onto the porch. 'I've just been thinking about my mother, that's all. Went to the graveyard to have a wee chat to her.' He looked at her, gently caressed her stomach and tugged on her t-shirt, pulling her in toward him, kissing her softly on the lips. He smiled again. 'I wish you had of met her. She would have loved you.'

'What, a British Agent?'

'Ex-agent, who gave me, her only son, something good to focus on.'

She kissed him. 'I know why you want to help Louise, and stop this mess in England. But once it's done, let's just take off and make time for us. Nothing else.'

'You want to see your sister first.'

'She can wait. Our sanity can't. I think us being away from this part of the world for a while is exactly what we both need.'

Brendan smiled at her.

'I've booked us flights for tomorrow morning.'

'You two need to come in and see this.' Mary shouted from the door.

Brendan looked over Lorna's shoulder, Lorna turned around.

'You've just made the headlines again.' Mary turned and went back into the house.

Brendan and Lorna followed her into the house. On approach to the living room, the sound of their names being mentioned was not really a surprise. As they stepped into the living room, the widescreen that was mounted to the wall had CCTV footage of both Brendan and Lorna walking through the arrivals terminal of George Best Belfast City Airport.

The reporter said. 'This image was captured within the last twenty-four hours. It shows Mr Cleary and Ex-British Agent Lorna Woodward passing through the arrivals terminal. Shortly after, they were seen following two undercover agents to the vehicle rental area, here, they are thought to have had a discussion with the two agents who's names cannot be disclosed at this time. What ensued after this is still unknown, but the agents have both been found dead a short distance from the airport. Both executed with bullets in the back of the head. Their bodies discovered on the Newtownards airfield.'

Brendan and Lorna both watched as the tv screen shot from the reporter standing on the entrance to the airfield to a full-sized picture of them both.

'Maybe it's better if you don't go to the airport, they'll be everywhere looking for you,' Mary said, turning the tv down. 'You know they'll kill the both of you. They've too much to cover up.'

Brendan nodded as he dropped himself down on the sofa. 'They can't afford to let us live.'

'They've silenced those two because they won't want any loose ends.' Lorna sat down next to him. 'Now they're trying to make it impossible for us to move around.'

'Look you two.' Mary sat down on the coffee table, crouched over resting her forearms on her thighs trying to get closer to them. 'You need to just get out of here. You both have a chance of having a happy life together. Why risk that?' She looked at Lorna, then Brendan. 'It's not your job to save the world.' She laughed without sarcasm. 'It wasn't your father's either, but I know the kind of person he was, and you're not much different to him, Brendan, love.'

'I can't just walk away, Mary. There are people over there that expect us to come back and help them. And that rat, Billy Moore isn't going to go through with this. Over my dead body will I allow that to happen.'

Mary sighed, then sat back again. Standing up she turned and walked towards the fireplace. She looked at a photo of Brendan and his father. Lifting it down, she inspected it closely, then looked up at Brendan. 'You'll have to get the boat over. But the government are watching you. You can bet your life that they'll have everywhere covered.' She turned and set the photo back up again.'

'There's only one place they'll not check, and it's guaranteed.' Brendan looked at Lorna.'

'Where?'

'We intercept one of the vans before it reaches the docks.'

Mary looked at Lorna, then Brendan. She laughed, but more out of astonishment than humour. 'Well, you really do like taking risks, son.'

'Do you have a better idea, Mary?' Brendan was quick to respond.

She didn't reply.

'I'll call Ivan. Once we know where the last couple of bombs are, we're intercepting a van. Greystone will be the one we take. I want the maker of these bloody things on the same transit as us.' Brendan reached into his pocket and grabbed his phone. Calling his uncle. He looked at Lorna, then Mary, shaking his head. 'The fucking government.' He looked down at the ground, paying an unnecessary amount of attention to the shoes on his feet. Well, his eyes were, his mind was elsewhere; perhaps a couple of hundred miles away in the midlands that was about to become a bombing haven, like a modern day 70s Belfast.

Ivan answered the call. 'Brendan, have you seen the news?'

'We have, Ivan. I need the whereabouts of Greystone. He's going to provide us our safe passage into England. It's not as if we can jump on a plain anytime soon and we need to get back there.'

'You've definitely got balls, son. And I can't talk you out of it, can I? Vanessa would kill me if I didn't at least try and stop you from going after them.'

Brendan smirked. 'I'm my mother's son, Ivan...but I'm also my father's son, and he'd be turning in his grave if I didn't take this opportunity to silence them.'

Ivan paused for a moment, then cleared his throat. 'Okay. They're leaving in the early hours of the morning. An overnight sailing. They're supposed to be making a switch. Changing vans two or three times before they reach their destination.'

'When's Greystone sailing? He's the only one we need for now. We can catch up with the rest once we get over there. I have a pretty upset English lady willing to give us the locations of all the targets.'

'Okay, I'll call you back in an hour.' Ivan hung up.

Chapter Thirty-Nine

IVAN CAME THROUGH. Greystone was due to leave the overnight sailing. A seven-hour swim across the Irish sea would have the last van heading for it's destination by mid-morning.

'Where would be the best place to intercept this transit?' Brendan said, as he scraped the plate dry, the evening snack prepared by Mary was something he'd enjoyed.

'The moment he gets into the van, we take it,' Lorna said, also scraping her plate. 'Mary, I'm going to miss your cooking. How about you come to England with us?'

Mary laughed. 'I've lived in this beautiful country all my life, and I'll die here, too.'

Brendan stood up and lifted their plates. 'Let's just make sure you don't die for a long time.' He brought the dishes to the sink. Pulling his sleeves up, he started washing. 'We'll need to go soon. Ivan said the van is parked in a rusty old barn shelter that hasn't been used in years. Greystone is to arrive in his own black Audi A6 and will arrive with only him in it.'

'Do you know the whereabouts of this barn?' Lorna said, getting up to help him with the dishes.

Brendan nodded his head. 'Got the address, but I know the area anyway so it should be easy enough to find.'

Mary joined them at the sink area. 'You can't leave without a cup of tea.' She grabbed the kettle and filled it with water from the fridge tap. 'Or do you want coffee? It's a long trek back to Belfast.'

'I'll have a double espresso,' Brendan said. 'And a long coffee.'

'God, are you planning on running back to Belfast?' Lorna playfully punched Brendan on the shoulder.

He smirked. He turned and looked at Lorna who was polishing the plates almost with purpose, she looked happy in that moment. 'You sure you don't want to go and see your sister before we take off somewhere?'

'No, I think it's better if we get away from this place for a while. I know a quiet little hotel on the white sandy beaches of San Andeas, Colombia. We can book in there for a few weeks and forget everything that's happened in our lives since we met.' She set the stack of three plates in the cupboard. 'If we don't take a long-overdue rest, were both going to collapse.'

Brendan looked over her shoulder at Mary. 'Where do you think you're going?'

Mary put her black suit jacket on, folding down the collar. 'I'm going back to Belfast. I'm not staying in his house all alone.' She checked her phone, then dropped it into her pocket. 'Anyway, I've got a shop to run, and there'll be a lot of angry people on the Antrim Road if they don't get their morning fry and cup of tea before they go to work.'

'They'll not feel any better if someone comes after you to get to me and they have to close shop permanently.' Brendan pulled his sleeves down, drying his hands on the bottom end of the cloth Lorna was using to dry the dishes. 'Just stay here, Aunty Mary, until it's safe. Please.'

'Brendan, son, I can't stay cooped up in this house...'

'Mary for God's sake,' Brendan raised his voice, his face reddening. 'If they hurt you I'll be back for them, and they know that. You're in danger if you go back there.'

Mary looked at Brendan then Lorna, then back at Brendan again. 'I'm not useless, love.'

'God, I know you're not, Mary. Christ, I wouldn't mess with you,' he smirked at he approached her. He gripped her softly at the top of her arms and pecked her on the cheek. 'Okay, why don't you drive us into Belfast. We can grab a car that can be dumped at the barn. Then you come back here.'

'Grab your stuff.' Mary turned and made her way out the door, through the hallway and towards the entrance.

Brendan looked at Lorna. 'You ready to go?'

'Let's go.' She left the room as fast as Mary did.

Brendan followed, reaching the doorway then stopped. He turned and glanced around the room, as if he were saying goodbye to the place where he'd been moulded into the man he was. The man his late father created. By training him, he carved and toughened him, becoming the Brendan Cleary the government would fear so much that they were willing to kill him to silence him. That's why Brendan hadn't handed himself in after clearing their names. They were innocent. What had taken place in Belfast on Bloody Thursday was all a lie. They were framed. Now he was dangerous enough to make them nervous.

He pulled the living room door closed and made his way along the hall towards the door. Spotting something beneath his coat that hung from the coat stand, he noticed it was Teodoro's skipping rope. Brendan lifted it and paused for a moment, looking at it, instantly feeling better about the young Romanian boy who Brendan had managed to help give a normal life to. He seen more his younger self in the young lad and in that moment, he looked up through the entrance of the front door out onto the porch, the sound of the car's engine starting up. He set the rope back down again and left, closing the door behind him. He got into the back of the car, Mary in the driver seat and Lorna acting as co-pilot.

As Brendan buckled himself in and got comfortable, he looked at his phone. A text message from Louise.

Brendan, there's been quite a bit of rioting tonight in both Nottingham and Leicester. A lot of the local Britain First hang outs have been targeted, burned to the ground. It's not just a couple of thugs or gangs doing this, these attacks are coming from Omar. And what happened to the tattoo artist is about to happen to a lot more. Social media is going crazy with people saying about how the poor people who'd been burned alive by those petrol bombs will not have died in vain and every member of Britain First will soon feel the wrath of the Muslim community. The crazy bastards think it's an attack on their religion and they think Allah will reward them for protecting his people.

'Allah is a fucking shit stirring cunt and if he were here he wouldn't be letting these dirty bastards get away with what they're doing.'

'But you know this is going to eat into the hands of the Muslim extremists. They've waged war on the western world, and will love all this shit kicking off.'

'Like Bloody Sunday,' Brendan said.

'What?'

Mary looked at Brendan in the reflection of the mirror as she guided the car along the winding Donegal roads, making use of the SUV's suspension and four-wheel-drive.

'Bloody Sunday was one of the biggest recruitment tools the Provisional IRA had for brining volunteers into it's ranks.'

'You're not comparing the IRA to the Muslim extremists, Brendan?' Mary said.

'No,' Brendan was quick to say. 'But the cause and effect would be the same. The Muslim people in England will feel threatened by the state that has provided them with home and jobs. A way of life they left their native counties for. Once the British state doesn't protect them, who are they going to seek protection from?'

'We need to stop these bombs from going off,' Louise said.

'Tell me something I don't already know, Louise.' Brendan sighed. 'We're on our way back to Belfast now. Greystone's leaving last for England. Lorna and me are going to take the van from him and once we get into England we need some people to help getting these bombs away from the mosques.'

'I can ask for some help from our Muslim friends,' Louise said.

'But you know we need to hand over whoever done that to Vanessa's brother? We need to if she's to give us any intel on where these bombs are headed.'

'I've already got the names of the bastards that done that. And don't worry those sick fucks won't be getting away with it.'

'Have you spoken with many of your crew?'

'Nope,' she said sharply, 'and I don't plan to either. They'll wish they'd never backed the losing team. I've noticed some dodgy people hanging around the bar. Definitely not locals. I'm thinking government.'

'Best stay away from the place.' Brendan put the window down in the back of the car. 'I'll let you know when we've intercepted Greystone's van and are on the boat.'

'Thank you for this, Brendan, really.'

'Don't thank me. We haven't done anything.' Brendan looked at his aunt in the reflection of the mirror again. He knew that look. Disapproval. 'I'll speak to you later.' He hung up the phone and set the phone down on the seat next to him. 'What's that look for?'

The moment he said this, Mary's eyes returned to the road ahead. 'You can't be the fixer of everyone's problems, love. You're going to get yourself killed.' She looked to her left at Lorna. 'And you, too, sweetheart.'

Lorna looked across at Mary, then back front. 'I know.'

'Then why don't you talk him out of this madness, running around playing superman.' Her tone changed. She became more emotional. She looked back up at him in the reflection at him, her eyes glazing over. 'I lost your father, I don't want to lose you, too. And dame our Damien for putting this on you, Brendan.'

'Don't speak like that about my father.'

'Your father, my little brother, Brendan. I knew him a lot longer than you did. I helped raise the little shit. He always wanted to do something big. "Make a difference" he always said. Well look where it got him. Taken away from you and Vanessa and an early grave.'

Brendan felt like arguing back, but what good would it have done? And she was right. He knew it. 'We'll send you a post card from our next place of holiday, straight after we're done in England. We're going to save Ramadan for the good Muslims that live in England.' Mary didn't reply. 'Just call me Ramadan Man.' Brendan watched as Mary's serious expression slowly stretched into a grin

Chapter Forty

MARY DROPPED BRENDAN and Lorna off in the city centre and knowing the chances of Brendan being killed were high, she forced her emotions below the surface and pulled him in for a hug, squeezing the air out of him. Lorna stood and looked on, fully appreciating the bond between Brendan and his aunt. She'd never imagine them to be so close. Brendan had never spoken about her for the first six months they'd known each other. It wasn't until the two had returned to Belfast to bury Brendan's past that Mary had become a topic. But as they both hugged each other beside the driver's door of the car, it was clear that she cared deeply about him, and the feeling was mutual. Perhaps to Mary, Brendan was the last thing left of her younger brother, the infamous global problem solver the world feared. Losing Brendan would be like losing the last part of her brother.

After an emotional goodbye, Mary waved as she took off. Brendan watched as the car created more and more distance.

'You'll see her again,' Lorna said, in an upbeat tone, trying to raise the mood. 'Let's go. Time to become the pain in Billy Moore's ass.' She pecked him on the cheek.

Brendan looked at Lorna. Pulling her in for a more intimate embrace, he kissed her like the time he'd seen her after she was kidnapped. 'Ivan said he can get us a car. And some weapons.' He gestured towards a late open café just across the road. 'Come on, we'll wait in there for him, I'm starving.'

As they stepped inside the café named The Seagull's Dinner, Lorna found amusement in the name. 'Guess seagulls have to eat too.'

Brendan entered first, the smell of fried fish and chips was a mouth watering experience for them both. 'You hungry?'

Lorna shut the door behind her. Taking her jacket off, she scanned the room. It was empty, which was good, given the fact their faces were all over the news again. 'Do you think it's wise, us being here?'

'I know the guy who owns it. He's not going to call the police, trust me,' Brendan laughed. 'They're the last people he'd call.' He went to the counter as Lorna went and took a seat. 'Michael Agnew.' He said the back of a man's head, whoever they were, they were busy cashing up the till. 'Don't close the till until I've ordered something.'

The guy set the knife down and turned around.

'Or are you going to give a free meal to an old school friend?' Brendan walked around the counter. 'Good to see you again, Mickey.'

The guy stood a few inches shorter than Brendan and as many inches wider. His salt and pepper hair and beard made him look almost twice Brendan's age, old enough to have been his teacher and not classmate. His expression was distant, his brown eyes emotionless. He tried to smile, but it was as if the muscles in his face wanted to do something else. His arms trembled as he reached out to shake Brendan's hand.

Brendan took his hand, then pulled Mickey in for a hug. 'Surprised I'm still alive?' He said, gripping his mate tightly. 'My brother from another mother.'

Mickey laughed, then his body started to shake.

Brendan put a bit of distance between the two of them and looked Mickey in the eye. 'It's getting worse, mate?'

'It's not getting better, that's for sure.' Mickey's face screwed up in his attempt to smile. He looked as if being behind the serving area of a shop with a knife should be the last place for him.

'You still drinking?' Brendan said, although he already knew the answer. He could smell it, and if Mickey was staying in the shop until late in the evening, it was his honest attempt to stay off the booze, and the trembling hands that looked as if they were about to go out of control were his body telling him he needed to few drinks to calm himself down.

'I'm trying to stay off it, Brendan.' He looked across the shop in Lorna's direction. 'She's beautiful, you're a lucky man.'

'Thanks.' Brendan looked around the shop, as if expecting to be approached by someone else. 'Where's your other half? She not helping you lock up?'

'Katie's gone around to her mums to pick up the kids, she'll be back soon to take me home.' Mickey looked across at Lorna again. 'Go and sit down, mate, I'll bring your usual over to you. What will your friend have?'

'She's like me, will eat anything.'

'I'll bring two over then.'

Brendan was about to turn around, but stopped and looked back. 'Mickey, do you need anything? You okay for money?'

'Seeing you're alive is enough for me, mate. Brings back all the old memories of the school days.'

'God, I wish I could go back to then, even for a day.'

'You're too busy being all over the news, wanted by governments. Brendan Cleary, the wanted man.' Mickey punched Brendan playfully on the shoulder.

Brendan smiled. 'It's good to see you, mate.' He pointed to the coffee machine. 'Can I grab us a couple of drinks?'

'Don't need to ask, your money is no good here.'

Brendan grabbed him and Lorna a couple of hot drinks and joined her in the corner of the room. She watched him the entire way across the room. He set the cups down, her eyes glazed over as he sat down. 'What's got you all thoughtful?'

She smiled and sat forward in her chair. 'Nothing, it's just nice watching you over there with your friend, I can tell he's an old friend. I'm thinking childhood, either neighbourhood or school, or maybe even both.'

He took a sip of his coffee. 'How could you tell?'

'I've been trained to read people, Brendan. It's a basic skill for anyone in the intelligence world.' She took a drink of her coffee, as her eyes followed Mickey along the front of the shop. 'How did I do?'

'Pretty well,' Brendan said. 'He's an old school buddy who also grew up in our neighbourhood.'

'He looks twice your age.'

Brendan looked back at Mickey. He looked happy, his facial expression was upbeat, a slight grin, and his eyes were wide and childlike. But his body was that of a frail old man. 'Yeah, he's been hooked on drugs and alcohol since we were fifteen.' Brendan turned back to Lorna. 'His dad was beaten to death in his home. Loyalists.'

'And he seen it?'

Brendan nodded his head. 'He was sitting at his dinner table with them when they came in the back door, straight in the kitchen, dragged his dad screaming out of his chair, crying like a baby because he knew what was coming.'

'They took him away?'

'No. They dragged him into the living room while a couple of them kept Mickey and his ma in the kitchen at gun point. He listened to them beat him to death.' He looked back over his shoulder, Mickey caught him looking and signalled with a thumbs up that he was coming with their food soon. 'Bastards may as well have killed him too. He's tried killing himself countless times.'

'Christ.' Lorna gasped.

'Well he's just another statistic to all the people impacted by the way of life over here back then.'

'Did they ever catch the ones that did it?'

'It's funny you should ask. They all turned up dead within six months. None of the paramilitaries claimed responsibility for their deaths. But Mickey's father and my father were as close as Mickey and I are.'

'You think your father did it?'

'Well, your government thought Damien Cleary was a professional problem solver, I don't know anyone who could have done what their killer did.'

Mickey came over with the food, his arms trembling as he fought to balance the plates. Lorna reached out and grabbed a plate as he handed it over. Brendan took the other. Mickey offered his hand to Lorna. 'It's nice to meet a lady that can finally put up with this one.'

'Piss off,' Brendan laughed, looking down at his plate.

Lorna shook Mickey's hand. 'He's okay when you know what makes him tick. And you seem to know how to gather his attention.'

Brendan looked up at her. 'You guys have all-day break-fasts in England.' He pierced a greasy sausage with his fork and dipped it into the orange egg yolk, bursting the bubble, watching it run all the way across the slimy white. 'This is our version.' He put the sausage in his mouth and pulled at face that done nothing but show his appreciation for the taste. 'You haven't lost your touch, mate.'

Mickey smiled and threw his dishcloth over his shoulder. 'Enjoy.'

'Nice to meet you,' Lorna said, watching him as he walked away. She looked at Brendan who appeared more interested in his meal. 'His mind is still sharp then.'

Brendan nodded and he forced a yolk smeared cut of potato bread into his mouth. He swallowed, washing it down with his drink. He pointed at her plate, are you not going to eat that? Because I will if you don't.'

Lorna lifted her knife and fork and quickly followed in Brendan's example.

Brendan's phone vibrated. He pulled it out and looked at it. 'It's Ivan. He said he'll be outside in five minutes. A silver Mercedes.'

'He's got weapons and an untraceable car?' Lorna said, cutting her sausage then dipping it into the ketchup.

'He wouldn't have come without them.'

'You sure you can trust him?' She looked up at Brendan, her eyes darting from his left to his right. 'I know he's your uncle, but there's no love loss between the two of you.'

'We'll be fine, don't worry. He's not someone we should be worried about.' He set his knife and fork down, sitting back in his seat, looking like he'd accomplished mount Everest. He lifted his drink and put it to his lips. 'Finish the best food you'll ever eat in Belfast.'

Lorna smirked as she made a sandwich with her bacon and two slices of potato bread. 'Thought your aunt Mary's food was the best in Belfast.'

'It's a tie for number one, then.' He stood up. 'I'm going to nip to the loo then say cheery oh to Mickey. Be back in a minute.'

Chapter Forty-One

THE MERCEDES ARRIVED outside the shop, the windows all blacked out. Illegal, but perhaps not the biggest offence being committed by Ivan. Lorna looked hesitant that the vehicle's occupants were unknown, behind the privacy glass. It wasn't until the car rolled to a stop, and the driver's window slowly lowered that they both knew it wasn't a set-up.

'You got the stuff I asked for?' Brendan said, as he dropped himself into the front passenger seat, Lorna sat in the back, directly behind Ivan.

Ivan nodded. 'Weapons are in the boot.'

'Thanks, Ivan.' Brendan fastened his belt and lowered the window halfway before Ivan stopped him.

'Let's leave the window up, kid. There's a reason I chose the car with blacked out windows.' He put the car in gear and took off. 'Your face is not something anyone should be seeing cruising around Belfast. We don't know who might see us.' He reached the end of the street. 'Just make sure you remind that son of a bitch Billy Moore Snr that he chose the wrong side, now he's got nobody to turn to now.'

'Except for his Neo-Nazi minions,' Lorna said. 'He's got them well and truly brainwashed.' She brushed a strand of hair out of her face then cleared her throat. 'Not like they didn't already need brainwashing; they just needed some more military leadership.'

'Well they've got that now,' Ivan said.

Loran didn't reply.

Brendan looked across at Ivan, he could see his uncles face turning a slight shade of pink, he looked stressed, and suddenly concerned about the words that he was to use. 'Ivan, meet Ex-British Agent, Lorna Woodward.' He looked behind him at Lorna who looked just as out of place as Ivan did. 'Lorna, meet the local leader of the supposedly disbanded UDA.'

'Can't believe I'm actually helping you,' Ivan said. 'I'll get killed if anyone finds out. Even the government will have my head on a plate if they find out I've helped in any way.'

'Look,' Brendan sighed. 'You can go back to hating me if you want the moment I get out of this car. 'You'll never have to see me again.' He looked across at his late mother's older brother.

'I don't hate you. I hated the fact your father was a leader of the Provisional IRA. If I had of got the chance I would have killed him.'

Brendan looked out through the passenger window, watching as the police Land Rover, fully armoured vehicle drove by. 'First off, I don't think you would have the chance to kill him, many people tried.' He turned and looked at his uncle. 'You would have had to kill me as well.'

Ivan smirked. 'You've defiantly got your mother's mind. She had the power to tame the infamous Damien Cleary.'

'If the governments had of done their jobs properly over here, there never would have been a war in the first place,'

Brendan said. 'But fuck it, it's in the past. We're moving on with things, apparently.'

'Where are you taking us to?' Lorna asked.

'To where your car will be waiting.' Ivan looked at Lorna on the rear view, but she looked like she needed more detail to the answer.

'It's an old disused farmhouse, covered in hedges and trees. It was perfect for our boys to leave their weapons when they were active. It's not been used for a long time. We've known it's where those bastards had been making their bombs, but we didn't do anything as we needed to find out who they were working for before we made our move. Now we know they're working with some government influence...'

'Meaning the police,' Lorna said. 'When the government controls the police, people who have their backing are pretty much free to do whatever it is they need to do.'

'Which is why we won't get involved,' Ivan said. 'I've spent many years in prison. I'm lucky to be alive when so many of my friends don't have the same luxury as me, because, that's what life is. A luxury.' Ivan looked across at Brendan. 'You've got some balls, kid.'

'It's not about having balls, Ivan. It's about doing the right thing, and the right thing is to stop any innocent people getting killed.' Brendan looked across at his uncle. 'And, I guess I'm too much like my old man.'

'You wish you were half the badass your old man was,' Lorna said.

Brendan looked back at her. 'One day.' He offered his hand to Ivan. 'I hope you can live the rest of your life in peace.'

'As long as the other side remains peaceful, we'll remain peaceful.' Ivan pointed across the disused land, a rusty old Renault Clio was parked, looking about as out of place a helicopter being there. 'That'll get you both to where you need to go. I've texted you the exact location. There is a can of petrol in the boot. Just burn it when you're done.' He unbuckled his seat belt and threw his door open.

Brendan got out and followed him, slamming the front passenger door behind him. He made his way along the passenger side of the car, watching as Ivan opened the boot. Brendan reached the back of the car. Looking in, he grinned as he looked at a black gym bag, inside it were two black handguns, pistols and a collection of pre-loaded clips. Ivan zipped the bag closed and lifted it out, handing it to Brendan. Lorna joined them at the boot.

'Neither of you mention my name again.' Ivan looked Lorna, then at Brendan. 'Have you both got that?'

'We know the drill.' Brendan offered Ivan his hand. 'Take care.'

'You, too.' Ivan shook Brendan's hand, then handed him the car key.

Brendan took the key, then looked over at the car they were moving off in. He looked at Lorna then at Ivan. 'You sure than rust bucket isn't going to die half way down the road.'

Ivan smirked. 'Let's hope for your sake it doesn't.' He nodded his head at Lorna then made his way back to the driver's seat. 'Make sure Billy knows it's my nephew that puts his lights out.'

'What, you're now glad I'm your nephew?' Brendan joked.

Ivan looked around and smiled. 'Good luck.

Chapter Forty-Two

SITTING IN THE CAR at the location, Brendan and Lorna waited patiently for Greystone to arrive. The good thing about knowing he was travelling, his time would be as accurate as feasibly possible. Greystone, being the bomb maker, and delivering the last parcel to England would be on time. Being late would bring unnecessary stress. And unnecessary stress when pulling of an operation like the one they were about to execute was as suicidal as playing a game of Russian Roulette. And from what Brendan knew about him, Greystone was not a stupid man. He was perhaps the most sophisticated in an army of knuckle draggers and bruisers. He was a thinking man, and that's why way back in the late nineteen eighties and early nineties when Moore's operations were at their highest, he was chosen by the UDA leadership, becoming the man entrusted in handling their heavy arsenal.

The darkness of the derelict land's stone covered entrance was broken by two blinding headlights. Both Brendan and Lorna jolted to full alertness.

'Let's go and sort this fucker out.' Brendan threw the driver's door open and lunged out, one of the pistols supplied by Ivan clasped tightly in his hand. He was grateful for Greystone's vehicle engine turning over, killing the sound of his shoes crunching on the gravel. Lorna followed, gripping her pistol tightly. Greystone's vehicle parked at the barn's entrance. The rear lights were like a set of red evil eyes sitting in complete darkness. As Brendan approached the rear, he neared the driver's side just when the sound of the driver's door opened, bringing with it the sound of Greystone's voice.

'Tell Billy I'm here now. The final package is about to be delivered.' He paused for a moment, humming to agree to what was being said from the other end. 'Okay, if the weather's bad overnight, I might be delayed, but nothing's been called off yet, so as far as I know, the ferry is still leaving at the normal time. But tell the men not to set off until I've spoken to them all again. They need to know exactly how to operate these things, unless they want to blow themselves up.' He hummed again as he listened to whoever the other person was. 'I'll call you when I'm in England.' The sound of his footsteps were crystal clear in the darkness, getting noisier as he approached the back, a tiny torch light was drawn along the ground. Brendan stood where he was, his gun pointed at head height, ready to meet the approaching head.

Greystone rounded the rear of the van, face first into Brendan's pistol. He gasped, then instinctively tried to moved, but Brendan clocked him on the side of the head with the pistol. He fell into the back door, then hit the ground. 'You sound like one of them Islamic State fucks. Except the blowing yourself up part, of course.'

Greystone threw a punch at Brendan's mid-section. Brendan stumbled back but found his balance and sunk his right knee into Greystone's head as he tried to get back to his feet.

'Get up and open the back door of the van and try anything else and the next blow you're going to feel will be a bullet to the back of the head. We don't need you alive but aren't in the business of killing people unless we have to.'

'Who the hell are you? MI5?' Greystone got to his feet, his hands in the air, 'you bastards have been feeding us all the intel on the targets, now you're turning on us?'

'I'm not government...'

'Yes we are,' Lorna quickly cut Brendan off, stepping around from the side of the vehicle. 'There's no point in lying to him now, we've got the piece of shit.'

Brendan didn't know what Lorna was getting at, but he knew she'd had something up her sleeve, so he let her carry on.

'Here.' Lorna activated the torch on her phone and tossed Brendan a packet of cable ties.

'Turn around,' Brendan said, while forcefully spinning Greystone one-eighty degrees, pushing him face first into the van doors. 'Put your hands behind your back.'

Greystone did so.

Brendan pulled Greystone away from the doors and walked him around to the van's side door. He pulled the sliding door open, revealing the bomb. 'You can keep your bomb company.' He forced Greystone inside then looked at Lorna. You want to drive or keep this piece of shit company.

'I'll drive.' She was quick to respond.

'You know when Billy gets his hands on you for this, you'll be begging for him to kill you,' Greystone said. It sounded more out of desperation than anything else. Greystone was an intellect. Not a hard man. He forced himself a weak laugh. 'I can't wait to see you try and stop both Billy Snr and Billy Jnr. Trust me, you wouldn't want to get on the wrong side of the young one, he's a nasty wee bastard.'

'Save your breath,' Brendan sighed, as he slid the van's door closed and sat down on the floor against the inside of the door. 'Billy Moore and Jnr are no longer your concern. Let us worry about that pair.'

Greystone shuffled anxiously in his seat as Lorna put the vehicle into motion. 'You're from Belfast. So you know what awaits you anyway when they find you.'

'Look, Greystone,' Brendan took his phone out, seeming distracted. He opened a text he'd received from Louise. 'They're both coming to a bad end. They've done too much to be forgiven.' He skipped through the text as he spoke.

'You're a cocky bastard, mate. Who do you think you are?' Greystone was smart. He was trying to get into Brendan's head. 'And you know those dirty Muslim bastards need to be wiped out. Did you see what they did to that poor bastard in Leicester. The tattoo artist.'

'Oh don't you worry,' Brendan said, 'I know who's done that, and they'll suffer the same fate as your gang.'

'Who are you, judge, jury and executioner.'

'I'm just here to help a few people.'

'Were you one of us? You have a grudge. Look mate, you can stop the operation. But you don't have to hand me over to the police.'

'Christ, you're not going anywhere near the cops. The dirty bastards can't be trusted. Just relax, mate. And this little idea you have of talking me around on the road trip is just a waste of time. If anything, it'll just piss me by insulting my intelligence.' Greystone didn't reply. 'I know you're an intelligent guy. And you can debate something with most people, you can maybe persuade people to see your point of view...'

'But not you.'

'Exactly.' Brendan got up from his seated position, slowly making his way towards the front where Lorna was sat at the driver's seat. He grabbed onto the back of her seat as the van built up speed. 'You know where we're going?'

She nodded. 'Will we just off him and do away with it.'

Brendan was taken aback for a moment. Lorna spoke loud enough for Greystone to catch what she'd said, but not so loud that it would make it obvious. Quickly, Brendan understood. She wanted Greystone to hear. She, like Brendan knew that a bomb maker, a thinker within the group was never trained on how to deal with the potential of being caught. Interrogation training would never have been given to Greystone. And thus, the thought of being shot and tossed out on the side of the road would perhaps be enough to scare him. It was surprising how well Lorna and Brendan could read one another. Send between the line messages in the company of others.

'What do you think?' She gave Brendan another nudge, looking at him in the rear-view mirror as the van flew down the M2 motorway towards the docks.

'I can be of help to you,' Greystone shouted.

Brendan smiled at Lorna as he kept looking at her in the mirror. His back to Greystone, now pleading for his life.

Brendan turned around. 'Why would you help us?'

'Because I value my life more than anything else.'

Brendan leaned against the van's side door, sliding back down to his seated position. 'You mean you wouldn't die for your cause?'

Greystone smirked. 'What cause? Combat 18?' He laughed. 'Bunch of fucking ass holes.'

'They why'd you do it?'

'A very nice sum of money.'

'That makes you an even bigger piece of shit.' Brendan stomped the heel of his right foot down the roof of Greystones foot, and by the screams of Greystone, breaking a few of those tiny footbones in the process. 'You're lucky that wasn't directed at your head.'

'Fuck you.' Greystone shouted.

'This is going to stop, whether you help us or not. We don't need your help. Our plan was just to take the van off you and pose as you until we meet up with rest of your crew.'

'Just put a bullet in his head and be done with him,' Lorna shouted.

'We'll dump his body close to the docks, the least we can do for him is to leave his final resting place somewhere in Ireland.'

'So you're a wee taig then.' Greystone was quick to say. 'Only one of those scumbags would refer to Ireland and not Northern Ireland.'

'I don't claim to be republican or loyalist,' Brendan said. 'I was raised catholic and protestant. My father was part of the Provos. My ma's brother's were founder's of the UDA.' Brendan smirked. 'You might have heard of my uncle. Ivan. Think he was in your little gang.'

'What a minute,' Greystone said. 'Cleary?'

'The one and only.' Brendan turned and pointed towards Lorna. 'And that beautiful English lady driving us is none other than one of the best MI5 operatives, well, former operatives. And I tell you something mate, she's got some nasty ways of interrogating people.'

'Stop it, you're making me blush.' Lorna shouted, as the car rolled to a gentle stop.

'Get yourself comfortable, mate. You've got a long night.' Brendan sat on the wooden bench that formed an uncomfortable seat, screw fixed to the back of the up-front seat. He pulled his phone from his inside pocket. A message from Ivan.

That van's being tracked, Brendan. Be careful. Ivan.

Brendan sighed as he forced the phone back into his pocket. A sleeping bag was at his feet. He lifted it, feeling it was damp he threw it back down again. 'Was going to give you this, but it's soaked. Don't want you getting a cold now, do we?'

Chapter Forty-Three

THE PROCESS AT THE docks was surprisingly smooth, in spite of the fact they had a bomb with enough explosive to destroy an entire city street, they got through without breaking so much as a sweet. Then came the wait, in a queue of around one hundred vehicles. With the engine off, they sat listening to the reports on the news about another night of riots in various different cities across England. A number of mosques has been targeted. Some spray painted. Some bricked and bottled. One in Leicester city centre and two in Nottingham had been set ablaze. Two members of the Asian community had been stabbed, left and bled to death outside one of their places of worship. The news reporter talked about the it being a contentious time of the year in England. When Ramadan was the religious celebration, the most important date on the Islamic calendar. Brendan laughed when they mentioned similarities between the lead up to Ramadan in England and the build up to the annual twelfth of July paraded a couple of hundred miles west across the Irish sea.

'Well, Billy Moore will love that little description,' Lorna said sarcastically. She started the engine to the sound of the eight vehicles in front starting theirs. The ferry was ready to board. As she followed directions from the docks workers, she spotted a familiar face. 'Christ, I should have know that piece of shit was involved in this somehow.'

'Who?' Brendan looked through the window. A middle aged man with a few extra pounds around his mid-section was thumbing them passed.

'Fuck.' Lorna hissed. 'He's government.'

'What?'

She nodded her head as the van carefully approached the ramp.

'Did he spot you.'

'I'm not sure.'

'What do you mean, you're not sure? It's a pretty big thing to be...'

'I'm not fucking sure, Brendan.'

Greystone sat sniggering to himself.

Brendan turned around, approached Greystone, crouched down and grabbed him by the throat. Squeezing his windpipe until Greystone passed out.

'Finally,' Lorna shouted. 'I'm tired of listening to that piece of shit.'

'He has to go, Lorna. The guy on the docks.'

'He followed us with his eyes the entire way as we passed.'

'We'll wait until the ferry sets sail, then I'll go and find him. You can watch sleeping beauty over there.'

'Take a weapon, you might need it,' Lorna said, as she followed a silver family wagon down the long narrow garage. The area was outlined with orange markings, designated walkways with passengers already disembarking, looking overly enthusiastic. She parked the van, making sure not to make eye contact with any of the hi-vis wearing parking attendants. The window was down, and the sound of Eastern

European accents bounced of the enormous tin can they'd be spending the next couple of hours. Then the sound of an English accent sounded over the top of the others, telling the rest of the men to hurry up and get down to the other end and help the rest of the vehicles ramp and get onboard.

'Was that him?' Brendan said.

'Yes. James Stingray. An eager to impress little fucking ass kisser.' She watched in the wing mirror, making sure the others were getting further away.

'How well do you know him?'

'Pretty well. We joined the agency together. Obviously, there was quite an age gap. I was twenty-one and he was thirty-eight,' Lorna grunted. 'Incompetent piece of shit said it was my firm ass and perky tits that bumped me up through the ranks.'

'Well, he's not wrong. You do have a great ass and tits.' Brendan reached over from behind the seat, pecking her on the cheek.

They sat there for anther twenty minutes. Every vehicle was onboard and securely locked down. The lights went out, and the silence was only shattered by the sound of the vessel's motors kicking in. Brendan's phone vibrated. It was a text from Louise.

Brendan, I've arranged a meeting with the ones who carried out the attack on the tattoo artist. Get the information from her and I'll gladly help her deliver their punishment.

'Great,' Brendan said, as he looked at Lorna, then back at Greystone. 'Louise has set up a meet with the artist's attackers.'

'Great,' Lorna agreed. 'Best contact Vanessa, find out where the drops are going to be.' She looked at her watch. 'How long is this sailing?'

'Seven hours, I think, give or take.' Brendan called Vanessa. It rang twice before she answered it.

'Hello.' Her answer was blunt.

'How's your brother?'

'He's fucked.'

'What do you mean?'

'I can't bear to see him like this.' She burst into tears. 'I went into his cubicle in the ward, and he started screaming and crying, shouting for me to get away from him. I don't know if he recognises me or is his head now that far up his ass that he thinks his own flesh and blood is going hurt him.'

'Jesus, Vanessa.' Brendan looked at Lorna, almost able to feel Vanessa's agony.

'I managed to calm him down, eventually. But he's like a fucking child. Tiring himself out, he cried himself to sleep in my arms, clinging to me.'

'I'm sorry,' Brendan said. 'I'd help you even if you didn't know the locations of the attacks. That shouldn't happen to anyone.'

'Thank you.'

'But I've something for you.'

'What is it?'

'A contact of mine has found out who they are and have arranged a meet with them. I will personally be there to help you if you need it.'

She cried. 'Thank you so much.'

'Just keep your head down and don't do anything silly until we get there, okay?'

'Sure.'

'I mean it, Vanessa. These are nasty people we're dealing with, and you won't be any help to your brother if you get hurt. And I can't help you from a distance.'

She didn't reply.

'You going to be alright?'

'I'll be fine.' She sniffed, then blew her nose. 'Thank you, Brendan.'

'Don't thank me yet. I haven't done anything.' He turned and looked at Greystone who was regaining consciousness. 'You ever met your boyfriends...'

'Ex-boyfriend,' she spat.

'Ex-boyfriend's mate, Greystone?'

'The bomb maker, yes. Piece of shit.'

Brendan smirked. 'Well, Lorna and I have got that piece of shit tied up in the back of his fan. We're on the ferry, crossing the Irish Sea as we speak.'

'You're travelling with a bomb?' She managed a tiny laugh. 'You're crazy.'

'I've been told that before,' Brendan joked. 'But Greystone isn't stupid, and he doesn't want to die. That's something I'm pretty sure of. So as long as he's here, the bomb and us will be safe.' He looked down at Greystone who gave him a mock thumbs up. 'I'll call you when we get to England. You can come with us, we'll take you to the people you're after.'

'I'd rather do it myself, if you don't mind. He's my brother.'

'And I told you these are dangerous people. I'm not sending you into something that can get you killed.'

She didn't reply.

'Take care, and we'll see you tomorrow.' He ended the call and rubbed his temples. 'Christ.' He climbed over the seats into the driver's cabin.

'How is she?'

'She's fine,' Brendan said. 'It's her brother that's a bit messed up. The poor guy cried himself to sleep in her arms only after tiring himself out.'

Lorna shook her head. Unresponsive. She looked in the wing mirror, her eyes glazing over as if in deep focus. Hawk eyed. 'The ship workers are leaving. They're heading up the stairs.' The lights went out, and the sound of a door slamming shut was followed only by the metallic clunk of a lock being engaged. 'Looks like we're all alone now.' She grabbed his hands. 'The sooner we can get away from this crap better.' She stroked his face. 'And you'll be able to relax a bit more.'

'I'm alright,' he said. 'Being able to help people in need of it is quite rewarding.'

'But you're stressed, Brendan. I can tell.'

'I'm alright.'

She looked at him, her eyes darting from his left to the right. 'Are you sure?'

He reached over with his head and kissed her. He was about to speak, when a voice broke through the silence. Someone was still there. Lorna put the ignition on, without starting the engine, and silenced the radio, allowing her to lower the window, getting a clearer understanding of what was being said.

'Yes, sir,' the voice said. An accent, sounding less southern, more of a northern accent. 'The van's here.' He paused, perhaps taking orders from the other end. 'Package had arrived. We are good to go,'

Lorna looked at Brendan. 'That's him, the slimy bastard.'

'Right, I'm going to get him.' Brendan whispered, shuffling across the seat towards the passenger door. He gently pulled on the door handle, wincing as if the glass was about to shatter. The lock released, opening the door an inch. He looked over his shoulder at Lorna. 'In ten seconds, hit the horn to grab his attention. I'm going to work my way down the line of cars and come up behind him.'

'Be careful,' she hissed.

Stepping out of the van, Brendan's feet slowly touched the ground. He pushed the door closed, but not fully engaging the lock, just enough to stop it from swinging open again. Taking his pistol in his left hand, he slowly made his way down the metallic line of vehicles. Looking through the lightly tinted windows of a black Audi A5, he seen the bright green of the hi-vis jacket the guy was still wearing. Ten seconds were up. The car horn honked.

There was a momentary pause. An almost deathly silence. Then the guy's voice came back. 'Hold on a second. Greystone is trying to get my attention.'

Brendan kept watching through the window of the Audi as the high-vis moved along the other side, in the direction of the van. He quickly rounded the Audi from the rear and followed him towards the van. His pace quickened as they got closer. It was obvious the agent wasn't expecting to see Lorna in the driver's seat. He was unarmed, walking without any consideration for his own safety. Of course, why would he, after all it was only Greystone in the vehicle. Or so he thought.

'What the hell are you blasting your horn for, you...' He stopped dead in his tracks when he arrived the driver's door. 'You? How the hell...'

'Good to see you, James,' Lorna joked.

'Don't say another word,' Brendan said, approaching him, his pistol pointed straight at his head. The agent turned around, looking directly at Brendan, a smug grin on his face, in spite of the fact he'd just been caught. 'You know the drill, I'm sure. Remove your weapons, and hand them over to Lorna. Try anything else, and you die, right here, on this ship and I'll see to it that your final resting place with be underneath this vessel, dragged into the mix of everything below.'

'Cleary. You're just everywhere, you little shit. Aren't you?'

Brendan lowered his weapon and grabbed the agent. He tried to wrestle, but Brendan gripped his hand, shattering every bone in it, taking the wrist bones next. The agent let out a loud cry, but the sounds coming from the ferry made it easily disguisable.

Lorna opened the door and stepped out. 'I know where this piece of shit keeps his weapons, and his backup.' She forced her hand inside his jacket, pulling out a Sig Saur. She slipped it into the back of her waistline and pointed towards his ankle. He leaned against the van and brought his right foot up to his knee, pulling his trousers up a few inches, revealing another weapon.

'It's good to see you, Agent Woodward,' he said, slapping the gun into her hand. 'Hoped you were dead.'

'Sorry to be the bearer of bad news, James,' Lorna said. She pointed towards his jacket again. He looked at her wondering what she was getting at. 'I know you have another.'

He looked at Brendan and sighed, pulling out a third weapon, fitted with a silencer. He handed it over. She checked the silencer was properly fitted then pointed it towards his foot, putting a bullet in it. He dropped to the ground, letting out a loud cry.

Lorna looked at Brendan, 'don't worry, these places a pretty much soundproof, nobody will hear him. And now we know he won't be running away anytime soon.'

'Bitch.'

'Brendan, meet Agent James Stingray.'

Brendan reached down and pulled Stingray back to his feet, hopping on the left foot, blood dripping from the wound. 'Don't worry, you'll live.' He pulled the sliding door open. 'In.' Brendan assisted the now moaning agent into the van, next to Greystone then slammed the door closed again. Lorna got back into the driver's seat. Brendan joined her in the front cabin, keeping his gun on the two in the back. 'Make yourselves comfortable, fellas. It's going to be a long day tomorrow.' He looked at Lorna. 'You want to get a couple of hours sleep and I'll watch this pair.'

'Sound's like a plan.' She shuffled around in her chair, making herself at least a little more comfortable. 'You thought about where you want to go afterwards?' She pulled her hands inside her sleeves and folded her arms tightly against her chest.

'Somewhere warm.'

'San Andreas is supposed to be nice. Very private. Nice beaches. And warm.'

'San Andreas it is then,' Brendan said, setting his pistol down on the dashboard.

'You won't stop this. I can promise you that.' The agent moaned. 'I can assure you, by the end of the week, the both of you will have died a very slow and painful death.'

'Get some rest, mate,' Brendan said, half listening, half scanning through his phone for any news updates about the situation in England.

Chapter Forty-Four

THE SAILING WAS ON time. Shortly after six in the morning, the crews opened the vehicle desk. The passengers made the return to their vehicles, many of whom were still half asleep, looking as if they'd slept rough. Red lines down the right side of a guy's face looked like he'd been sleeping on it for the majority of the journey across the Irish Sea.

Lorna started the engine as the cars in front shuttered to life. The huge ramp slowly dropped, allowing the sunlight to flood in, temporarily assaulting their sensitive eyes. The heating blasted, sending the smell of rubber and fuel through the vents.

Brendan put the radio on. BBC Radio One was playing the final ballad of a morning hip hop show when, approaching the half-hour news bulletin. He looked around at the two in the back. Both looked exactly as they should: two guys who'd slept rough, with the worry of what their future was going to be. 'We'll get to land then we'll get you both some food.'

'Fuck you,' Stingray said.

Greystone smirked and shook his head.

'Fair enough,' Brendan said, turning back to face front. 'Well I'm getting something for breakfast, I'm starving.' He looked at Lorna. 'What about you?'

'Oh, I'm having something,' she spoke loud enough for the two in the back to hear. 'Take a good meal while you can. I hear prison food is terrible.'

'Probably still nicer than the taste of food in hell.' Brendan joked, as the vehicles in front slowly started to creep towards the sunlight.

'We'll see who has the last laugh,' Stingray mumbled.

Lorna followed the vehicles towards the ramp. Brendan called Louise, but there was no answer.

'Probably still asleep.' He chucked the phone down on the dashboard next to the pistol. 'She doesn't seem the type that would be up early.'

'Nobody's up as early as you are,' Lorna said. 'You take the piss.'

Before Brendan had a chance to respond to her comment, his phone rang. He looked at the screen. 'Looks like she's awake.' He answered. 'Morning, you're up early.' He smiled at Lorna.

'Only because you've bloody woken me,' Louise groaned. 'I guess you've got here alright?'

'We're just getting off the ferry. We've got ourselves another passenger. An old colleague of Lorna's. They just happened to be guiding the van onboard, making sure the parcel had gotten on ok.'

'If there's an agent onboard, there'll be more of them around,' Louise said.

'I'm guessing his phone's going to ring soon, a confirmation call, to check everything's good.' Brendan looked back at Stingray.

'We've got a busy day ahead.'

'Hopefully, it'll be the last busy day I'll have for a long time.' Brendan said, looking at Lorna, she was nodding in agreement. 'Can you meet us somewhere, a vehicle that we can change into until the meet with Moore and the rest of the gang.'

'Where?'

Brendan just thought for a second. He knew government were going to be all over them, especially if Stingray didn't check in. He wanted Moore and the rest of them stopped before they turn the midlands into a war zone. 'I think we need to bring some of these bad guys together.' He looked behind him at the two in the back. 'I'm going to send you a text. I don't want what I'm thinking being heard by certain people in the van.' Brendan hung up and started sending a text message.

We can use our Muslim friends who carried out the attack on Vanessa's brother. Can you tell them that we've got some bombers that are looking to target Mosques tomorrow for an explosive celebration of their annual Eid hoopla.

Louise replied. *Is Vanessa coming with us?*

Brendan replied. *After what she's described his state to be, someone innocent, I'm tempted to leave them in the same state.*

Okay, I'll deliver the news to our Muslim friends in the area, but Brendan you know they're not going to like it when they find out their leader and a few of his men have been taken out.

I don't give a shit what his scumbag pals think. We're stopping these attacks not to save them, but the Muslim community. The normal, decent Muslim community. Find a place our

Muslim friends can store Agent Stingray and Greystone. We'll head for Nottingham. I'll call you when we're close.'

Brendan hung up just as the vehicle came off the ramp. They'd officially arrived on English soil. The sun was shining. Even for the time of the morning, the bright blue, cloudless sky advertised it to be a scorcher. He put the window down, embracing the cool air coming in as the van built up speed, following the other drivers towards the gates. 'Head towards Nottingham. Louise is going to find a place for us to leave the packages.'

'I think there's a service station not far away. We can stop off and have breakfast. My stomach is bloody rumbling.'

The service station was full. An overwhelming mix of morning commuters, waiting impatiently in their queues for a pump. Keeping his head down and his anonymity in check, Brendan went into the shop. Paying for a full tank of diesel, he then ordered four breakfasts to go. As he stepped out into the sun, a family of four walked past him, looking like they were excited to have reached Eid for anther year. They consisted of a man, a woman, and a boy and girl, neither of who were a day over ten. The man of the family looked at Brendan with nothing less than contempt. Of course, Brendan, being white and looking as he did, would have fit the stereotypical mould of a member of Moore's gang of thugs, and would be just as quick to spit on the family if they were on fire. The smell of fried bacon and sausages in the foam plates looked like it had caused extra offence as the man looked at Brendan as if he were a catalyst to all his worldly problems.

Brendan crossed the carpark towards the van, Lorna smiling at him. He guessed she'd understood the passing of the family.

'What are you grinning about?' He said, as he handed her across the food then climbed up into the front cabin.

'If only that guy new what you were doing, Ramadan Man,' she giggled. 'He wouldn't be looking at you like you were nothing but the shit on the bottom of his shoe.'

Brendan removed the cover from his plate and gave it a good sniff. 'I'm just happy to have some proper food in my belly.' He lifted a sausage and dipped it into the egg yolk, bursting the yolk, sending the yellow stuff all over the food, like an erupted volcano. He put the radio on. BBC Radio Midlands was now playing an urgent news bulletin from Leicester. The local hangout for Combat 18 and Britain First, including the homes of former leaders of the organisation were said to have been destroyed, leaving some people injured but none of them had life-threatening injuries.

'Very lucky,' Brendan said sarcastically.

He looked back at the two in the back. 'You sure neither of you want something to eat?'

'Fuck off, Cleary,' Greystone said.

'Fair enough.' Brendan turned back to finish his meal.

'What are the chances these attacks are from Omar's crew?' Lorna said, imitating Brendan with the sausage.

'Very good, I'd say.'

'Or do you think they've done it by themselves to make what's going to happen tomorrow, at least half justifiable.'

'It's possible, I suppose.' Brendan appeared more interested in the food in front of him. 'You anything to add?' He shouted back to the pair in the back.

'All will become clear, when the times right,' Stingray said.

'What's that supposed to mean?' Lorna shouted back, making a sausage and egg sandwich with two slices of butter-soaked toast.

'You'll see.'

Brendan looked at Lorna, then back at Stingray. He knew by now, people like Stingray, working for the government, had a contingency plan for the contingency. But without carrying on, they'd not know what it was. They were walking into something. It was only a matter of time before they knew what. Brendan considered the fact that Stingray and Greystone didn't want to die. It wasn't their way. They were doing their part simply for the cash. The big pay day. Of course they weren't going to put themselves in any danger, in spite of the fact there was a bomb only feet away from them.

Chapter Forty-Five

ONE HOUR DOWN THE M1 towards Nottingham, Stingray's phone sounded. His hands were bound and he had no chance of picking up.

'We'll need to come off at the next service station,' Brendan said. 'I'll jump in the back and return that call.'

'We passed a sign for services a few miles back. There'll be one coming up soon.' Lorna reached across towards the radio. More attacks were reported on the streets of Leicester, Derby and Nottingham. Three of the cities populating the East Midlands, up in flames the night before, with attacks on Islamic places of worship. A religious leader for the local Muslim community was asked what he could say to the wider Muslim population that could perhaps steer them away from any retaliation. The leader, Abdul Mohammad said it was not up to him to tell people what to do or what not to do. But he did emphasise that, those ready to bring in the end to the year's Ramadan celebrations, should remember the teaching from Allah, and should act based on those teachings.

'What a load of bollocks,' Stingray said. 'Those bastards are all "peace and love thy fellow human for the lord" in from the camera. Hiding behind their Quran. Holding their little book with one hand, with a blood-stained meat cleaver in the other.'

'It was the same the same in Belfast, during the troubles. Fuckers hiding behind the cloth. Abusing their authority,' Greystone said.

'As much as it bothers me to do so,' Brendan shouted back. 'I'm inclined to agree with you.'

'So how much were you getting paid for doing this?' Lorna shouted. 'MI5 not paying enough these days?'

'Unless you can look good in an office suit, it's always going to be harder.' Stingray grunted. 'That sweet ass and perky rack of yours is what got you so far, Woodward.'

Lorna looked at Brendan who was sniggering to himself with his eyes closed, shaking his head. 'I suppose it had nothing to do with the fact I beat you in all of the exams in basic training?'

He didn't respond.

'Or the fact I killed you every time on exercise, you didn't even manage to get me once.' Lorna laughed, indicating to come off at the next service station. 'Guess it was my sweet ass and perky tits that made all that happen, too?' She pulled into the service area, parking the van in the corner of the carpark furthest away from any other vehicle.

Brendan jumped out and got in the back. He pulled the sliding door behind him again as he climbed in, pointing his gun at the pair. 'You're going to give me access to your phone, now, and...'

'Fuck you, Cleary.'

Brendan slid against the side of the van into a squatting position, still pointing the gun. 'I'm sorry you feel that way, but you're still going to do as I say.' He looked up at Lorna who also got out of the van. 'Look, I really don't give a shit whether you live or die. You're screwed either way. But if you play ball with us, then at least it will run a little smoother for you.'

'Very considerate,' Stingray mumbled. 'Thanks.'

'You're very welcome, now...' Brendan pulled a flick knife out of his back pocket. 'This can be for cutting your throat, or to cut the cable ties, freeing your wrists. Which will it be?'

'I've found something,' Lorna shouted, slamming down the driver's seat. She held her hand up. A tracking device in her hand. 'Bastards know where we are.'

'Okay.' Brendan pulled Stingray forward, cutting the cable ties from his wrists. 'Give me access to that phone.'

Stingray thumbed in the four-digit combination and handed the device to Brendan. A voicemail was received immediately after the last call. Brendan played the messaged on loudspeaker so they could all hear what was being said.

'Call me back as soon as you get this message. There's been a slight change of plans. I need to know Greystone has arrived in England. The tracker says it's in the Midlands but the incompetent twat hasn't called in. Moore is starting to have a fit. He likes his orders to be followed through, and if one hasn't been, he starts to think something's up.'

Brendan smirked as the message ended. 'We wouldn't want Moore to get a little stressed now, would we?' He gave the phone back to Stingray. 'Call him back. Tell him you spoke to Greystone before he left the ferry and you confirm he's in the van, making his way towards the meeting.'

Stingray did as he we told. Brendan took the phone back off him, and cable tied his hands again.

Lorna got back in the driver's seat.

'You want me to drive for a while?' Brendan said.

Lorna shook her head. 'It's not far now.' She fastened her belt and started the engine. Lowering the window, she tossed the tracker into the road. She put the window back up then put the vehicle in gear.

THIRTY MINUTES AND sixty miles south east, they arrived in a rundown part of Nottingham. Whether it was a good choice or not, the fact they were going into a heavily populated Muslim council estate while being non-Muslim, was sure going to attract a few stares from people. The time was shortly after one in the afternoon. Louise had pulled through and had organised a meet with the group who'd kept English detained. Their meeting place – the VIP room of Omar's classy nightclub. If ever they'd seen the definition of a diamond in the rough, this was it.

As Lorna led the car onto the gravel covered carpark, Louise stood leaning against her black Range Rover, smoking what looked to be a joint. But judging from the crowd of Asian's she was stood with, she was smoking more to fit in and please them than really wanting to. The group all watched as the van pulled up next to their cars. Next to Louise's SUV sat a row of vehicles that looked like a scene straight out of a Fast and Furious movie. A blue Subaru Impreza sat next to a white Mitsubishi Evo, which was alongside a Mercedes S Class AMG.

As Lorna shut the engine off, with the window down the local slang could be heard coming in. The group stood around Louise were young wannabe thugs, probably smoking weed and listening to gangsta' rap while looking at their posters in the bedroom of their parent's house.

Brendan cast a quick glance at the group, thinking of how his cousins used to act, hanging out on the street corners of West Belfast. He smirked as one of them kept checking to see if his white gold chain was still sat correctly over the Nottingham Panthers NBA jersey.

'Bet you were just like that when you were their age,' Lorna said, playfully punching Brendan on the shoulder.

'I wish,' Brendan said, taking his eyes off the group, looking at Lorna. I was too busy trying to keep my mother off the drink,' he said then turned his gaze back them. 'A lot of good that did. She drunk herself to death anyway.' He paused, watching as one of them caught his eye, trying to stare him out. Brendan looked away, turning back to Lorna. 'But my aunt Mary's sons were exactly like that.'

Lorna looked across him, out through his window. 'He thinks he's just got one over on you, staring out the infamous Brendan Cleary.'

Brendan smiled. 'Let him have it. I've got nothing to prove here.'

'If they could walk a mile in our shoes.'

Brendan put the window down, letting some air into the van. 'Somehow I don't think they could. Or maybe if their father schooled them as much as mine did me, they'd take it all in their stride.'

'You're a hard man, Cleary,' Greystone said from the back, Stingray sniggering.

'You'd know, wouldn't you Greystone?'

Greystone didn't respond. Neither did Stingray. Brendan pushed the passenger's side door open. 'Let's get this pair inside. I need to stretch the legs after all that travelling.' As he stepped out, his shoes crunching down on the gravel, the rowdy chatter from the group who were entertaining Louise died down, leaving only a few mumbles between a few. He pulled the side door open and stepped in. 'Up you get. Both of you. Come on.' He pulled Stingray to his feet, then Greystone and directed them out. As they both got out, Louise approached. Brendan pushed the two in front of him, in the direction of Louise. 'Take us inside, there's no time to have this pair out in public view.'

'Follow me.' Louise led them toward the clubs side door.

Louise stepped up the three stairs. 'You three fuck off and make yourselves useful. I'll call you later when we need you.' The three did as she said, descending the steps, all of them glaring at the group of whites who they all now seen as their enemy.

The one that stared Brendan out, had another go. This time his eyes were met with Brendan's, and this time Brendan didn't look away.

'You looking at something, pal?' The lad said.

Brendan carried on up the steps.

'Yeah, that's right, walk on, boy.'

'Just ignore him, Brendan,' Lorna said, 'the fucking little ass hole isn't worth the energy.'

'Fuck you, sweet cheeks. I'll gut you like a fish, a laugh at you as I watch you bleed out.'

Brendan stopped, looked at the ground shaking his head. He turned and went back down the steps again. The lad pulled a six-inch blade and stood looking at Brendan.

'What you going to do, white boy?'

Brendan took the pistol out of his jacket. The lad's face dropped. Brendan handed the pistol to Lorna. 'I'll hardly need this.' He turned to the lad who's confidence had returned partially, but not fully. 'I know you have some hard man image to uphold, which is why, in spite of the fact your shiting yourself inside and wish you didn't open your mouth you...'

'Fuck you!' One of the others pulled a knife out, followed quickly by the third.

The instigator speered his knife holding hand towards Brendan's stomach. Brendan caught his wrist, shoving the lad's hand back in the opposite direction straight into the attacker's stomach. One of the others slashed Brendan's cheek then took a second swipe. Brendan caught the lad's wrist, and using his own momentum, sent the blade straight through the lad's left eye. He dropped to his knees screaming, crying at the top of his voice.

'Get out of here now,' Omar shouted from the top of the steps. 'Get them to hospital, and don't bring any questions here. This did not happen here.'

Brendan stood looking at the third who looked like he was about to cry.

'You're dead, Irishman.' The one who took the blade in the stomach shouted.

'You're not the first person to say that.' Brendan turned and walked up the steps towards Lorna and Louise. Lorna handed Brendan his gun back. He looked at Omar. 'You sure these two are secure here?' He gestured at Stingray Greystone.

Omar nodded. 'We'll have plenty of fun with them.'

'No you won't.' Brendan was quick to say. 'We need them alive until this is all done. Otherwise, we'd have been better killing them and tossing them overboard into the Irish Sea.' His phone rang. He looked at the caller then at Lorna. 'You take them inside.' The ringing stopped and a text message came through.

Meet me in half an hour. Just around the corner from Mc-Gregor's club in Nottingham.

Brendan looked at Louise. 'Can I borrow your car?'

Louise tossed him the key.

'Is English still alive?' Brendan said.

Omar smirked. 'Just about.'

'Make it stay that way. None of them die. I'll be back in an hour.'

'I'm coming with you.' Lorna followed Brendan down the steps and towards the Range Rover. 'Give me the key, I'll drive.' She opened her hand bag. Pulling out a packet of tissues she pulled him closer. 'Come here.' She softly dabbed the cut on his face. 'He could have taken one of those beautiful eyes out.'

'That's why he's now one eye down.'

She kissed him. Then pulled away, looking directly into his eyes, from the left to the right. 'We've got to walk away from this life. I can't lose you, Brendan.'

'I know.' He kissed her hand as it continued to stop the blood from running down his face. He handed her the key. 'Let's go.'

Chapter Forty-Six

MCGREGOR'S WAS BUSY. Lorna parked in one of two remaining parking spaces on the red bricked victorian era road, just around the corner from the club. McGregor's was a strange place for meeting Vanessa. But Brendan gathered there was a method behind everything in life. He guessed it was something to do with the news she had on Moore.

'Did she say where exactly to meet her?' Lorna said, checking her pistol was loaded.

'She didn't say.' Brendan pulled his phone out. 'I'm calling her now.' It rang three times before being answered. 'We're just around the corner from McGregor's. Where are you?'

'You're in the Ranger Rover?' She said.

'Yes.'

The sound of a car door slamming behind them gave them both a start. Brendan gripped his pistol and stepped out. Lorna followed.

'You're probably wondering why I chose to meet you here.' She locked her silver Audi A8. She was wrapped in a long leather coat that ran all the way down past her knees.

'Hope we don't get the weather you're expecting,' Brendan joked. 'But yes, why here? Most people would think you were trying to set them up.'

'And you didn't?'

Lorna stepped around from the front of the car. 'You've no reason to set us up,' she stepped up next to Brendan. 'And for what it's worth, I'm sorry about what happened to your brother. If it were my family, I'd want as much blood as you do.'

Brendan looked at Lorna then at Vanessa. 'This is Lorna.'

Lorna offered her hand. 'So, let's figure out why you've decided to meet us here, perhaps it's something to do with your boyfriend and his father's new crusade.'

Vanessa pointed towards the derelict block the joined the health club. 'That's where they're meeting is.'

'What time are they meeting?'

'Once Greystone makes contact with them. They will gather so he can check over the bombs one last times before they go out.'

'So we need Greystone to come along before it all goes down.'

'Not necessarily,' Vanessa said. 'That's plan A. If you were part of a plan this big, would you not have a plan A, plan B, plan C, probably half the bloody alphabet?'

Brendan looked at the building, nodding his head agreeing that Greystone was only one. But an operation that has potential to write itself into history books, that could potentially produce a generation of hate throughout a country like England that prides itself on being so multi-cultural. On one day, that could all be wiped out.

'Can you get us in?' Brendan said.

She dangled a key in front of them. 'When we last spoke, I knew it was going to lead here. So instead of beating about the bush, I hoped a good will gesture would help convince you to hand over the soon to be living the rest of their lives in agonising pain bastards who tortured my brother. But all of the work you're doing is something good so I'm happy to help regardless.' She snapped the key back and dropped it back into her pocket. 'Let's go. You'll be surprised how much stuff they've got locked up here.'

She led the way across the road, towards the front of the building. It looked as if it would fall down at the first hint of wind. The single pane windows rattled as she shoved the key in the door. The paint was red and flaking. Cobwebs on every corner give the building that Halloween ghost hunt feel.

She opened the door and led the way in. They stepped inside. The door creaked as Lorna closed it behind her. Once the alarm shut off, they made their way down a dark, narrow entrance, stained glass office windows were on either side. Perhaps a once bustling office full of enthusiastic employees.

As they reached the end of the corridor another wooden door with flaking red paint was locked. She unlocked it and held the door open. 'Don't switch the lights on in,' she said.

Brendan stepped into the room. An arsenal. A mixture of automatic and semi-automatic weapons sat neatly lined up as if on display.

'Christ. It looks like this guy's planning a war,' Brendan said.

'He is,' Vanessa said.

A printed map was taped to the wall next to a desk. As they got closer, they seen there were pins, in what looked like strategically placed locations.

'What are these?' Lorna said, pointing at the pins.

'Those are the locations of the biggest mosques in the area. The more people, the more casualties. The more casualties, the more impact the attacks will have.'

'These guys are going all out, aren't they,' Lorna said, stepping closer to the map. 'We need people on these points.'

'Do you have people that can be at these locations?' Vanessa said, looking at Brendan, then at Lorna.

'We're using some associates.' Lorna said.

'How are we going to do this?' Brendan said. 'If we catch them at the meeting, we catch them all together. We catch them on the locations, we pretty much catch them red handed.'

'Moore won't be stupid enough to have them all gathering at the same place,' Lorna said. 'I think he'll operated an electronic meeting.' She looked around the room. 'I think this will be his storage. Where he can come for more weapons. A weapon's depot.'

Brendan laughed, 'a conference call to discuss a massacre.'

'It's the way of the world now, I guess,' Lorna said.

'Moore's holding a meeting this evening, here. He said tomorrow, he wants to be the one at the biggest Mosque in Nottingham. Where did all this hatred come from?' Vanessa said.

'Moore has been involved in that much bloodshed over the years, he simply can't walk away from it now,' Brendan said.

'He's meeting with the person who's funded it all from the English side.'

'Do you know who this guy is?' Brendan said.

She shook her head. 'But I know he was the one that cooked up this plan and from what it sounds like, it's personal to him.'

Brendan looked at Lorna. 'Do you recall anything from your days in the agency?'

She shook her head. 'No, but I can dig into it a little, see what I can find.' She looked at the computer across the table. 'Can you get access to any of these?'

'Do you really want to be hanging around this arsenal?' Vanessa gestured around them.

'Safest place in the world,' Brendan said. His phone rang. It was Louise. 'Louise.'

'Brendan, we've got a problem.'

Brendan sighed and looked at Lorna. 'Why doesn't that surprise me.'

'The girl you're with, she's been followed and had led them to you, you're all about to be...'

The noise of cars screeching to a halt outside the building was followed by doors opening and closing.

'Shit,' Lorna shouted, 'we've got company.'

Brendan looked at Vanessa. 'You've been followed here.' He still had his phone to his ear. 'Louise, where are you?'

'I'm in Nottingham, I've managed to squeeze some info that piece of shit Steve. I'm sending people over to help you.'

'It might be a bit late. A carload of them have just arrived.' He ran over to the arsenal. On the ground, next to a collection of AK47 assault rifles was a box of armoured vests. He snatched one out and tossed it to Vanessa. 'Put this on.' He lifted one of the AKs. 'Any idea how to operate one of these?'

'Yeah, because my dad was fucking Rambo.' She put the jacket on.

'Don't panic,' Lorna said. 'We've only heard one car arrive. I'm pretty sure we can hold them off for a while.' Just as Lorna said this, flashing blue and red lights slowly crept passed the window. 'Police are here,' she looked at Brendan, shaking her head. 'Great. Fantastic.'

'Don't you panic,' Brendan said. He pulled his phone back out. He called Louise back. She answered almost immediately. 'Louise, tell your guys not to come straight here, the police have just arrived.'

'How the fuck are you going to get out of that?'

'We'll think of something.'

Lorna looked at Brendan. 'This has been a set up. Get us here, cook up a bollocks story, and while we're in custody, the bombings get underway.'

'That's not going to happen,' Brendan said. He looked at Vanessa. 'Do you know your way out of here? Another exit.' Before she had a chance to respond, the sound of a door beign forced open, echoed through the room. 'Looks like it's too late.' He grabbed the gun and ran to the door. Stopping next to the door, he peered around the edge. The sound of footsteps clapping. He turned around, Lorna was looking through the window. 'You found a way out?'

She turned and shook her head. 'Let's go,' she gestured with her hand, waving for him to move.

'You two go first, I'll hold them off.' Brendan hissed, as the sound of footsteps grew louder.

Lorna opened the window and climbed out. Vanessa followed.

'Don't fucking move,' the first person who entered the room shouted. 'Not another fucking...'

He was silenced, Brendan grabbed him from behind, wrapping his left arm around his throat like an anaconda squeezing tighter, he dropped his gun, struggling, but the tighter Brendan squeezed, the weaker the guy's fight became, finally, he passed out. The sound of more footsteps running along the corridor. With the guy now sleeping in Brendan's grasp, he backed closer to the door, kicking it closed with his right foot, but before he was shut fully, the next person came through the door. He raised his gun, Brendan spun the guy in his arms around, using him as a shield. The guy didn't fire a gun, but he knew who he was dealing with.

'Cleary, you've been caught. Give it up,' he said. 'Nobody has to die here,' Brendan snatched the unconscious cop's gun from his holster, pointing it at the agent.

'You give it up, you're not going to pump your friend here full of lead. I know it. And you know it. Now drop your gun.'

Reluctantly the guy set his gun down.

'Now close the door and slide the little bar across so no more of your mates can get in.'

The agent did as instructed. He turned and raised his hands.

'Now sit on the ground against the door.'

As the guy sat down, he looked up at Brendan. 'Do you think you can stay in here forever, Cleary? You're going to have to leave eventually. He laughed, sounding as if he'd gotten one up on Brendan. 'Any moment now, they'll all be at this door.'

'That's what I'm hoping for.' Brendan threw the unconscious agent to the ground, next to the one doing all the
talking. He moved cautiously towards the window, smirking
when he seen what Lorna had done. The officer that was at
the cars was now unconscious and cuffed to their own vehicle. She was waving for him to hurry up. He turned and ran
over to the guys on the ground. He pointed his gun at them.
'Cuffs.'

The guy that was unconscious slowly came around. The
other tossed Brendan his cuffs. Brendan tossed them back
and ordered him to cuff himself to the copper piping that
ran adjacent to the door frame. Then he approached the other cop. 'For what it's worth, sorry.' He shot him in both feet,
bringing him scream out of his daze. Brendan ran across the
room to the window. Bangs were coming at the door. Someone on the other side was driving what sounded like a steel
toe cap boot into the other side. Looking out the window,
Brendan seen that Lorna was now in the Range Rover, and
had performed a three-point turn, pointing the vehicle in the
opposite direction. Brendan pocketed his gun and climbed
out onto the ledge. Hearing gun shots blow holes in the
door, he took one look back, one of the agents now lay there
dead from the friendly fire, not doubt pinning the blame
for that on Brendan. Brendan turned back and went for it.
His eyes scanned the area, his ears listened for anything that
would tell him that he was in danger.

'Hurry up, Brendan,' Lorna shouted from the car.

Brendan made a run for it as the door to the room was
shot through. He sprinted across the rundown surrounds of
the old building, straight for the car. Reaching the vehicle,

he pulled open the rear driver side door and jumped in, then he ran back to the two cars that sat with all four doors of each wide open. Shooting the tyres out of the passenger side of each car, he ran back to the Range Rover and hopped in. Lorna stomped on the accelerator, the SUV flying along the street, making the surroundings pass by in a blur.

'How the hell did they know we were there?' Vanessa said.

'That's what I'd like to know,' Lorna said. 'Someone's been watching you.'

'Oh my god, Mark.'

'Nothing's going to happen to your brother,' Brendan said.

'I've got to get to Leicester to see him.'

'Sorry, we're not letting you out of our sight for a while,' Brendan said. 'Just get us back to Louise's house. We need to know what the hell's just happened. Ramadan's tomorrow and we have none of these bombs in sight. Louise's secret house it the only location we can go to now. Get us there. I'll tell her to meet us there.'

Chapter Forty-Seven

THE HOUSE WAS EMPTY when they'd arrived. Louise was on her way. After what happened – contact with the police and government officials, it was highly probable that Moore was likely to be in the loop. He'll have been drip-fed the information about Brendan and Lorna being up to something. And an operation that wasn't only going to ruffle a few feathers in the country, but change the entire social and political landscape in England, the powers that be that were funding this, would not be willing to let the son of a former hitman for world leaders and an ex-MI5 agent stop their campaign.

They quickly entered the house, not wanting to stay in public view for any longer than they had to. Lorna led the way into the living room, closing the blinds then switching the light on. 'Where's the bloody remote control,' she frantically searched the white leather sofa, then the two matching recliners. The device fell out from the side of the seat closest to the fireplace. She pointed it at the tv and turned it on. Sky News was the channel the tv was set at. The news was a continuous stream of reports, played over and over again. The current program was broadcast live from Leicester. There was a mass knife attack on a group of skinheads who'd gotten rowdy and started hurling abuse at the establishment's Muslim majority. According to the report, the attack had gotten out of control, and when security attempted to eject the skinheads, fighting had broken out, which is said to be linked to four men and two women being stabbed two streets away. One dead, two in critical condition and the rest being treated in Leicester General. Social media accounts have exploded. People in support of the Muslim population commenting on how it was coming, after all the attacks on the Muslim population. Other's posted hate videos aimed at the Muslim community.

Brendan sat down on the sofa, draping his right leg over the left, watching it all unfold. 'If Moore knows there are people trying to knock their little campaign out, they'll have resorted to plan b to make sure the bombs get delivered to the spots, ready to go off.' He looked up at Lorna, then at Vanessa. 'Any suggestions?'

Lorna sat down next to him, not taking her eyes off the screen. The news was going on to say how people in the Muslim community were being threatened, warned not to go anywhere that will put themselves in danger. But some angry protesters claimed they would be going about their Ramadan celebrations, no matter the threat.

'You're just right, mate,' Brendan said to the tv, as if the guy could hear him.

'Think I might know who's behind this.' Lorna jumped up and marched across the living room towards the dining room table. She pulled her laptop out and took a seat at the table. Brendan got up and joined her at the table. 'Remember the IS bombings two years ago, at the music concert?'

Brendan hummed to agree. 'I remember.'

'There was a lot of bad feeling floating around the intelligence offices. How we didn't pick up on the attacks.'

'It's kind of hard when they're everywhere. It's not as if you can start watching everyone.'

'Yes, but someone quite high up who was supposed to be looking after national security. He missed that one, and not only did many innocent people die at that concert, but his nine-year-old daughter was one of the victims.'

'She was killed in the explosion?'

Lorna nodded while tapping on the keys of the laptop.

'Jesus. And he was in charge of this? Poor bastard.'

'Yes, well if it is him, that poor bastard is about to kill many innocent people. Which won't make him feel any better about his daughter.'

'Who is he?'

Lorna flipped the laptop screen around so Brendan could see the man in the image. A middle-aged man with a long, thin face, pointed nose, chin and ears. Next to the lady in the photo, he looked like a giant. The photo was taken outside Buckingham Palace. The man in the photo was the current Lord Mayer of London, who after the sickening attacks on ethnic minorities, wanted to clean the streets of London, and to Brendan it became clear why this particular guy would have so much hatred towards Muslim extremists.

'Loosing a child is one thing, and if I'd lost someone I loved that much,' Brendan looked at Lorna, 'like I almost did in Italy, I'd want revenge. But he can't start a campaign of ethnic cleansing on the streets of one of the most multi-cultural countries in the world.'

'He's always been very eccentric. In his politics, the way he carries himself and how he portrays himself to the world. But that's also what's got him to the position he's in. The lovable guy who wanted to clean up the streets of London. Nobody would think it was him.'

'Christ, he's going to create a massacre.'

The sound of a car engine starting outside snatched their attention away from the laptop. Vanessa was gone. Brendan jumped up and ran to the window, catching only the rear of Louise's car as it passed through the gates, disappearing from view.

'She's gone to get her brother.' Lorna stood up closing her laptop. 'We've got to get after her. She's not thinking straight. She'll get herself killed.'

'I'll go. You stay here and wait for Louise to get back.' Brendan went to the mantel, snatching a key to another of Louise's cars. An Audi A5. He turned and rushed towards the door.

'Brendan...'

He turned and looked at Lorna.

'Don't go anywhere without this.' She tossed him his gun.

'I'll see you soon.' He quickly said then left.

BRENDAN KEPT THE RADIO on as he sped towards Leicester. Fighting against the urge to smash the speed limit in the four litre Audi, the control of the engine's horses was tempting, but overruled by the fear of being stopped and pulled over. He was starting to realise this was a life he and Lorna were not going to remain in for long. If they wanted to have a long, happy life together, then they'd need to live normal lives, somewhere private. Perhaps build a family. One day he'd hope to be the father the late Damien Cleary Jnr once was, minus the mistakes. But being a good father, would not involve being in prison or eventually getting killed. Therefore, the idea of taking the money his father had accumulated over the years was at the forefront. Just beyond the desire to help the lady who'd been going through the same as him. Loosing her father in a similar fashion had drawn Brendan to Louise, not in a sexual way, he had an unbreakable love for Lorna, but he was drawn to Louise, and helping her was almost like he was helping himself again.

As he approached Leicester city centre, Brendan's phone rang. He didn't recognise the number, but the fact he had as many fingers to count with as numbers in his contact list, that wasn't as unnerving as it would to most. The voice that was on the other end, however, did put him on edge.

'The infamous Brendan Cleary,' the English accent spoke in mock humour. 'Your father was just as big a nuisance. Looks like you've taken over for the late Damien Cleary.'

'Who's this?' Brendan said, pulling the vehicle over into a bus stop.

'This is the man who needs you to walk away from whatever it is you're planning to do, before it's too late. You're putting your loved ones in great danger. If we can't get our hands on you, which I think is perhaps an accurate assumption, after all you're father was impossible to trace, I'm guessing you're going to be the same, but we will go after those you love.' He cleared his throat. 'Like that lovable aunt Mary of yours back in Belfast.'

'You've already mentioned the fact my father was, well, what he was. And with that said, you clearly know I'm not going to stop and let you kill innocent people. If you had half a brain, you'd call this off and forget all about your little Ramadan celebrations.' Brendan knew his aunt Mary was smart and would know she'd be in as much danger as he was; she was as good at ghosting herself as anyone, so he didn't have to fear her being dragged into something dangerous. 'My family are safe. They're not stupid, and while we're on the descriptive word – you'd be very stupid to think I won't come after you if you target any of my family.'

'Where do you get the nerve to speak to someone like me in that way, you little shit.' The man's voice became deeper, more aggressive. He was losing his cool. 'How much do you think it would break poor little Agent Woodward's heart if her sister and weird excuse for a son came to a grisly end?'

Brendan's eyes shot open, not paying enough attention to anybody else other than his own family members. He didn't respond. He felt as if he'd just been gripped tightly by the balls and led back out of the country again while the rest of the country explodes in a ball of racist anti-Islamic smoke.

'Nothing to say?'

'It's the same as if you come after my family – I'm coming for you.'

'You know when I mentioned your name to Moore and his son, their expressions both grew into those of lottery winners. They seemed to be very keen on getting their hands on you. It appears, Mr Cleary that there are a lot of people out there thirsty for your blood.'

'That's something I've gotten used to all of my life, and the Moore family have had plenty of opportunity to make their feelings known to me all their lives.'

The voice laughed. 'Perhaps now that the infamous Damien Cleary is well and truly dead, they know he'll not be coming back. You've no daddy to come save you now, my boy.' He laughed. 'Now walk away from this. Leave England and you and that bitch Woodward will live to see another day. If not, I'll make sure the deaths of her sister and nephew will be so grotesque is will royally fuck her up. She won't want to live after she sees the way their bodies are left. And trust me, this will be all over the news. You've been warned.' He hung up the phone, then a text message came through. A photo of Lorna's sister and nephew tied to chairs in a dark room.

'Fuck.' Brendan thumped the steering wheel with his tight gripped fist.

Chapter Forty-Eight

GETTING TO THE TATTOO studio, Brendan caught a glimpse of some movement coming from the flat above. Louise's car was parked just fifty yards around the corner. He checked his pistol was loaded then got out, slowly shutting the door, pushing it closed until he heard the click.

The roads were quiet, two taxis parked on the other side of the road, outside the depot was the only other sign of life. Both drivers were both stood having a coffee, one of them smoking. Both looking at him. He needed to attract attention like he needed a bullet in the head. He ignored the fact he was who he was and made his way towards to narrow alleyway that separated the shop from the newsagents to it's right. Pulling his phone out he quickly sent a text to Lorna, telling her he'd arrived. He then called Vanessa, and as expected, she ended the call after the first ring. Approaching the building, he could hear a lot of movement coming from the open window. She'd knocked something over, perhaps distracted by the phone call, but at least she was smart enough to keep the lights off.

Brendan went down the alleyway, the building's door was left open. Her voice escaped out into the alleyway. She sounded as if she were in the middle of a debate, but it was only her voice on the waves. Whoever she was talking to was not in the room. He slowly pushed the door open, hoping it wouldn't creak. It didn't. He closed the door behind him and locked it. Making his way up the staircase, he continued in silent prayer for his arrival to continue going undetected. He'd no idea who she was or whether she was feeding information to Moore or not. He believed he was a good judge of character, but there was something about this lady he just couldn't put his finger on. And the way she was acting was putting them all in unnecessary danger, regardless of it being an honest mistake or not.

'I don't know where he is now, but if he finds out what I'm doing, I'm dead,' she hissed, as she continued to rummage around the room. Brendan stopped in the hallway, remaining where he stood, wanting to catch more of the conversation. 'I've found it,' she whispered, sounding victorious. 'We've got to get out of here. I'm coming to get you. I'll see you soon.' Her footsteps grew louder as she got closer to the door. She stepped out into the hallway, walking right into Brendan's silhouetted outline, face first into his gun. She gasped, dropping her bag, raising her hands in the air.

'What's going on?' Brendan said. 'You're feeding them information about what we're doing?'

'What?' She lowered her hands again, her entire posture relaxing upon hearing Brendan's voice. 'No, of course not, Brendan. What the hell are you doing here?'

'Well you kind of left abruptly, we thought you'd been a fucking dumbass and gone after your brother. But now I've caught a bit of that conversation you've just had, I'm left wondering whose side are you on, because it sure as shit isn't clear.'

'Fuck you, Brendan. I'm on my brother's side. And that's who I was on the phone with. I've got to get him out of here before those bastards come back and finish him off. They'll think tomorrow's attacks will be linked to him. I'm not going to let that happen.'

'Those bombs are not going to go off, tomorrow,' Brendan said, lowering his weapon.

'Yes, they will. It's the bloody government that's doing this, the dirty bastards are as crooked at the next guy, and...'

Brendan grabbed her by the wrist. 'Come on, we've got to get out of here. We haven't got time to debate this here.' He turned and led the way down the stairs, back out into the alleyway, rushing out onto the main street. Three males stood, blocking their way to the car.

'Brendan Cleary,' Sam said. 'Looks like Louise made a mistake thinking you were on our side.' He stood there, Reg and Tesh on either side. All of them looking as if they were ready to get busy with their fists.

'It's not what you think,' Brendan said, 'and trust me you guys do not want me to be kept back from what I'm in the middle of.'

'We don't give a shit about you, Cleary,' Sam looked past Brendan, as if he were irrelevant, 'we've came here for that bitch.'

'That's out of the question.' Brendan pulled her behind him. He pulled his gun out. Pointing it at the three. 'All of you back away.' Before Brendan could say another word, a loud crack echoed through the air. He felt a sting in his neck, his hand instinctively jumped up to where he felt it. He went dizzy then went to sleep.

WAKING UP IN THE BACK of a van, Brendan felt groggy. Naturally, he tried to move, but the plastic cable ties cut deeply into his skin. Vanessa was next to him. Mascara smeared all over her face. A red line of blood run from her left nostril down her face. The van had stopped, and the front door slamming was what had woken them. The sound of club music grew louder as the sliding door was pulled open. Light drops of rain blew in. They were in a side entry. The driver pulled Brendan out first then Vanessa. Standing in the narrow entry, Brendan recognised the street out towards the front. They were at the club where they'd brought Davy English.

An emergency exit had it's green doors held open by two members if the door security. Both Asian. Both Muslim looking, who'd have been hungry for too long, and were now looking at a white man with the same accent and from the same city as the father and son who'd woken the dormant Combat 18 in line with the increased attacks from the Muslim extremist group calling itself the Islamic State.

Brendan looked at Vanessa. She was looking at him as if he had the answer she was looking for. He didn't. They were caught, and now at the mercy of some very angry, very dangerous people that all but killed her brother simply for being that – her brother. 'Don't worry, if they wanted us dead, we'd already be.' He turned and led the way up the steps, in through the evacuation doors, heading towards the room they were taken to when they'd captured English. As they stepped into the room, there he was. Omar. Sitting there carelessly, his right leg draped over his left, smoking with his right hand, his left hand pointing a remote control at the TV. The news was blaring.

'Come in,' Omar said, his tone light, full of joy, but perhaps more at the fact they'd caught some influential people and not what was being shown on the TV. 'The Irish Ramadan Man.' He tapped on the black leather sofa he was sprawled across. 'It seems you've been playing us all, Louise included.' He repeated the taps on the sofa. 'Join me, see what's happening out there, those streets have become very dangerous.'

'I'll stand,' Brendan said, he looked back at Vanessa, she was nearly crying.

'Sit the fuck down.' Omar spoke through gritted teeth, lifting a pistol off the sofa, pointing it at Brendan.

'Fuck you. Shoot me then,' Brendan spat.

'I heard you were a smart man, Mr Cleary. Your late father's reputation has given you a lot of street cred. Don't tell me he was the only Cleary with some smarts.'

'You want to get smart?' Brendan strolled across the room, carelessly. He was running out of bargaining chips. He was about to cash them all in. 'You cut us both loose and let us stop what's going to be the biggest nationwide massacre that's hit this country since the world war.'

'What are you talking about?'

'There is a plan to set off a number of bombs tomorrow during your precious Ramadan celebrations.' Brendan looked at Vanessa, then around the room. 'She has been posing at Moore Jnr's girlfriend for some time now, simply on my request, so that she could get close to them and figure out what exactly those inbred Neo-Nazi fucks plan to do.' He lied, looking at her, hoping she'd catch on to his story.

'She looked very much in love with him, from what we've seen, they've been very cosy,' Omar said.

Brendan walked back over to her. 'That's because she's that good an actor. She had you fooled. She had them fooled. Christ, she almost had me fooled.' Brendan's lie was that good, he was almost believing himself.

'Where are these bombs going off?' Omar stood up and pointed the gun at her. She flinched, and started gasping for air, as if suffocating on her own nerves. 'Tell me or I'll blow your pretty little head off.'

Brendan stood in front of the gun. 'You shoot her, and you'll never find out. And I'll make sure the entire Muslim community know you were the one that prevented us from stopping it.'

Omar looked around the room, lowering his weapon. He paused for a moment. 'You lie to me, and I'll come after not only you, but your family in Belfast will all come to a bad end.'

'That's an empty threat,' Brendan said, 'a lot worse have come after my family before and they didn't live to tell how it worked out for them. But I'm not in this depressing city for the fun of it. I'm here because a man that once created mayhem in Belfast is about to do the same to the good people of England.'

'We'll be coming with you.'

'We travel alone,' Brendan said. 'You can keep your distance. We're meeting with Louise and Lorna. Then we decide who's going where.' Brendan looked around the room. 'But we could use some of your men. We need numbers. You have numbers? People who aren't afraid to get involved in this?'

'We've got numbers.' Omar tossed his pistol down on the sofa. Reaching into his shirt pocket, he pulled out a joint. He took a lighter from the coffee table and lit it.

'We'll need a car.'

'We've got a car.

Brendan looked at Vanessa. 'Let's go.' He looked back at Omar. 'We'll be outside. Get us the car, we haven't got time to mess around.'

Chapter Forty-Nine

BRENDAN HAD BOUGHT them time, but it was running out. At least they'd been given a little time to plan their next move. Two black Mercedes SUVs followed their lead towards Louise's house. She'd not answered the phone the last two times Brendan tried. Coming within a twenty-minute drive from the house, they needed to know who was on the way.

'She needs to answer this bloody call,' he said, as they stopped at a set of traffic lights. He looked in the rear view, the vehicles right up behind him, towering over them like over-powering bullies, itching to throw their weight around. 'This isn't the time for...'

'Brendan, where the hell are you?'

'Louise, we've ran into a little bit of trouble. Your Asian friends had arrived and were about to do the same to Vanessa as they did to her brother. But Omar's let us go. I've told him what we're doing, he's offered to help with numbers. We're going to need a few bodies that will come at the drop of a hat. People who'll be directly involved in these attacks.'

'Where are you now?' Louise said. 'I'm with Lorna. At the safe house.'

'We're on our way there now, but after tonight you'll need to find yourself a new safe house as we're coming with extra company. A bit of insurance that Vanessa doesn't feed info back to the other side.'

Louise laughed sarcastically, 'nothing's simple with you, Brendan is it?'

'Life would be very boring if it were easy.' Brendan past the sign for Nottingham, he looked to his right. 'There's something else next door to McGregor's that can be useful in stopping these attacks tomorrow.'

'Lorna's told me about the weapons. We have the map with the destinations. I know there are nine targets. Nine bombs. Four in Nottingham. Two in Leicester. Two in Derby and one in Walsall. Nine. They were very precise about there being nine.'

'Wasn't she nine years old?' Brendan said.

'Who?'

'Mayor Tailford's daughter?'

'Coincidence?'

'And where were the bombers from?'

'Nottingham, Leicester, Derby and the leader was from Walsall. Hold on, Lorna wants to speak with you.'

'Brendan, he's been planning these attacks for some time. He's been to all of these locations an unusual amount of time in the past twelve months. He's gone to these places in a bid to extend his hand in friendship to the community he now holds directly responsible for the death of his nine-year-old daughter.'

'At least we know where we're going to,' Brendan said. 'It'll save us a lot of time. Now we just need to find out who's going where.'

'I'm thinking if the leader of these attackers were from Walsall, then the bomb in that location is going to be the biggest and most important one for him.'

'That's where Moore will be then, guaranteed. Moore Jnr might go with him, but definitely Moore,' Brendan said.

'How can you be sure?'

'Because no matter how loyal his comrades were, he always relied more on himself than anyone else to get the job done right. And if he's being paid handsomely for this job, then he'll want to make sure the job's done right. And I want to see the bastards face when we arrive there and rain on his little parade.'

'So, I'm guessing you're nominating yourself to go to Walsall?' Louise said.

'Does a bear shit in the woods?'

Lorna laughed. 'We'll both go.'

'That's right, I'm not letting you out of my sight ever again. We're going for a long holiday after this one,' Brendan said.

'Music to my ears.'

'Right, we'll see you all soon. We need to have a quick chat together, just you, me, Louise and my co-pilot here. There are some things we need to discuss without certain ears listening in.'

'See you soon.' Lorna ended the call.

The moment the call ended, Brendan knew what was coming next. Vanessa would want to know when she would get her hands on Omar. He looked across at her. 'I know what you're thinking. And you'll have Omar before you next see your brother. You can tell Mark you've got them for him.'

She didn't respond. Folding her arms defensively, she looked out the window as if she couldn't even look at him.

'I think we should bring them all together. Take them all out at the same time.'

'What do you mean? How can we bring Moore and Omar together? They'll just kill each other.'

Brendan shrugged. 'That's not such a bad idea.' He put the window down, letting some air in. 'But Omar sees himself as the leader of this community. If an attack like this is going to be foiled, he'll want to stop it. We can allow Omar to be the hero, go in after Moore, save the day, then when they're all together, we let them all have it.'

'I'm not sure it'll work.'

'You got any other ideas?' Brendan looked at her as the car stopped at a set of traffic lights. She didn't respond. 'I've just bought us some time. We're lucky to be alive, Vanessa. We're out of time. The Ramadan celebrations start tomorrow. This is our last chance.'

'I want to be up close and personal when we take them both out.'

Brendan sighed. 'You're going to get me killed.'

'You can stay at a distance. Watch through a lens.'

'I'm not going to stand from a distance and watch you walk into something like that.'

'Then you'll you'll have to come with me then. But I want to look into his eyes when he takes his last breath.'

Brendan looked in the rear view mirror, the two cars still behind. He cast a quick glance over at Vanessa then back to the road again. He sighed. 'You're going to get me killed.'

DEAR PROOF-READERS. Thank you all so much for your support. How would you guys like this final chapter to play out? Does Brendan die, or does he live on and continue the series? Please email me your thoughts to paul@siranipublishinglimited.com I hope you've enjoyed it so far ?

Chapter Fifty

About the Author

'I'm simply a guy who wanted to write his partner a book in her language, it's just got way out of hand!'

P.M. Heron was born in Belfast and spent the first 27 years of his life on Irish soil before moving to Loughborough, England to finish his study in sports management. He completed his degree in May 2012, which was, to say the least, an inspiring time to be in Loughborough. That summer, the university hosted Team Japan and Team GB for the 2012 Olympic Games in London.

At that time, he met his partner who came to England from Italy also to study sports management. Quite a summer to remember. Obviously graduating wasn't too bad either!

Later that year, he decided to teach himself to speak Italian. As a way for him to practice what he had learned, he began writing in his work diary - in Italian - and this was how he discovered a love for writing.

In March 2015, he decided to write his partner a book - in Italian - for their 3rd anniversary.

So, after 6 months, he managed to finish that book: a story titled "La Storia Della Mia Vita" which is Italian for "The Story Of My Life".

So, he fell in love with writing but didn't know how to continue. Until Sunday 11th October 2015, while talking to a friend in a leisure centre which he had been managing at the time, he came up with the idea for his first fictional series. It's simply snowballed from there!

Read more at pmheronauthor.com.

Printed in Great Britain
by Amazon